For K, D, J & S

CHAPTER 1: INVITING TROUBLE

I acquired a taste for secrets from a very young age. The thing about secrets is that each has its own distinct flavour, no two are the same. Some can be thrilling, others even poisonous. Your secrets will always taste different to other people's — sometimes they can be used in ways you never quite imagined.

I suppose my rather secretive nature does encourage suspicion. That and the fact that I seem to attract death. I've been accused of seeing more than my fair share of dead bodies, as if that is a crime in itself. In my experience, death is never fair. Perhaps I have seen more than most, but, as Mother always says, it's less than an undertaker. Mother doesn't do tact.

Maybe it's more the manner of the deaths circling above my name, in every article little black words like *slaughter*, *stabbed*, *poisoned*, *drowned*, *impaled*. They do tend to give the impression that I invite death.

But, until we visited Greystone, I'd never seen anyone killed by a cannonball, nor a body wedged in a priest hole, and I'd definitely never seen medieval waterboarding before. It's the *nature* of the death that brings it notoriety, or so Mother explained to me when she wrote a gruesome article about each of the deaths we experienced on this fateful trip to Black Towers, or 'The Tower of Death', as she renamed it. But as Mother never tires of reminding me, death sells. And to be fair to her, she wrote our friend's obituary first and that broke all our hearts a little bit.

It's the details, the moment of death, the motives and mystery that I find captivating. Which does, I realise, make me sound a little too fascinated by death to be healthy or well-adjusted. But those are two things I've never been accused of.

The picturesque village of Greystone is like any other quintessential English village that is about to play host to murder. Behind the chocolate-box beauty and seeming tranquillity simmers a pot full of jealousies, resentments and greed. But most of all, those drystone walls and country cottage gardens hide secrets. All manner of secrets — some darker than others, some long since forgotten, some that refuse to die.

When Mother discovered she had been invited to a weekend at Lady Marsha Black's, she almost died right there and then. It was to be a weekend at their castle on Dartmoor, which looked down on everyone else in Greystone. Perfect for Mother. The 'save the date' email came months in advance, affording Mother plenty of time to tell everyone she knew and spend vast sums of money we didn't have on buying outfits for every occasion. She was like a child about to embark on their first residential trip, packing all manner of unnecessary paraphernalia in anticipation of a multitude of conceivable and inconceivable situations. There were to be many of both on this trip — sadly Mother didn't have a suitable outfit for any of them. But then I'm not sure exactly what an outfit would look like that was designed for multiple murders. Wipe clean, perhaps.

Among Mother's extraordinary weekend wardrobe was a riding-themed outfit (she can't ride but likes an 'equestrian look'), a shooting-themed outfit (again, she doesn't shoot but likes a 'field sports look') and several evening dinner outfits (she doesn't eat dinner but more than compensates for it with wine, although a 'boozer's look' isn't something she really aspires to). Essentially, Mother had contrived to look like an extra on *Downton Abbey*.

So it was a great disappointment to Mother when the actual invitation finally arrived. There was to be no shooting, riding or any of the other pursuits Mother has never done before. There wasn't even going to be a sumptuous dinner with multiple courses and shocking announcements. It was, in fact, billed as a 'safari supper party'. The image in my mind of Lady Marsha Black also changed when I saw the quick biro-scrawled note on the back. 'Bring sturdy boots and something warm. All very casual. Will be fun!'

It had the ring of a command to it.

'Safari supper?' Mother looked as if something dirty had landed on the breakfast table — like food. Neither of us does breakfast. Just coffee. But we can't sit at the coffee table, as it's covered in aspirational lifestyle magazines and cookery books. 'Sounds like something that dreadful Cameron man would do with a load of filthy animals.'

She hadn't looked this disappointed since she'd been told the Marmadukes hadn't invited her to their boat party. It's well known that the Marmadukes have a visitor book on their boat which isn't for guests to just sign after a visit but is where they are asked to write their recommendations for potential invitees. It's based on all the things they recognise as extremely desirable in a guest — wealth, a desire to ingratiate themselves with anyone they see as remotely important and a large number of Instagram followers, so they can show the boat to as many people as possible with a variety of filters.

Mother does in fact have quite a lot of 'friends' — virtual ones, of course. She doesn't do real friends anymore. But this new-found fondness for 'likes' is all based on her profile being that of someone personally involved in multiple murders rather than anyone's need to invite her to their rapacious social climber parties. Which is a shame, really, because the one thing Mother does do is obsequiousness, especially around people she sees as important (rich). She's more what you'd call an 'ingratiator' than an 'influencer'. Unfortunately, her humble bragging, virtue signalling and Coachella vibe is slightly overshadowed by the body count attached to her name.

She now attracts those who inhabit the shadier borders of the internet as a result of her 'true crime blog'. It's called *Death Smarts*. She, Pandora Smart, writes about various situations where we, the Smarts, have been involved in near-death experiences. She makes some money from adverts that appear on the blog about stain remover, high-powered room spray, kitchen knives and rat poison. Alongside that, she sells salacious stories to anyone who'll pay, documenting our time in the Slaughter House, where four people were murdered, our trip to an Outer Hebridean Island that also resulted in four deaths and, when she wants to give them a bit of emotion and 'show a more human face' — difficult given the amount of filler — she writes about her husband dying. It seems hard to believe, especially if you know my mother, that she had no hand in any of these deaths. But that part is true. She was actually an innocent bystander, if 'innocent' is the correct word for someone who sells the stories afterwards to make money.

Mother and I have, improbably, survived two horrific near-death experiences and the loss of Dad. When I thought I'd found someone in the wreckage of our last trip, we managed to navigate our way through him abandoning me. But even Mother doesn't write about Spear. Not yet, anyway.

Some people might be brought closer together, but so much drama can actually 'stultify emotional growth', as Bob the Therapist used to say. I should say that Bob the Therapist isn't dead, he just needed to take a break last year from hearing about the various murders we'd seen. The last we heard, he was in a Peruvian jungle experimenting with legal highs. Mother was appalled that he'd chosen to be somewhere with no phone signal, given that she used to speak to him roughly six times a day and more at night. He'd suggested many times that she should become more dependent on the voice in her own head. But Mother placed a gagging order on that years ago.

Mother was even less impressed when Aunt Charlotte appeared at our house later that day, clutching a similar invitation to the one we'd received from Lady Black.

'Why the hell would she invite you?' Mother squinted at the invite distrustfully as if she was examining a possible forgery. She has some knowledge in this area. Fake invites have worked for her a couple of times, most notably Ann Widdecombe's book launch. Sadly though, not for Meghan and Harry's wedding, where, if you look very carefully, you can see her in the bottom section of one photograph being forcibly ejected from Windsor Castle.

Aunt Charlotte stood proudly holding out her invite. 'It was me who introduced Marsha to book club in the first place, if you remember.'

Book club was killed off after that weekend away at the Slaughter House ended in four body bags, one of which in fact contained an actual member of book club. But she deserved an untimely end. Which may sound callous or even a little like I murdered her. But I didn't. Someone else got there first. I thought about it, but no one ever went to jail for imagining someone's death. After Dad died, I *imagined* murdering a lot of people, but so far that's just been a bit of a mindful distraction.

Mother did that quick head-and-shoulder shake she does when she needs to shake off everyone else's opinion, like a dog shaking itself dry. 'Marsha only came to a couple of book clubs. You put her off with all your talk about *Gone Girl*.'

'That was nothing to do with me!' Aunt Charlotte drew her chin back and tried to look insulted. She very rarely is. 'She lost interest in book club after she married Lord Elzevir, that was all.'

I snorted. '*Lord* Elzevir bought his lordship.'

'What does that matter?' Mother flicked her hand, swatting away the idea like a fly. 'He's a lord and bloody Marsha Mould is now *Lady* Marsha Black.'

I laughed. 'Shame she didn't go for the double-barrelled.'

They let their eyes come to rest on me, watching me with their usual confusion, trying to figure me out.

'Marsha had a lot on with the castle renovations, that's all. How could she carry on with book club? There's no time for books when you've got an ancient library to demolish.' I couldn't tell if Mother was intending irony.

'Well, she certainly expects us all to be there. Look—' Aunt Charlotte held out the invitation — 'it says quite clearly that I should make sure all the old book club gang are together and that my lovely niece Ursula comes, and her mother too if she wants to tag along.'

Mother's face puckered up like the ready-meal film she always forgets to remove before cooking. She looked down at her invite, which wasn't her invite at all. I could clearly see my name on the top-right corner with 'plus one' written next to it. Mother turned the envelope over in her hands. It was addressed to Miss U. R. Smart. She shot me *The Look*.

I widened my eyes as if to say, 'Don't blame me.' I am to blame though. I've spent a lot of time liking Marsha's renovation pictures, even the one of the library being ripped apart to house a gym. I can be morally ambiguous sometimes too. I'm just quieter about it than Mother.

'I don't believe this.' Mother closed her eyes.

'Breathe, Pandora. Have you been doing your mindful colouring?' Aunt Charlotte slung an unwelcome arm around Mother's shoulder. 'We're all going on a little holiday.'

'Fun and murder for me and you?' I tilted my head to the side, searching Mother's face for a reaction. I counted it off on my fingers. 'Number one, the Slaughter House. Number two, the Isle of Death. What next, Castle Kill?'

'Don't be ridiculous,' Mother sighed. 'Tower of Death sounds much better.'

'Ursula!' Aunt Charlotte looked shocked. 'Don't invite trouble!'

'Invite trouble? People don't start killing just because I'm there.'

'It has been suggested a few times on my blog.' Mother folded her arms.

'I'm sorry?'

'Yes. If you ever bothered to read it, you'd know. It was a piece called "Murderous Magnetism — do some people attract killers?" I did a little case study on you. I kept your name out of it though.'

'What?' I let the word out letter by letter.

'It got a lot of likes. I mean a lot. I got the Oxy Power Booster cleaning ad out of it.'

'I can't believe you've written about the horrors I've endured.'

'Yes, you can, Ursula,' Aunt Charlotte said distractedly. 'We're all grist to your mother's mill. She did a piece on sibling rivalry last month entitled "How to cope if your sister is an emotional vampire." I'd only asked her if I could borrow the Vax.'

Mother looked defiant. 'You can't blame me for embroidering on my tatty relatives. I need to market the blog. It needs sensational, clickbait titles.'

'Oh, you mean,' Aunt Charlotte leaned in conspiratorially, '*young men.*'

I frowned. 'No, Aunt Charlotte, that's jailbait.'

She didn't have the look of someone who understood the difference.

'Mother, all these catchy little murder names, interviews and articles are denigrating what we went through. And let's not forget the endearing memes you put out for Mothers' Day, with our police photos and shots from the papers with the lovely line, "Who said a weekend away with Mother would be dull?"'

Mother cast me a nonchalant look. 'Well, your so-called Tragedy Poetry isn't going to put food on the table or clothes on our backs.'

'Not if you always insist on wearing Chanel and St Laurent.'

Aunt Charlotte nodded. 'I'm afraid I agree with Pandora, darling. I do like their clothes. They're so durable, and with a casual fit.'

'That's *St Michael*, Aunt Charlotte, and M&S haven't used that name in years.'

'Charlotte hasn't bought any clothes in years.' Mother sipped her coffee. 'I don't know how you hope to fit in with the country set.'

Aunt Charlotte looked confused in tweed, a signature look. Her shirt was crumpled and her hat battered as if she'd been on a 1930s expedition and travelled back in her trunk. She shifted uncomfortably. 'I shall fit in like nuts in a squirrel's pouch, my dear.'

Mother laughed. 'You may well be aiming to look like a rodent's nuts, but Lady Marsha is renowned for her fabulous style.'

Aunt Charlotte sighed deeply. 'I know how she feels. It can be a terrible burden.'

Mother put the coffee cup down with a decided crack on the glass table. 'I've been looking forward to this weekend for months.' She watched Aunt Charlotte's face begin to fall. 'I love you but . . .'

Three of the best words in the English language instantly transformed by the simple addition of 'but'.

Fortunately, Aunt Charlotte doesn't care to examine the finer nuances of Mother. 'That's settled then. Greystone here we come! Now, Pandora, you'll have to decide whose plus one you want to be.'

Mother's eyes fired. 'I am not, nor will I ever be known as "plus one". That term is reserved for partners no one wants to name.'

I held up my hands in a 'pause' sign. Mother needs visuals sometimes. 'I'm sure it won't matter.'

She was defiant. 'You'll have to decide who's taking Mirabelle.'

'No one's taking Mirabelle!' My mouth hung open as if I had something more to say. I didn't. Mirabelle is hateful, and if it was going to be up to me, I'd make sure Mirabelle wasn't coming.

Mother has dragged Mirabelle around with us for years like a comfort blanket, unpleasant to everyone but her. She couldn't bear to be parted from Mirabelle.

'She's already got an invite.' Aunt Charlotte sounded uncharacteristically apologetic.

Mother adopted what I call her 'cattle prod' face. This is when I imagine how she'd look if someone used a cattle prod on her.

'What, Mirabelle as well?' Mother said flabbergasted. 'She never mentioned it. Who's she taking?'

Aunt Charlotte looked at the floor.

'Well, come on. Who?' Mother leaned forward.

Aunt Charlotte cleared her throat. 'Bridget,' she said quietly. 'They've . . . they've . . .'

'What?'

'They've moved in together.' Aunt Charlotte looked at Mother as if there might be a slim chance of mercy.

Mother was silent, which is never a good sign. Finally, she drew herself up as if gathering all her energy. 'Mirabelle hates dogs.'

'Bridget's got a cat now. A sphinx. It's completely bald so there's no problem with hair. Mirabelle's allergies—'

'How long has this been going on?'

'A while I think,' Aunt Charlotte said sheepishly. 'They wanted to keep it secret for as long as possible.'

'Secret? Who from?'

Aunt Charlotte didn't respond.

'How could she? She knows how much I detest secrets!'

Which isn't entirely correct. The only secrets Mother doesn't do are other people's. She has plenty of her own. Almost as many as me. And Mirabelle's failure to mention her new living arrangements was not the only secret that was going to be revealed on that fateful weekend.

CHAPTER 2: THE MOOR

Mother drove in a ferocious silence until we finally hit the borders of Dartmoor. She likes to 'get the drive done', which always requires relentless driving with no stopping, small talk or music. But rather than making the drive pass quickly, it somehow made time slow down. A cloud of anxiety settled over the car about ten minutes into the journey and grew darker with every hour. It was like sitting an exam entitled, 'How to travel with Mother' and the only word that would surface was 'don't'.

As we crossed into Dartmoor, the road seemed to rise and twist. It was disorientating at first, both sides flanked with thick, high hedges, as though we were being over-whelmed by the landscape.

The light was already beginning to dwindle. The only strip of sky I could see rolling out on the road ahead seemed to take on a new steely edge. As the road widened and the hedges ended, the vast stone landscape opened out. Great crags rose up from broken earth and met the sky in dark, crooked lines.

There was so much movement here. The mist travelled in smoke clouds over the cold dusk. Wind twisted trees bent against distant outcrops of rocks. Clouds were driven fast across the dark sky.

Granite boulders were piled randomly, some cracked and worn into vague faces and shapes. The holes of their eyes watched our car drive by. Gorse ran in wild yellow streaks across the open, bleak land.

As we rounded another bend, the world seemed to end and fall away down into a steep valley. Mother braked hard and surface water sheered up and away from the sides of the car.

'Maybe we should stop,' Aunt Charlotte murmured.

'We'll be there in half an hour.' Mother drove on.

'I need to eat.'

'You always need to eat.'

The shadows were drawing out across the thin, grey road. There were no street lamps. The occasional small house we passed reflected on our car window. Sheep ambled round in small, lost groups.

'Look!' Aunt Charlotte pointed in awe. By the side of a roughly paved car park, just nestled beneath a string of gnarled trees, stood the dim lights of a small mobile café. On the opposite side of the road, rising steep, was a broken granite tor lifting up into the low sky.

'Hound Tor,' I read from the small sign. 'This was online. It was supposed to have inspired Sir Arthur Conan Doyle!'

'To do what?'

I turned and looked at Aunt Charlotte, who had colonised the entire backseat. I didn't attempt to explain.

Mother sighed and drew into the car park next to the van. I looked up at its faded sign: *The Hound of the Basket Fills*. Below was a notice explaining that they provided small picnics of four items with a choice of ham or cheese sandwiches, crisps, an apple or orange and a small biscuit in the shape of a large dog with red eyes. It was all in takeaway cartons designed to look like cardboard baskets.

Mother, Aunt Charlotte and I stood by the side of the car looking out at the grim dusk. Layers of grey drizzle blew across the jagged granite cliffs. The moor's air was peaty and rich with the smell of damp grass, sharp and astringent. The thin, watery light drifted across the far hills. It was a stark sky. Puritan grey. It seemed strange to come so quickly from the cosy villages and main roads into this ancient world of crags and moorland where time was set into the rock in such distinct layers. There'd been only one small sign to mark our entrance into the moor, but it was beginning to feel like we'd crossed a much greater boundary.

There was no silence here. Water ran over moss covered boulders. Birds called and flitted through the high branches of the trees above. Far beyond the crags, I could see the shapes of ponies racing across the moors.

We sipped our hot tea and picked at the cling-film-wrapped food.

The woman at the sandwich bar watched us as she wiped a tea cloth slowly round the rim of a mug. She wasn't just looking at us, she was studying us. Carefully.

'We got stone rings.' The woman said it as though she didn't expect a response.

'Ah, I sympathise.' Aunt Charlotte took another bite of the limp sandwich. 'I'm a martyr to them.'

I gave the woman a weak smile.

She pointed at the vast array of boulders. ''Ound o'Baskervilles.'

'Yes, thank you.' Mother managed to be far more dismissive.

'Sherlock 'Olmes,' she nodded.

'Who?'

The woman looked at Aunt Charlotte in confusion.

'Be quiet, Charlotte. We're heading for Black Towers. Lord and Lady Black's home. Perhaps you know of it?'

The woman's face soured. 'You should go. Get on there. Fast as you can. Dark's coming.'

'Oh, perhaps we could finish—'

'Go. Rain's coming.' She sniffed deeply and drew her tongue across her bottom lip tasting the air. 'Go.' And she closed the front panel with one decisive movement as if she was quite used to telling people to leave.

'Looks like shop's closed,' Aunt Charlotte spoke with a mouthful of food.

'We should go. The light's fading and I don't like the look of those clouds.' Mother threw her unopened cardboard basket into the bin as she walked towards the car. 'I can't see why we needed to stop. We're going on this safari supper in a few hours.'

'We hadn't eaten today!' Aunt Charlotte looked affronted. 'You might be able to survive on air and irritation, but we can't.'

Mother was already climbing into the car with a face that said there was a lot more irritation to come on this journey.

The endless, stark landscape rolled out on both sides of the car. Grey-white stones were broken teeth across the dark mouth of the moor.

The first spots of rain started almost as soon as we pulled back onto the main road leading through the moor and it gathered pace, falling faster as we drove into the dusk.

At a small crossroads was a low stone mound in the shape of an oblong next to the road. It was thick with moss and a withered bunch of flowers had been laid on it. There was clearly a headstone at one end. I folded out the map at the back of the guidebook.

'We've got the satnav,' Mother sighed.

'Doesn't tell you about Kitty Jay's Grave though, does it?' I flicked through. 'Says it's the grave of a young girl who committed suicide. She couldn't be buried in consecrated ground. She had to be at a crossroads so her spirit couldn't find its way back to people.'

'That's so sad,' Aunt Charlotte said in a low voice.

'Utterly terrifying, if you ask me,' Mother said. 'I don't know why you always insist on telling us these frightening little tales.'

'It's part of the folklore. It's important. It says here that fresh flowers continue to be put on the grave and no one knows where they come from.'

'Utter nonsense,' Mother speeded up a little.

'They're everywhere,' Aunt Charlotte leaned through the gap between the front seats. 'Look over there.' She pointed towards a group of stones clearly arranged in a circle. They dotted the landscape, some small, others wider with larger stones. Time-worn arrangements half buried in the grass.

I glanced down at the map. So many strange and ancient names — Coffin Stone, Hexworthy, Bonehill, Five Wyches Farm and Gibbet Hill. The area was littered with stone circles, cairns and hidden mires. This was a place filled with all manner of lurking dangers. In the darkness they'd be impossible to see.

A mist had fallen so quick it obscured the distant crags already. Perhaps the old woman had been right — we should move on as fast as we could. I felt Mother accelerate.

The lights from houses were sparse and distant, individual pin pricks glowing in the landscape until we came to the edges of the village. The small sign announcing Greystone was overshadowed by a tall, twisted tree bending itself away. The name was worn and barely visible anymore.

Wind buffeted the car. The road behind us had already sunk into the mist. The wipers flicked fast and the windscreen sparkled momentarily with the lights from each house we passed catching on the raindrops, our wheels scything water up high on both sides of the road.

The road slipped round unlit turns and jarred us with sudden deep potholes. I looked at Mother and could see the concentration starting to pain her face. Even Aunt Charlotte was quiet in the back now.

Finally, as the road rose up from the valley, we could see a cluster of lights ahead and the ominous shape of a large castle against the dark mottled clouds.

'This must be it,' Aunt Charlotte leaned eagerly between the two front seats. 'It's a castle!'

'Well done, Kirstie Allsopp,' Mother murmured.

'Who?'

We don't explain that sort of thing to Aunt Charlotte anymore.

As we neared the low outer wall, I could see the spire of a church against the wet slate of the sky. It was on the opposite side of the road to the castle and another large house stood close by. Lights were on in some of the windows of the house, and I thought I saw a shadow pass quickly through the light of a downstairs room.

The car rumbled over a wooden section of the driveway with two large chains lifting up from either side.

'Oh my God, it's even got a drawbridge!' There was a childlike glee in Aunt Charlotte's voice, her face lit from the side by the large flame of a torch.

'If you're going to be such a keen little puppy all weekend I will have to drown you in the moat immediately, Charlotte,' Mother said wearily.

We passed through the gatehouse and below two heavy portcullis gates. Cannons flanked both sides as it opened out into a torchlit central courtyard. Mother drove straight towards a large open door over the other side where a lone figure stood with a hand raised.

Lady Marsha Black was framed in the light of the entrance to the castle, her slender arms spread wide with a whole spectrum of rings flickering across her fingers. She was the very essence of groomed. I'd seen her a few times, but since I was decidedly not a member of book club, I only ever saw the women arrive before hearing the raucous laughter as more Prosecco was opened. Lady Marsha looked very much like she'd moved on from all that. There'd been a strange, imperceptible shift that came with this new status and environment. She was a lot more Champagne than Prosecco now.

CHAPTER 3: THE CASTLE

The castle was every inch the vision of a dark fairy tale. We stood in the great courtyard staring up into that bruised, old sky. The turrets, arched windows, arrow slits and towers looked down on us like we were peasants waiting for some bread. It wasn't hard to imagine Lady Marsha Black dismissing us all with a simple, 'Let them eat cake.' Her pink little twinset and immaculate, smooth brown hair was utterly untouched by the squally air. Mine instantly covered my face the moment I opened the car door, the wind thick with the scent of rain.

'Welcome to our humble abode!' She held up her hands and gave a simpering smile. 'Black Towers.'

'Like the wine?' I enquired with a smile.

'No.' Lady Marsha tightened her mouth. 'We have an "s".' She dropped her hands. Her voice had a weary tone to it as if I wasn't the first person to have said this.

Mother gave me *The Look*.

'Oh, it's marvellous, utterly marvellous, Your Ladyship!' Mother fawned. Numerous torches studded the castle walls, the flames apparently impervious to the wind-driven rain. The fire light glanced off the thick wax of Mother's brand-new Barbour jacket. She lunged forward, displaying a level of desperation I'd only ever seen her employ at the John Lewis sale. But Lady Marsha was already turning into the hallway, leaving Mother to quickly disguise her move with a little skip forward.

We walked through the great oak doorway and I looked up into the stony shadows above. The rough walls seemed to be hewn from the same stone we'd seen at Hound Tor, dark and scarred by weather and time. A lone flag hung limp in the rain and was caught for a moment on a gust of wind. Its emblem fluttered out into the darkness — a large cannon aimed up into the sky flanked either side by a large cannon-ball. In the darkness it could easily have been mistaken for something a little cruder.

I caught Aunt Charlotte's eye and she was smirking. 'Looks like a—'

'Yes, Aunt Charlotte, I see it.'

'Please let my housekeeper take your . . .' Lady Marsha looked me up and down with obvious distaste. 'Your coat and bags.' She was pointing at an older woman, bent and squat as if the life was slowly being pressed out of her.

'Oh, thank you! Thank you!' Mother struggled out of the greasy new Barbour.

I wasn't sure how I was going to cope if Mother was going to be this grateful for everything during the weekend. Mother doesn't usually do gratitude. This had a distinctly nauseating edge to it.

I handed the woman my small, damp rucksack, which she dutifully held at arm's length. I wiped back a strip of long wet hair in an effort to look a little smarter. 'Thank you, Mrs . . .'

'Abaddon,' she snipped. 'It's biblical.'

'Oh, that's nice.' I smiled.

'A destroying angel, I believe.'

Mother and I paused. I heard her take a sharp breath. Lady Marsha looked first at me then Mother, then Aunt Charlotte, who was standing with her mouth hanging slack. An awkward silence weaved its way round as memories returned of those grisly deaths from a different kind of destroying angel we'd all witnessed at the Slaughter House. Each of us looked away in turn.

'Mrs Abaddon, take the coats please and send Miss Morello to serve drinks, if she's not too busy.' There was a definite note of sarcasm in Lady Marsha's tone.

She cleared her throat and turned to us. 'Well, let's get a drink, shall we? We can show you to your rooms later.'

Mother nodded frantically as if she was trying to dislodge something. Sadly, it didn't shift her great big ingratiating grin.

'Mrs Abaddon, any sign of His Lordship?' Lady Marsha had a very obvious look of distaste.

'No, Your Ladyship, I'm afraid not.'

'How unsurprising.' Her eyes were cold.

We followed Lady Marsha through the stone hall. The ceiling was high, but the room still felt darkly oppressive. It could have been down to the distinct lack of lighting or perhaps the vast array of weaponry on every wall. As Marsha walked, she randomly commented on huge displays of pikes and swords set out in over-sized, deadly flower arrangements above thick oak tables. Dark varnished chests were placed at random intervals like a strange display of old coffins. I was tempted to lift a lid and look inside, but the party was moving on at speed and this was definitely not the sort of place to get left behind on your own. Or fall into a large chest.

We passed a closed door on our left with black metal strips similar to bars running the length of the aged wood. As I looked up, I saw a white face peering from above the frame. I let out a quick high-pitched note. The party stopped and turned, almost as one.

Lady Marsha laughed. 'Don't worry, just a death mask. One of the old Lords. Not the current one though.' She sounded disappointed.

I stared at its closed porcelain eyes. 'Oh, that's comforting.'

But the group were moving on at pace down the vast, stone corridor. I hurried after them.

Large, modern, gauche-coloured paintings that screamed expense were hung beside suits of armour, somehow cheapening both. Everything was mismatched as if this new decor might have been specifically chosen to insult the building. It was like dressing a stately grand dame as some sort of cheap, withered Barbie doll. My eyes landed on Mother, who was eyeing me suspiciously.

Lady Marsha flicked her wrist towards various rooms, explaining how they'd renovated and redesigned aspects that hadn't been touched for centuries. It had the sacrilegious feel of someone explaining how they'd rearranged Stonehenge to improve its feng shui.

There was a flippant, almost careless manner to this woman, as if this wasn't even her home. She was acting like a disinterested tour guide. I walked alongside her and Mother, trying to look like I was solemnly appreciating the grandeur — a sort of Stephen Fry visits Chatsworth kind of face.

'So how old is the castle?' I adopted a clipped voice to try and give myself extra gravitas.

'No idea. Wait—' Marsha turned to me — 'you're Ursula, aren't you?'

I winced a smile. In my experience, it's never good when people say that.

'I read your mother's interesting article about how you seem to attract murderers like . . . wait, what did you say, Pandora? "Like *Most Haunted* attracts the disturbed".'

I paused, giving Mother my *really?* face.

'Let's hope your magnetism takes a rest this weekend.' Lady Marsha grinned. 'Don't want any killings at the castle now, do we?'

It was just another moment when I wanted to blend into the air.

'But listen, the article said you guys are a regular little Famous Five—'

'I didn't say that exactly,' Mother interrupted.

'I'm not a mother myself, but using your own daughter to write about murderers, is just . . . so *fascinating*.' She said

19

it in that way where 'fascinating' can easily be substituted with a number of other words — *disgusting, distasteful, repulsive, grim, odd.*

Finally, we ended up at the door to a large sitting room. Marsha told us to come into the parlour, like a spider might invite in flies. It had taken me very little time to stop thinking of this woman as Lady Marsha. Simple Marsha already seemed more appropriate.

As we walked into the vast, velvet-festooned room, I immediately saw there were already some visitors caught in the web. Mirabelle and Bridget.

'And look,' Marsha announced. 'Here's the rest of the little gang you write about.'

Everything about Mother tightened as quickly as if she'd just been vac-packed and put in the *sous vide* machine she'd bought last Christmas and never used.

'Pandora!' Bridget chimed. 'How lovely to see you. And your charming daughter.' She laughed, her thin mouth a wound slowly opening up. 'I've not read that article, I'm afraid. But I haven't really read any of the little things you write.'

Mother's smile spread like a crack through a sheet of glass. 'I've not read any of yours either.'

'I don't write any . . .' Bridget's voice fell away.

A sharp little scream of vicious laughter came from somewhere above us.

I looked up quickly.

'Oh, don't mind Dupin. He's nothing to worry about.' Marsha spoke dismissively and threw out her hand. She rolled her eyes. 'Another of Elzevir's ridiculous ideas.'

'Dupin, *du vin*, du . . .' Aunt Charlotte saw Mother's face and her voice petered out.

Sitting on a thin perch, at the end of the room, was a sharp-faced little monkey with russet-coloured fur. He had a lead round his ankle that tethered him to the wooden beam. Although his mouth looked something like a smile, the rack of teeth on display was far more disturbing. He watched us with two keen, polished eyes. There was an astuteness in the way he surveyed us all, almost mockery. He pinched his eyes together and let out another scream of delight, dancing on agile, little feet.

Marsha gave the animal a spiteful glance. 'Don't worry, he looks smarter than he is.'

'So does Charlotte and it doesn't stop her causing trouble—' Mother stopped as her eyes landed on Mirabelle. Since she found out about it, she hadn't mentioned her beloved Mirabelle moving in with the hateful Bridget. And it's always a sign of trouble if Mother isn't talking about something. Mother doesn't do enigmatic silences.

'Well, we all know each other, so let's get down to it,' Marsha said. 'Who'd like a cocktail? Now, I seem to remember you guys are partial to a bottle or two of Prosecco, so I've had some specially brought in. None of that Champagne nonsense for you, eh? I said to Lord Elzevir, "Zavvy darling, they'll be such good house guests. They really don't need any of the finer things in life. They're such simple, home-spun ladies. It'll be fun *and* cheap."'

As she walked over towards a large sideboard, her laughter and rich spiced perfume rippled along like an expensive car passing by.

Marsha didn't seem to drop the act once. She conducted herself as if the kind of men who would describe her as 'fragrant' were watching at all times. There were no cracks in her armour, at least none that I could see yet.

I stayed close to the door. I like to maintain a secure escape route when I'm in unfamiliar places these days. Mother sat down without speaking and kept her eyes firmly on Mirabelle. She hadn't looked at Mother yet, resolutely staring straight ahead at the large leaded window framed by layers of dark pink velvet curtains. As the table lamps shone across the folds, a rose glow lit the room. The deep sofas were also pink, the fringed lampshades blooming with large, salmon-coloured flowers. The whole effect was quite saccharine and very much at odds with the stark stone walls bristling with shields, crests and swords.

I was distracted by a strange scratching sound near the sofa.

Marsha raised an eyebrow. 'She brought her cat.'

The monkey hissed and screamed again, its eyes fixed on the floor next to the sofa.

'Come on, darling.' Bridget leaned down and picked up the small, wrinkly animal. It was completely hairless and as pink as the furnishings. 'Come on, my little Schrodinger.'

'Wait, you called the cat Schrodinger?' I said doubtfully.

'It seemed appropriate.'

'Why, because you're a pretentious arse?'

Bridget shuffled indignantly in her chair like a twee, uptight librarian. 'Let me tell you something—'

'There is nothing you could tell me that I could possibly want or need to hear.'

Mother settled further into the large flesh coloured armchair.

'Oh, I beg to differ.' Bridget smiled. 'I'm living with Mirabelle and she understands me. She's told me a lot.'

Mother was practically vibrating, a tense ball of anger that might combust at any minute all over the pink velvet. She was staring at Mirabelle, who still wouldn't look back at her.

The monkey clapped eagerly in excitement.

'We're friends, that's all,' Mirabelle said heavily, as if the words were a burden. Her eyes flicked towards Mother. 'I needed a friend. You were so busy with all the interviews and articles and your *daughter*, that . . . that . . . well, I just felt a little . . . *unnecessary*.'

That is Mother's great skill, making people feel unnecessary. One day, maybe she'll make herself feel that way.

'All these years, Pandora.' Mirabelle was barely audible.

Bridget placed the bald cat onto the sofa beside her. Its colour matched the material so perfectly that in the dim light it blended in, leaving only a pair of sharp, dark eyes lingering next to her. She stroked the reluctant animal, dragging thin rolls of the animal's loose skin down its back until those eyes bulged like marbles.

'You just took Mirabelle for granted. She needs *nurturing*.' Bridget made it sound like she was going to consume her, savouring every last morsel.

'Mirabelle,' Mother breathed. '*I* could have nurtured you.'

The monkey laughed.

'Quiet, Dupin!' Marsha handed us our drinks and the monkey fell into immediate silence.

'Now, let's not sound so desperate, ladies. You don't want to ruin the weekend before its even started now, do you? Shall I run you through the itinerary? There's also a document in each of your rooms that outlines the schedule and what we expect of our house guests. Our cleaner, Lucy, is utterly incompetent, so we don't like to rely on her for anything.'

Marsha's newfound refinement seemed to be slipping a little. A coarse, sharper edge was cutting through. 'At the end of your stay you must strip your bed, wash the sheets, pillowcases and towels, dry them and put them back in place exactly as they were. I recommend taking a photograph on your phone so you know precisely where everything should go.' She smiled. 'Miss Morello, Lucy that is, will show you where the washing machine and drier are, if she can remember.'

I stared at her in astonishment. 'I don't think I've ever stayed anywhere that expected house guests to do all that.'

Marsha analysed me until I was very aware of my awkwardness. I sat down on the edge of the over-stuffed sofa.

'I don't think you've ever stayed anywhere I'd be familiar with either, dear,' she drawled.

I looked towards Mother for moral support. I couldn't imagine she'd be too happy about stripping beds and washing sheets. She hadn't shown any inclination towards it before.

But Mother and Mirabelle were still locked in eye combat. They didn't look like they'd taken in anything apart from most of their drinks.

'The safari supper starts at eight, so we'll reconvene just before then. It's going to be enormous fun.' Marsha's tone suggested she thought entirely the opposite.

A violent gust of wind seemed to rock the stones around us, howling its way in disapproval down the chimney and circling the room.

'We move around the village and have a course in each house. Everyone starts here with cocktails and fizz and then we move to . . .' She unfolded a map that she'd picked up from the small side table. 'Verity at the Vicarage first. Jocasta MacDonald and her husband, Ron, are meeting us here.'

'I'm sorry?' I spluttered my drink out. 'Her husband is Ron MacDonald? *Ronald* MacDonald?'

'They're pagans.' Marsha said it as if that was all we needed to know. 'They live in the Lodge. You'll have seen it on your way in. It's all wind chimes and stone mushrooms.'

This was perhaps the first sign that the sleepy village of Greystone had a lot more going on behind its cosy windows and floral drapes than might first meet the eye.

'Then we're moving onto . . .' She scanned the hand-drawn map of the village. It was incredibly detailed and had obviously taken somebody a long time to compile from a lot of careful observation.

'Did you make the map, Marsha?' I asked without thinking.

She looked at me disdainfully. 'I don't have time for that sort of thing! I don't know who drew it up. It just landed on my mat one morning. Then Verity came up with this idea of the safari supper and suggested we use the drawing that had been sent. What does it matter who drew it?'

'May I look?'

She seemed doubtful for a moment then, spotting her own empty glass, handed over the map before moving back towards the long sideboard and the bottle. She watched me distrustfully as though I might be about to set the piece of paper on fire. I've not done that since I got my A level results and Mother couldn't be bothered to look at them. They were good, but the only way I could get her attention was to create a little blaze over her silk woven rug. Life has just carried on in that vein ever since, really — setting fires to get her attention.

I studied the map. There was a lot of detail. Whoever had drawn it had enjoyed being quite meticulous. It seemed like a lot of effort to go to just for a supper party. It was intricately drawn and each house had a name next to it. The castle was clearly marked. I could see the vicarage Marsha had mentioned, and the Lodge, complete with its fast-food pagans. The church was next to the vicarage, and the name Reverend Vert was written next to a small structure at the back of it rather than the vicarage.

There were, in total, ten dwellings in Greystone, including whatever structure was behind the church and, of course, Black Towers. Someone had also found it amusing to leave the 's' off when they'd compiled the map, and someone else, presumably Marsha, had petulantly added the missing letter in red ink.

I'd been completely absorbed by the intricate little map for quite a few minutes when a strange and unnerving grinding noise drew me back into the room. Slowly, the voices petered out, the scraping sound growing louder as we fell silent.

CHAPTER 4: INSTRUMENTS OF TORTURE

On the furthest wall of the room, near the large full-length window looking out onto the lawn, was a tall, wide metal box. The whole front was slowly swinging open on hinges. As I looked more closely, I could see that there were two black holes driven through the metal and the shape around them was that of a loosely drawn head. The structure was shaped like an oversized human body with its hands folded across its chest and its mouth sealed shut.

'Please excuse our iron maiden.' Marsha gave a simpering smile. 'It sometimes does that.'

'Oh, I quite like them.' Aunt Charlotte bounced her leg up and down and nodded her head repetitively as if in time to a rhythm only she could hear.

The upright metal coffin continued to open with a dramatic, cold groan. We fell into a tense silence.

Bridget gasped and clutched the cat closer. 'Dingerling, have courage.'

In one last violent surge, the door opened and a large, limp object slumped against the inside of the door before collapsing onto the floor.

It was a body.

No one moved. I felt eerily calm in those opening moments.

We were staring transfixed at the unmoving form of a man.

'Oh my God!' Aunt Charlotte breathed.

'Elzevir?' Marsha said in disbelief.

A scream lit up the other side of the room.

I turned to see a young woman standing at the door, her eyes bulging and mouth slack with a trail of loose spit dangling from it.

My head was filling up with panic, the pulse surging against the sides of my skull. I looked back to the body. Pin holes of blood started to seep through the caramel-coloured jacket, blooming out across the material in two perforated lines. His strange, gingery-brown hair had fallen at an odd angle to his head. His arms were both beneath him.

The iron maiden stood open, looking down disdainfully at where it had spat him out. The great spikes were dripping with sticky trains of blood.

'You've. Killed. Him!' The woman at the door panted out each word as if she was blowing them at us.

The angry pools surfaced in a blotted pattern down the man's back.

'Elzevir.' The name came out of Marsha slowly in a quiet stream. It had a dreamlike sound to it. Her face was entirely expressionless. It was as if she was looking through what we could see at something else entirely.

'You murderer!' the woman at the door shouted. Her furious reaction stood in stark contrast to Marsha's coldness.

The body lay so still it could have been a very natural pose, resting as though the man had just stumbled a little, and this was merely the pause before he got up and everyone asked if he was all right. The blood stains down his back told a different story. A much more savage one. A brutal death was staring back at us.

Slowly, I began to stand, each of my movements making this seem more real. More believable.

There really was an impaled man lying dead on the sitting room floor. His body was there, right in front of us. My mind hadn't just invented the last few seconds. I wasn't just imagining this in an idle moment at a drinks party, bored and conjuring up dead bodies on the carpet.

Marsha placed her glass down with careful movements, taking a long breath. She began to move towards the bundle of clothes thrown on the floor. Everything about her had the self-conscious action of a person who knows their every move is being watched.

My head felt dull, as if I was watching all this underwater, the movements fluid, the noise muffled. I couldn't close my mouth. My breathing was short, fluttering. There was a dead man. There was a murdered man on the floor. Right in front of us. I couldn't take it in. There was no space inside my head.

'Mother?' I stuttered, the light dizzying in my eyes.

She moved closer towards me. I swayed and looked at the body, leeching out into the pale carpet.

'Don't you touch him!' the woman at the door cried.

'Be quiet, Lucy.' Marsha spoke in a crisp, efficient voice. It echoed in my head. I saw a strange look of confusion pass over her face — almost annoyance, as if a child had spilled something, nothing more than that.

I could feel my heart desperately jittering away inside my chest.

'Touch nothing, Your Ladyship.' Bridget hurried across the room clutching her cat as though there was still a threat, an imminent danger. 'Forensics will be all over it!'

Marsha paused.

Mother had moved close and was at my side, her eyes still on the dead man's outline. She threaded her fingers through mine without looking at me.

I thought I heard Marsha whisper, 'How?' or 'Now?'

It did seem impossible that this had happened just at the moment when we had all gathered here. It was already starting to have a very pre-planned feeling to it, a drama that was timed to perfection and intended to go off at that very second. The door slowly opening to reveal the dead man just as the party had gathered. It all felt very staged.

I caught sight of our reflection in the long, black windows. Rain stippled the image of each person carefully positioned around the dead body.

Aunt Charlotte had adopted a resolute face. 'We need to get help.'

Marsha looked to the door. 'Lucy, fetch Mrs Abaddon.'

The girl didn't move. She was shaking as she watched Marsha with blazing eyes, tears pooling in the bottom lids.

'Now! Please, Lucy.' Marsha had a controlled authority to her that seemed to have surfaced quite naturally and quickly.

The girl let out a small noise of anguish before running from the room.

Marsha moved closer to the body, her eyes pinching into a wary look. She took careful, precise steps, as if she thought the body might leap up at any moment.

It did.

CHAPTER 5: RESURRECTION

In one great explosion of bloody clothing and confusion, the body was on its feet, shouting words I couldn't unpick. The face had a frenzied grin. The arms were spread wide.

'Save us!' Bridget threw herself into a chair, clutching the bewildered cat, her eyes tight shut.

My heart hit the front of my chest. My jaw instantly clenched so hard I felt sure I heard my teeth crack.

'Ah-ha!' the manic face shouted out into the stunned room. 'Got you, you buggers!' A sense of unrestrained glee radiated from the man. He held his arms out rigid on either side as if soaking up the adulation. There was none.

I felt a sharp pain stab right through my chest, the blood all rushing into the centre of me in great surges.

He had a thin trickle of carefully applied blood down one side of his chin. The dark stains that pierced his light-coloured jacket were mirrored on the front as well.

Marsha was nearest to him but hadn't moved. She didn't make a sound but watched him with incisive eyes.

He gave her a bold look in return. 'Not dead yet, m'dear!'

Everyone else was frozen in position, scared to burst this moment's bubble. We all just stared in horrified silence.

When Marsha spoke, each word was meticulous and cold. 'So it would appear.'

She took a sharp breath. 'Ladies, *this* fine specimen is my husband. Lord Elzevir Black.'

Aunt Charlotte was making strange, blustering noises, barely able to hold in her obvious rising anger. 'What the hell are you playing at, man? You could have scared us to death.'

Mother looked as though he had, her face the colour of curdled milk. She held her hand to her chest, as if struggling to hold everything in there. 'I can't . . .' She trailed off. Her other hand gripped mine tight.

A cool voice brought another shockwave to the room. 'Miss Morello said Your Ladyship required my presence as His Lordship was dead.' Mrs Abaddon was at the door looking glacial and grey. 'It would appear that is no longer the case. Should I remain to serve the drinks?'

'Elzevir?' The hysterical girl stood wide-eyed at her side.

Mrs Abaddon gave her a sharp look. '*Lord* Elzevir to you, girl.'

'You're alive?' The girl said it as though she thought it was impossible. 'I . . . I . . .'

Lord Elzevir laughed excitedly, finally lowering his arms to casually take off the now heavily stained jacket. 'Blood capsules.' He pointed to the inside of his jacket. 'Took ages to get them all in the right place.' He gave an indulgent smile.

I could still feel the panicked blood racing through my head. I tried to control my breathing.

Mother's hand was still in mine, and it was hard to tell who was gripping tightest. 'OK?' she whispered.

I nodded once. But every part of me still rippled with the shock like electricity frazzling through to the ends of my fingers, sparkling in my head.

'What kind of freak show have you got going on here?' Mother's anger had surfaced.

The man's expression fell. 'Welcome to my home, madam. And you would be?'

'Pandora Smart.'

31

A cruel little smile appeared on his face. 'Oh yes, one of the so-called Smart Women. Thought you'd love this. You're all about the murders, aren't you?'

I frowned. 'We're not "all about the murders."'

'Not according to your mother's blog.' He paused as if struggling to remember and then gave a laugh. 'Death Smarts.'

My eyes flicked to Mother.

The monkey clapped along. He'd been suspiciously quiet till then — presumably he'd seen the trick being set up and understood too well what was happening.

Lord Elzevir cast an assessing eye over us all. 'Well, ladies, I'm charmed to meet you.'

Aunt Charlotte let out a sharp, dismissive noise.

The monkey screamed in response.

'Can't you keep your bloody monkey quiet, Marsha?' Lord Elzevir Black looked around the room. His slightly beaked nose and the flinty shine of his eyes gave him a hawk-like air; an indulgent smile crept over his face before his eyes finally landed on me.

'Pleased to meet you all.'

A film of sweat had settled on his face leaving it with the pale, greasy look of lard. He stepped out into the room and started to brush himself down. He held up his hands and wriggled the fingers to show us he had nothing up his sleeves. 'Little trick I've been preparing for our newcomers. I like to keep my guests on their toes, don't you know?'

'A comforting thought for the rest of our time here,' Mirabelle muttered.

He pulled a spotted handkerchief from his top pocket in the manner of a cheap magician. In fact, his whole demeanour had a little of the carpetbagger about it — as if there was some trickery to him. He was well dressed but in a way that suggested someone had told him that was how he should dress for this scene. A yellow cravat was bunched unnaturally around his neck and pushed inside his shirt. He threw the blood-stained jacket onto a large wooden chair. 'See if you can do anything with that, Mrs Abaddon.'

She nodded.

The girl beside her was still weeping in great stuttered breaths. The strange, detached way everyone else was responding made her emotional reaction seem out of place, when in fact it was the only genuine acknowledgement of what had just happened. It was a very disorientating picture.

Mrs Abaddon turned to the girl. 'Lucy, take Lord Elzevir's jacket and go and calm yourself down.' She spoke as if the girl's shock was completely out of proportion with what we'd just witnessed.

'I can't believe . . . I—'

'Be quiet girl! Go!'

The girl darted across the room and snatched the jacket up. She paused to look at Lord Elzevir. 'You didn't tell me. How could you?'

He shrugged at her, dismissively.

'Get out!' Marsha barked.

More loud tears broke from the girl as she ran out of the room.

Lord Elzevir appeared utterly unmoved. Nothing was very comfortable about this man. A distinct feeling of unease followed him. He just carried on wiping the smears of fake blood from his hands and chin.

'How very funny you've been, dear. Now, come and let me introduce you properly.' Marsha still looked irritated rather than amused, or relieved that her husband wasn't dead. Perhaps it was just that his tricks had worn very thin, but something about her seemed to suggest there might be more to it than that.

'Ah yes, Champagne all round, I see! Bit of Bollinger or La Grande Dame perhaps?' It was unbelievable how flippant he was being. He was acting as if faking his own death was a daily occurrence here. Perhaps it was.

'This is ridiculous.' Mirabelle looked down when she spoke. 'We're just going to have drinks now, are we?'

'Oh be quiet,' Bridget sighed. 'We've had enough drama.'

Lord Elzevir grinned. 'And who doesn't love a bit of theatre, eh, m'dear?'

The cross-currents of emotion were utterly bewildering.

'Can't beat a bit of fizz, eh? Should really be having Black Tower though, I suspect!' There were traces of an accent on the edges of his voice that he'd obviously worked very hard to conceal. Here was a man struggling to keep something disguised.

Mother slowly let go of my hand. My palm was damp with sweat, but I didn't know if it was mine or hers. I could feel my heart fluttering away like a desperate moth against the inside of my ribcage. I fell into the nearest chair, my head still swimming.

'I do wish you wouldn't be so crass. I hate it when you make that joke. We live in Black Towers, with an "s".'

'You were the one who wanted to rename it. Greystone Castle seemed good enough for centuries of knights and lords.'

They'd moved on so naturally from his gruesome death.

'It's Prosecco, anyway.'

'Ah, yes, the cheap ladies you told me about.'

'Be quiet, Zavvy, and come and say hello properly.'

Mrs Abaddon moved towards him and handed him a drink. He didn't say thank you or even acknowledge her. He took a mouthful and looked around at our stunned faces. I suspected he often looked very pleased with himself. He laughed. 'Come on, ladies. Just a bit of fun! Stop looking so stony faced. After all, no one died.'

CHAPTER 6: THE PLAN

Lord Elzevir downed half of his drink and let out a long, satisfied sigh. 'Marsha, come on. It was just a—'

'Let's not dwell on it.'

He smiled, enjoying her obvious discomfort. 'Oh, I'm so sorry, dear, but you know how I love to slip out of a maiden before I greet my guests.'

He gave an odious grin before taking a large enough mouthful of his drink to leave the impression it was quite badly needed. He wiped the palm of his hand down his mouth and chin like a man more accustomed to downing a pint of lager in a pub. 'Well, I've not seen this many pretty ladies in one place since I took a trip down that road in Amsterdam.'

'For God's sake, Zav,' Marsha sighed.

Aunt Charlotte bent towards me and whispered loudly, 'He means prostitutes, dear.'

'Yes, thank you, Aunt Charlotte.'

Mother had sat back into an overstuffed pink chair, the cushions rising up so high around her that it gave the impression it was swallowing her.

Lord Black leaned awkwardly over the back of it. It made neither His Lordship nor Mother look particularly comfortable. The lights seemed to flicker on command as another gust of wind circled the castle.

'Welcome to Black Towers.' He drained the rest of his drink, then held the glass out to Mrs Abaddon without looking at her.

Marsha's expression of cold rage hadn't moved. She pressed her lips together until they were ringed with a white line.

Mrs Abaddon poured without looking at Lord Elzevir. The only sound was the trickling of the liquid into the glass. He took another deep swig and let out a long, satisfied breath. 'Now ladies, has Marsha brought you up to speed with all this madness?'

Mother's laugh was joyless. 'No. Funnily enough, she was a little preoccupied with her brutally slain husband.'

'Oh, that wouldn't put Marsha off her stride would it now, dear?'

To be fair, he did have a point. Marsha hadn't seemed overly distraught.

I looked at her now, with her vinegar smile.

'I'm Bridget.' Still squeezing the cat close, Bridget held out one hand in the manner of a queen, as if expecting him to bend and kiss it. He did, and she giggled her way through every note of an octave and then back down again. 'Oh, my Dingerling, did you see that? He's not dead after all.'

It was surreal how everyone except me and the hysterical girl seemed to have slipped back seamlessly into some version of normality when a dead man had just been resurrected before our eyes.

'Goodness me, fine Lady Bridget.' Lord Elzevir looked down at the bald cat. 'I take it this is your . . . Dingerling.'

Bridget smiled coquettishly.

He turned his head to the side and looked at Mirabelle. 'And who might this be?'

'I'm Mirabelle.' She sounded guarded, almost apologetic. Her eyes went quickly to Mother and then looked away. Nothing had been the same since our trip to the Hebrides. We nearly died — and lots of other people did.

Mirabelle thought it would be the ideal environment to tell me that, far from being a saint, my beloved father had been a philandering arsehole. She'd kicked a hole right through me, and Mother doesn't like anyone doing that except for her.

'So—' Lord Elzevir fell into a large chair near Mother — 'what's the plan of action then?'

I watched bemused as he continued to wipe the traces of fake blood from his mouth like it was no more than a little sauce rather than the vivid remains of his recent non-death.

'You know very well, Zav, and don't pretend otherwise.' Marsha remained standing. 'The safari supper—'

'Safari supper,' he spluttered and leaned closer towards us. 'Did you ever hear of such a thing?'

'It's quite common these days.' Marsha stared at him. 'If you're under sixty, that is.'

An awkward silence passed through the room.

The monkey clapped again.

'Control that bloody animal, will you?' Lord Elzevir snapped. He seemed to swing so quickly between different moods.

'Quiet now, Dupin,' Marsha said wearily. 'Perhaps he's had a little shock.'

I listened to the rain tapping away at the large, black windows and watched Marsha. Her little jab about age had been quite right. She did indeed look at least twenty years younger than the mottle-faced man opposite. Needle-thin veins wormed through his cheeks in a way that suggested not every decision he took was a healthy one. The whites of his eyes had a dirty, tarnished colour to them, as if they'd seen too many things they regretted. Each of his teeth was outlined with a dark brown stain. He gave the impression of someone wearing make-up to age them and seem more dishevelled than he actually was.

'We're setting off at eight. So be ready for then. We're stopping at Verity's first—'

'Ah,' Lord Black interrupted again, 'murder at the vic-arage! What, ladies?'

Marsha sighed wearily. 'We live in hope, dear.'

'I think we've had enough death for one night.' Mother sat starch stiff in the chair looking pointedly at Lord Elzevir.

He ignored Mother — which is never a good idea.

'Wait.' Lord Elzevir's smile faded. 'Is Verity involved in this nonsense?'

'You know very well she is. It was her idea.'

'I didn't know she'd be hosting anything. Are you sure she'll be all right?' his voice had a more genuine note to it now. He took another large mouthful of his drink. 'Poor love.'

He swung round to Marsha again. 'Do you think she's really up to all this. I don't want—'

'Your sister will be absolutely fine. She asked for the staff to go down there to help. We don't need them up here again tonight, and it looks like Miss Morello might need a little break from your antics.' Marsha's laugh was hollow.

'I've got Mrs White to go over there and sort out the starters. She's there already cooking some sort of mini wellingtons and crab cakes. Verity asked if Mrs White could stay on to help clear up and I've said she can just go home after that. Mrs Abaddon will lay everything out. Verity's actually very excited.'

'Well, if you're sure she'll be—'

'Yes, Zav, I'm sure.' Marsha turned to us and smiled as if we'd suddenly been readmitted to the conversation. 'You'll meet Verity later. She's the first house on our route.'

I was still holding the map. Verity Black's was next to the Vicarage.

'Zavvy just worries,' Marsha continued. 'Verity had a riding accident a few years ago and finds it a little hard to get around. We take care of her.'

She's only doing nibbles. We're off to Tony's for starters.'

'Oh God.' Lord Elzevir threw himself back heavily into his chair and looked around at us all. 'Greystone's very own Paul Daniels.'

'Who?'

Lord Elzevir flashed a confused look at Aunt Charlotte.

'Tony's a magician,' Marsha said. 'Used to be quite big until . . . well, I don't really know what happened. Came down here to get over it all, whatever *it* was. Probably cut someone in half. Anyway, calls himself the *Seer of Greystone*. Hosts all these séance evenings and Ouija board sessions. Very popular with the WI, I'm told.'

I consulted the map. Aunt Charlotte pointed out Greystone Lodge across the road from Lord Elzevir's sister. 'Pagans *slash* fast-food clowns here,' she said. She moved her finger to the house opposite on the map set just a little back from the road. 'Disgraced magician here.'

'Let's hope he can magic a bit more space in that little dolls' house of his.' Lord Elzevir seemed mesmerised by Bridget's rhythmic stroking of the hairless cat. 'Full of voodoo nonsense and spiritual hooey.'

'My, my, Lord Elzevir.' Bridget smiled. 'What a lot of godless characters you've got here. Magicians, voodoo and pagans. Whatever next? The Devil himself?'

'He's already here.' Marsha downed her drink. 'At least that's what the locals say. Over at Widecombe they say they saw a man drinking beer, and when it ran down his throat, they heard it sizzle and saw steam rise out through his mouth. There's a lot of superstition out here on the moors.' Her eyes never left Lord Elzevir.

Another taut silence fell.

I watched as the monkey reached out with his nimble little fingers towards Lord Elzevir's head. From the back, the little animal carefully lifted the edge of what was clearly a toupee before dropping it down again. Lord Elzevir frowned and, not realising what had happened, smoothed his hand over his head. He took another drink. The monkey clapped and gave me a cunning little smile. Marsha winked at the monkey.

'It all sounds like a lovely, fun evening.' Mirabelle said in a flat voice. She gave a weak smile, trying so hard to be nice that it was positively nauseating. I preferred her before when she was leering at me from Mother's side and judging my every move. Mother was studying Mirabelle.

'Yes,' Marsha began, 'on to Greystone Cottage for the main course.'

'Oh Christ.' Lord Elzevir was beginning to sound like a petulant teenager faced with a family Christmas. I should know. I'm twenty-seven but I still have the urge to be surly, especially living with Mother and the family Christmases we have to endure. They've never been any good since Dad left — well, died.

'The Bradshaws.' Marsha raised a knowing eyebrow at Lord Elzevir, as if she was somehow intending to provoke him. 'Harriet and Gerald are Greystone's resident historians, self-appointed protectors of our village's heritage and a general broadsword in our side. They have blocked and objected to every single piece of work we've wanted to do on the castle. The fight over the murder hole nearly turned very nasty indeed.'

'Murder hole?' Aunt Charlotte repeated slowly.

'Hmm. It's a hole they used to pour boiling oil out of onto invaders and attackers.'

'I'll have to look into getting one,' Mother said tartly.

'Bloody waste of time and a lot of money. We literally had to preserve a hole in the roof! Unbelievable.' Lord Elzevir grunted. 'And I had to pay to make it safe! Safe, I ask you! It's called a murder hole. What's safe about that?'

The monkey did a little back flip on his perch. He reached out towards Lord Elzevir's wig again and gave it a cheeky little flick. Lord Elzevir frowned and drank as if he was inhaling it. The little monkey was getting bolder, and it was beginning to have the distinct flavour of a well-practised routine.

'Oh, the murder hole debacle was all done with ages ago.' Marsha swept the idea away with her hand. 'Joseph fitted some sort of extra-strong glass up there. You could jump up and down on it and you wouldn't go through.'

The monkey jumped up and down as though he could understand every word she was saying.

'And you'd know all about jumping up and down with Joseph, wouldn't you?'

There was a pause. Marsha gave Lord Elzevir another challenging look before she continued with the outline of our tour.

'The last stop is the Peacocks. Millicent and her partner Cassandra live at the far end of the village in Rose Cottage. They are a little . . . well, they don't come out much.'

'In the daylight,' Lord Elzevir scoffed.

'For heaven's sake, Zavvy. We're doing this and that's it. Look, my lovely old book club's here and everything. Let's try and be more . . . inviting.'

Lord Elzevir laughed. 'And you're so very inviting, aren't you, dear?' He smiled round us all, but no one was smiling back.

'You're just sore because you've got to go to the Peacocks. My dear husband still owes them for work their interiors shop did here at the castle over a year ago.' Marsha smiled as if she'd scored a point.

'*Inferiors* shop, more like. The bloody stuff was shoddy and badly made. Hardly suitable for a residence such as this.' He quaffed back his drink and held out the glass again. 'Looked like they'd salvaged it all from the cemetery.'

Mrs Abaddon refilled his drink, carelessly slopping it down the sides of the glass until it dripped onto the man's moleskin trousers. She hadn't given the impression, until now, of being a careless sort of person.

'Watch it there! Cordings' finest, these.' He wiped down the legs of his trousers and rearranged the Tattersall shirt. He looked every inch the man playing the part of the country squire.

'You need to go and change.' Marsha drained her glass. 'We're going in an hour and I don't want us to be late.'

'Oh, for God's sake.' He looked down at the dark splashes on his trousers. 'What does it matter? We'll be soaked to the skin soon anyway.' He gestured at the large windows running with rain. Our blurred figures were all still set out across the glass like a stage set with all its actors carefully placed, poised for the start before the lights go up. 'It's belting it down. How are we supposed to move around the village in this? The road'll be treacherous. Think about Verity.'

'I'm always thinking about Verity,' Marsha sighed. 'She doesn't need to come if she doesn't want to but she's very keen. She'll have Cook and Mrs Abaddon. If we didn't go out when it was raining, we'd never go out at all. Put some boots on and a coat. We can dash between the houses. It'll be fun. Remember that? *Fun?* Something we used to do.'

Lord Elzevir paused. He seemed to be considering his next words very carefully. 'Will *he* be there?'

'Who?' Marsha had turned her back to the room but, from her tone, it was very obvious she knew the 'who' Lord Elzevir was referring to.

'You know who I mean. Him.' His voice was flat but not emotionless.

Our eyes swung back to Marsha, who still hadn't turned. I glanced back at our image reflected on the long, dark windows.

'Greengage.'

Marsha didn't move. 'I don't know what you mean, I'm sure.'

Bridget stopped stroking Dingerling. 'Greengage. It's a type of plum.'

'I don't know if he's coming. Perhaps,' Marsha said slowly. 'How should I know? And what does it matter if he does anyway? He lives in the village. He has every right to come.'

Lord Elzevir imitated choking. 'I think he forfeited his rights when he decided to dip his nib in the village ink well.'

Marsha turned, her face flushed. 'It isn't the time for this.'

'Oh, I think we should warn the ladies what kind of man lurks in the bushes of Greystone. Still hasn't mended my portcullis either.'

'It's not broken. You've just lost the remote control. *Again.*'

'Remote control?' Aunt Charlotte interrupted. 'You have a remote-controlled portcullis?'

'Zavvy's idea.' Marsha lifted her glass to her lips and let it linger there as she watched Lord Elzevir.

Mother cleared her throat. 'I think I might need to freshen up after the little incident.'

Aunt Charlotte frowned. 'Have you let yourself down?'

Mother shot her *The Look*. 'I meant Lord Elzevir's near-death experience.'

'Oh.'

'Perhaps we should head to our rooms.'

'Good idea.' Marsha slammed her glass down and turned towards the door. 'Mrs Abaddon, I'll take them up. I could do with some fresh air!' She looked pointedly at Lord Elzevir. 'You can stay and clear up Lord Elzevir's mess.' She nodded towards the bloody iron maiden.

Mrs Abaddon raised an eyebrow but said nothing — as if this wasn't the first time she'd been asked to perform a strange, random duty.

'That's right.' Lord Elzevir seemed to stagger a little. 'You go and have a good natter with them all about Joseph Greengage and what you get up to in an afternoon.'

'We *get up to* talking through all the maintenance jobs you want doing and your bloody stupid portcullis.' Marsha turned to us as we all began to wander behind her. 'Elzevir wants his portcullis to be like a garage door.'

'Bloody good idea, it is.' His words were blending into one another a little too much now.

'It's never worked. You've had to sit in the car for half an hour or more trying to get the bloody thing to work. When it's up it should be down, when it's down it should be up.'

'Greengage knows all about that sort of thing . . . Carrying on with young Scarlett Bradshaw as well now, isn't he?'

Marsha looked stung.

We started to file out of the room, our heads bowed, almost as if it was us who should be in disgrace. I glanced back at the room and the open iron maiden, still dirty with fake blood. The incident felt so distant, and both Lord Elzevir and Marsha had acted so indifferently that it seemed now as if it couldn't possibly have happened at all and I'd somehow imagined the whole thing. Which I'll admit has happened before — but I don't do that sort of thing anymore.

I paused for a moment and looked back at Lord Elzevir. 'Wait, Lord Black?'

He raised his head, but the saggy piece of skin that bulged over his eyelids hung too low over his eyes to allow much movement. They had a hooded, weary look to them. But there was still a hint of something dishonest lurking there.

'What's your cook called?'

'Cook? Why? She's dreadful . . . Theresa White. Or as I like to call her, Theresa *Sh*—'

'So you're Lord Black.' I picked up the map. 'The vicar is Vert or "green". There's Greengage the plum, Mrs Peacock, Miss Scarlet, and your cook is Mrs White?'

'Can't imagine cook is married, must say,' he slurred.

'Where's Colonel Mustard?'

'Who?' Marsha was at the door looking equally bemused. 'There's only Lee left, if that's what you're asking, and he's not in the military. He's a farmer. Or will be until Zavvy evicts him. Why, do you know him? Lee Colman?'

'Can we just get on?' Mother turned and walked out.

Marsha waited for us in the hallway. 'Sorry about all that with Zavvy.' She said it in an off-hand way as if he'd just made a small faux pas rather than staged an elaborate and bloody murder scene. 'He drinks too much and thinks he's being entertaining. He gets a little . . .'

She paused and stretched her mouth apologetically until her lips were very thin. Her eyes glimmered in the dull light as if a new sheen had just washed over them. 'He doesn't mean anything by it when he's . . . Anyway, yes, let's get on. Ignore him.'

But her anxious eyes seemed to say that she couldn't. I looked at her hands, so beautifully manicured, yet the tell-tale edges of each nail were bitten away and picked until they were raw. She adjusted her thick string of pearls and they clicked against one another. I caught a glimpse of a livid, circular bruise on the side of her neck. It was small enough and deep enough to have been made by a thumb. This woman had the worrying signs of someone who might be too entrenched to fight her way out.

But who can say what goes on behind closed doors?

What was certain, even then, was that this safari was possibly going to be a little bloodier than we'd first imagined. Just how much bloodier would be a surprise to us all.

CHAPTER 7: THE SAD AND THE DEAD

The tension lingered on Marsha's face even though we'd left the room, and Lord Elzevir, behind. She was a lot more self-conscious, as if she'd just remembered we were guests and not just people who happened to be there while they had an argument.

'You mustn't mind us. Always a lot of *banter* here.' She smiled, looking for expressions of acceptance and understanding. 'He doesn't mean any of it. Well, he might about that little tramp, Scarlett Bradshaw.'

'Scarlett Bradshaw,' I repeated slowly and looked down at the map.

Marsha seemed surprised that I still had it. She placed a manicured finger on a house halfway down the road from the castle. 'The Cottage. She's Harriet and Gerald Bradshaw's daughter. They're not our favourite friends.'

'Doesn't sound like many people are.' Bridget let the cat down, and for the first time, I noticed it was wearing a collar with a lead. The hairless cat ambled about, looking strangely naked crawling across the flagstones.

Marsha began to walk on ahead as she talked about the villagers. 'Harriet and Gerald Bradshaw are our resident archaeologists and history buffs. All very Sealed Knot and metal detectors. Drives Zavvy mad.' She shook her head slowly. 'You know. About the castle. This should be preserved. That should be preserved.' She turned and smiled. 'We're so preserved sometimes it feels like we've been pickled.'

'Quite a lot of the time, I should imagine.' Aunt Charlotte turned to me and mimed downing a glass of something.

Marsha looked unamused but continued. 'They'd get a preservation order on toilet paper if they could. Always complaining about our renovations.' She waited and passed a glance over us all. 'You know what it's like.'

Clearly, we didn't.

'To be honest, it sometimes feels like we're living in a museum.'

'Oh, Marsha, you're not that old!' Aunt Charlotte smiled.

Marsha tilted her head.

'Not sure about Lord Elzevir though,' Mother murmured.

'It means we're left with all manner of nonsense and paraphernalia we have to conserve.' Marsha held out her arms to the walls. From the number of lances, shields, pistols and rapiers set in great swirls and spiked designs, they could have hosted a full-scale battle in this place, which is always useful when Mother comes to stay.

'Look. Just look at this.' She guided us over to the side of the corridor and pulled back the corner of a large, threadbare tapestry.

'A wall,' Aunt Charlotte nodded. 'Very nice. Good stones.' She patted them heartily.

Long oak beams, their grain darkened with age, were set into the wall. Marsha ran her fingers down the edge of one plank, and just before she reached the stone floor, she started to pull. She glanced up at us and raised an eyebrow before turning back and dragging the wood towards her. It opened like a small door.

I bent and peered into the small stone cave hollowed out of the wall.

'A priest hole,' Marsha whispered conspiratorially.

'A priest's what?'

Marsha looked at Aunt Charlotte.

We were silent for a moment staring into the dark cupboard in the wall.

'It's where priests hid if people were coming to the castle,' Marsha said quietly.

Mother turned to Mirabelle. 'Oh, you know, Mirabelle, for when people are trying to hide where they're living!'

A large crease gathered between Mirabelle's eyes, and the frightening thought occurred to me that she might just be about to cry. I looked away quickly.

'Let's not be jealous now, Pandora,' Bridget sneered. 'Friendships change.'

'Bloody hell,' Aunt Charlotte's voice echoed. She had most of her head inside the small hole now, and I could only hope she wasn't considering wedging all of herself in there. 'How on Earth did they fit inside? You can't swing a cat in here.'

'We could try.' Mother looked down at Bridget's feet, where Dingerling was crouching like a small, shaved familiar.

Marsha nodded solemnly. 'Many died.'

'What, cats?' Aunt Charlotte peered back at her from inside the hole, her eyes glistening out of the darkness.

'No,' Marsha looked puzzled, 'priests. Many priests died from starvation or asphyxiation in priest holes. There's tell of a local priest, here in Greystone — the Bradshaws told us about him. The village was full of Roundheads, sweeping the area. They were crawling the streets in search of a Jesuit father, Richard Wyatt. They sent out the priest hunters to track down those in hiding and on the run.'

'Right.' Aunt Charlotte's face lit as she pulled herself out from the hole. 'I get you. Kind of like *Nuns on the Run* but with priests . . . and more deaths.' She had an intensely serious expression on her face.

Marsha frowned but continued. 'The old lady of the castle was Catholic and had the priest sheltered here for months. She was good at hiding him. Very good. Nicholas Owen himself built this priest hole.' Marsha nodded towards the tiny stone chamber.

Our faces remained blank.

'Nicholas Owen built many of the priest holes and tunnels. He was the principal priest hole creator at the time of Elizabeth the First. They lead all over. Smugglers used them after that for a while.'

'Good title.' Aunt Charlotte nodded, still with an intense look of concentration. 'Principal Hole Creator. The Creator of the Principal Hole. Hole—'

'Enough!' Mother snapped.

'Fiendishly clever, some of them were.' Marsha parroted the words with pride but it sounded distinctly like borrowed knowledge. However disparaging she was about the people fighting to save the history of the castle, she'd definitely memorised these snippets of historical significance about her home.

'Nicholas Owen was tortured and killed though, of course,' she added flippantly. 'He's the patron saint of escapologists and illusionists. So Tony tells me, anyway. Very appropriate, given my husband lives here. His Lordship's very good at sleight of hand and trickery.' There was a bitter note to this final comment.

We all busied ourselves looking at the hole in the wall.

'Well, that's according to Tony, anyway. I don't know how much of it is true, but they say the ghost of an emaciated priest drags itself from this hole in the night and is so starved its bones crack and clip against the stones.'

A thread of cold air passed down my neck.

'Tony?' Mirabelle glanced anxiously into the hole as if he might still be in there.

'Tony Voyeur, remember? Our resident magician. You'll meet him later. He's doing a very controversial gazpacho.'

'Are we all expected to join in?' Aunt Charlotte looked worried. 'I'm not very nimble.'

'Soup, Aunt Charlotte,' I explained quietly.

'Yes, cold soup.' Marsha began to walk away down the long stone corridor. 'Not enough effort, according to my husband. There's been a lot of emails.'

A solemn air had settled over our group. In single file, we climbed a narrow staircase that circled round. I could hear Aunt Charlotte behind me, breathing quite heavily.

The stones were worn and the lighting poor. More than once I saw Mirabelle's foot slip as she walked ahead of me. She seemed very unstable, and it occurred to me how much more fragile she was generally. I didn't know what was more disturbing, the thought of her falling or the thought of her falling on me. She still hadn't spoken much and was avoiding Mother. This was a definite thunder cloud waiting to break.

As we surfaced at the top of the staircase, the room opened out into a long corridor lined with dark wood panelling. There was an undisturbed feel to this part of the castle as if Marsha and her husband did not come here as much. There'd certainly been no renovations. The thick black handles on the windows were rusted and didn't look like they'd been used in decades. It would have taken a huge amount of strength to open those now. The window frames were riddled with holes and a few panes of glass were cracked. It was such thick, distorted glass that it cast an oppressive light that suggested we were no longer permitted to see the outside world very clearly. As if we were being sealed in.

The walls were hung with various portraits.

'Family?' Aunt Charlotte panted.

'No idea who most of them are,' Marsha said dismissively. 'All look pretty miserable though, don't they? They say this corridor is haunted by a lady who was murdered by her husband.'

We let the comment hang in the air. Marsha smiled self-consciously. 'Lady Greystone is said to have been beaten and held hostage by her husband. I think we've got a painting of her somewhere.'

'Could this be it?' Bridget enquired. 'The one with the brass plaque below saying "Lady Greystone"?' She gave Marsha a self-satisfied little smile.

'Oh, how clever of you, Bridget!' Marsha lifted the corners of her mouth but no one could have described it as a smile. 'Lord Greystone was her fourth husband. He married her for the money, you see. Legend is she killed him as well.'

'What do you mean "as well"?' Mirabelle spoke hesitantly, staring at the sombre painting.

'She killed all four husbands.' Marsha leaned in conspiratorially. 'They say she rides out across Dartmoor down towards Tavistock in a carriage made of her husbands' bones, a skull of each one on the corners. She travels with a great black hound with blood-red eyes.'

'Aha.' Bridget made a noise that she presumably thought made her sound intelligent. 'Yes, I believe that might be the origin of *The Hound of the Baskervilles*.'

'Gosh, Bridget,' I said wide-eyed. 'You *are* well-informed. What made you think that? The fact that we're on Dartmoor and there was a massive hound with red eyes?'

Bridget glared at me, before thrusting her chin up. 'Come along, Dingerling. You too, Mirabelle.' She used the same voice for both of them.

Mirabelle still seemed very cowed. I could even have started to feel a little sorry for her if I hadn't managed to store up so much anger for her over the years. Mirabelle and Bridget walked on behind Marsha and I caught Mother's eyes following them suspiciously.

'Let them be, Pandora,' Aunt Charlotte sighed. 'They're happy.'

'They don't look it,' Mother snapped.

'Since when were you an expert on that?' I couldn't help myself.

'I'm considering a career as a well-being and life coach, if you must know.' Mother pursed her lips in defiance.

'You?'

'Yes, me, Ursula.'

'You hate coaches, Pandora,' Aunt Charlotte said. 'Remember that trip to—'

'I don't care what you think of it. You're not going to stifle my journey.' Mother shook her head and walked on after them.

I looked at Aunt Charlotte, who just casually shrugged. 'It was Pontypridd, August 1997. Dreadful trip. The tour guide was a bigamist from South Shields.' She nodded towards Mother and Mirabelle. 'Best not to get in the middle of that though.'

She was right. Mirabelle and Mother's battle was not mine. Mother doesn't do *friendly* fire.

Marsha glanced back towards us. 'Ladies, shall we get you to your rooms?'

We followed her down the long corridor, lined each side with the portraits of yet more beautiful, wealthy women with sad eyes. It looked like one of Mother's drinks parties.

One was a painting of a girl about my age, wearing a high, white wig. She was so delicate and looked out at me with a melancholy that seemed to suggest she never got much older. There was a small bird at her feet and a dog. Her pale blue dress had the sheen of silk and was so voluminous it made her seem even more doll-like. Her hands emerged from the vast cuffs, ending in slight little fingers that were barely bigger than a child's.

'She's beautiful,' I said quietly.

'If you like that sort of thing.' Marsha turned down the corners of her mouth. 'We want to freshen this up. Elzevir thought we might put up a few Banksys.'

As we walked along the dark red strip of carpet, our muffled feet seemed like such an intrusion on this sacred little world. Marsha and Elzevir Black must have felt like this every day. The fake lord and lady who'd taken up residence somewhere they so clearly didn't belong.

A door was at the end of the corridor on the right. Marsha opened it with a flourish. The first thing I noticed was that there was no lock. Locks are very important to my family. My old therapist, Bob, used to say Mother and I should open the doors to each other more often. We should see each other as a lock and key that fit perfectly. We've tried for a while to replace Bob since he embarked on his monastic journey of self-discovery, but after the fifth therapist left we stopped looking. We've finished with therapy or therapy has finished with us. Now I just talk to Dad.

'Ursula, I've put you in here. It's quite Gothic. I thought that would suit you.' I couldn't tell if Marsha was being sarcastic or not.

Usually, Mirabelle would offer up a snide little comment at this point, but she stayed silent. It was becoming quite unnerving. I almost wished that the vicious old Mirabelle would resurface from the quiet little shell she'd retreated into. She just seemed so replaced.

'This is nice, isn't it dear?' Aunt Charlotte cast a doubtful eye over the room. She was concerned. Again. Aunt Charlotte spends most of her life being concerned about things she has no intention of fixing.

'I'll be fine, I promise,' I murmured to her.

Marsha frowned. 'Is everything—'

'I'm fine. Please don't worry.' Somehow, every time I try to reassure people, I manage to make it sound like I might have some lurking issues. I do. But Lady Marsha Black didn't need to know about them.

'Right, well if you're sure you've got everything you need . . .' On this occasion, I was fortunate. Marsha was the kind of woman who had no wish to know anything about other people's problems. She seemed to have enough of her own. And Mother would be able to fill her in amply on how difficult I am.

Aunt Charlotte gave me another 'Are you OK?' face and I nodded.

Their voices disappeared quickly down the corridor, as if they were making a hasty exit.

I was alone.

CHAPTER 8: THIS CASTLE HAS A GHOST

The room was quiet, peaceful except for the sad whine of the wind at the windows. It sounded so forlorn, so pitiful that it was easy to imagine pulling back those thick folds of curtain to see a bone-white face at the glass, the fine skull of the abandoned priest or the vengeful eyes of a cruelly treated wife waiting solemnly. My thoughts landed on Marsha and her disorientating switches between the self-possessed, gauche wife of Lord Elzevir and the barely disguised, anxious victim, consigned to whatever fate she was enduring. She seemed to inhabit two different personas at the same time.

I walked further into the tired room, dust sighing out with every step. The four-poster bed, in the middle of the room, was hung with heavy rose-covered drapes as if a great garden had sprung up around it to engulf Sleeping Beauty. The curtains were open but fell in such vast swathes of old fabric down each side of the window that they covered a large section of the opposite wall. The vines and creepers were beginning to overwhelm the entire room.

Another desperate-eyed portrait glared out from the wall. This woman looked pallid with fear, giving the very distinct impression she might even have been walled up behind the painting. Everything smelled of a room that had just been opened up, freshly disturbed, but the scent of neglect still clung to it. Perhaps Lord and Lady Black hadn't renovated quite so much of the castle as they liked people to think. Only the areas that were regularly seen had been played with, and even then it seemed like quite superficial work. The bones of it were still the same — all faded carpets and old-fashioned furnishings. They'd been at great pains to blame the Bradshaws for frustrating their grand design schemes, but I wondered if the tales of Lord and Lady Black's vast wealth were running a little dry. A place like this had to be a money pit. Mother had been very vague about how Lord Elzevir made his money, which is unlike Mother. She likes to know everything about a person's finances before she starts to assess how much they are worth to her.

This room certainly hadn't been subjected to any kind of programme of renovation. It was stifled with swathes of ancient fabric, badly worn by age, and dark wooden furniture bruised by time. Even the light was jaded. This room wasn't just neglected. It had been forgotten. It was the sort of room that makes you doubt that you'll emerge unscathed in the morning.

There was a small stand in the corner with a little china wash bowl and jug that looked purely ornamental. At least, I was hoping there would be a bathroom. My bag had been carefully positioned at the end of the bed on a small stand. It looked dirty and worn even here. I heard another fierce wave of rain batter against the window and the curtains seemed to sway out into the room. The dim side lights flickered.

I sat on the edge of the high bed. It was hard and didn't give much beneath me. There was a small bedside table with a few books propped up against an old lamp, all of which looked like disturbing bedtime reads. Titles such as *Richard Branson: Finding My Virginity*, *How to Be More Downton Abbey in the Bedroom*, *Think Yourself Rich — Think Yourself More Hair* and *Unleash Your Inner SAS* gave away the fact that Lord Elzevir might occasionally sleep in this room. There'd been a nod towards this being a guest bedroom as someone had added a few tattered classic books that looked as though they'd been bought from one of those companies that sell books by the foot for home décor rather than for reading. But *Moonfleet*, *Rebecca* and *The Complete Adventures of Sherlock Holmes* certainly didn't look comfortable nudging up against *How to Swear Like Gordon Ramsay and Really Mean It*.

There was only one book I was really interested in at that moment. I unbuckled the side pocket of my bag and pulled out the battered old Bible. I held it close. Its leather was worn soft and black as a priest's robes. The thought of that hole hidden behind the tapestry crawled into my imagination and the poor devils left to rot in a small stone tomb downstairs, forgotten, abandoned by all but their faith. Their belief, a dirty secret to hide away.

I ran my finger along the edge of my father's Bible. Secrets are a necessary evil.

I opened it and there, in the hollowed-out pages, was my father's hipflask. I unscrewed it and took a great mouthful of the brandy. It passed over my tongue and burned its way into my chest. A feeling of life rushed through me. A transient feeling but worth the moment of illusion. Everybody needs their slipstream in life.

That was the first time that I saw the dark figure here. It was in the corner, watching me. I didn't move.

Its head was bent and shoulders curved over as if a great weight rested there and never left him. I should have felt something — fear, shock, sympathy even. But I'm immune. My heart is numb now.

'Dad.' I took another drink. 'You decided to come then.'

The figure lifted its head. His ivory eyes locked with mine.

I don't tend to mention that I see my father's ghost. Not straightaway. It colours people's impression of me. They become a little more . . . *distrustful*. A little more wary round me. He's always there, even if he's out of sight. Even if I can't see him, he still pierces little holes into my brain that just won't close ever again.

His death is a silent weight now, just as he is a silent spectre. Death robs people of their voices but their actions still reverberate. That's what speaks for him now. What he did. He is shame, standing in the corner of my room. And I am anger. I can't let go of that anger. Maybe if I did, I'd let go of him too.

I passed him another dismissive look so he knew that all my rage was still alive. Festering with the thought of his betrayal. Sometimes I feel like I'm becoming the ghost in the corner, but he's still there to remind me I'm not. He remains.

His shape drifted in the corner as if we were drowning together without a care in the world to save ourselves. It's very easy to become mired in grief, a great quicksand that will pull you under the surface of life. Just when you think you've found safety it drags you back under, not enough to completely smother you, of course, but just enough to make each breath a struggle.

He doesn't speak. He never speaks. Perhaps I should be grateful for that at least. I don't even know why he turns up anymore. Not after I found out the truth last year. He'd been an icon to me, something to worship in my darkest hours in my own cramped, broken hiding place. He didn't used to bring happiness but he did bring a stillness, a calm from the great raging tide of grief that he left behind. I still cherished that sense of kinship even after he died. I was thirteen when I felt the life slip out of him, as easy as air from a balloon. His untethered soul just floated away and left.

At least I thought it did until he started to appear again as if he had unfinished business. Which was true. Last year I found out he wasn't quite the martyred soul I thought. Not quite the patron saint of me. More a fickle soul in torment seeking forgiveness. He morphed so easily from saint to sinner.

There'd been another woman when he died. He'd cheated on Mother, cheated on me, and then just left us all with the pain of his death. For years, I'd painted Mother as the guilty party, the dark shadow in my loneliness. But I'd been wrong — misjudged their souls. I suppose that's worthy of punishment too.

I don't talk about it very much to Mother. Her grief is a closed book. She doesn't do self-pity. She doesn't do pity at all. And I don't talk about it to Dad. The vague, smoky shape just stands there with that look of the damned on his face.

I took another dose of the brandy. 'I don't know why you bother to come anymore.' I screwed the lid on nonchalantly. 'I should just give you your forgiveness and then you can disappear.' I looked at the pathetic outline in the corner. His head lifted and, for a brief moment, his eyes pierced me. I turned away.

'But I'm not going to do that. That's too easy. So you just carry on floating around and I'll ignore you. Seems like a simple punishment for us both, I'd say.'

His face clouded over. He was trying to figure me out but he never could. I know that now. I know my desperation and loss had distorted everything. That toxic blend of love and grief squeezed me tight, like a hug that starts to become unwelcome. Sometimes the angle that grief takes can distort everything else.

'Here's to punishment.' I held up the flask to him then aggressively drank.

Knock, knock.

'Ursula, who are you talking to in there?'

It was Mother. She doesn't leave me on my own for long these days. Perhaps she should have considered the implications of telling me the man I worshipped, who died in my arms, was a cheat and a liar. But Mother doesn't do forethought. To be fair, it was Mirabelle who leaked the information first, but she looked like she was getting more than her share of punishment now.

'I'm coming.' I pushed the Bible into a small bedside draw and shut it. Someone had hung my coat on the back of the door. It was the kind of house where other people's belongings were easily interfered with in the name of assistance. I took the Bible back out of the drawer, went over to the door and took down my coat. I slipped the Bible into a large inside pocket. I didn't look back at the shape of Dad. I didn't owe him that.

Mother stood at the door, dressed in another country-based outfit that involved a lot of velvet-trimmed tartan. She looked like she'd fallen out of *Country Life* magazine's Hogmanay special. The telltale smell of her own hipflask announced itself loudly. A present from me last Christmas, and I'd even hollowed out a copy of *Gone Girl* especially to house it. It did actually raise a smile from Mother and, more than that, she uses it all the time.

'I had the radio on,' I said. We both looked back into the room. It was very obvious there was no radio.

I walked on ahead down the corridor, my footsteps muffled by the thick, red carpet. I could feel Mother's eyes on my back watching my every move closely as if she might have to describe them in detail at some later date. Mother is always trying to open me up as if she's attempting to see inside me. She's always looking for the secret of me. Secrets are so fascinating to people.

CHAPTER 9: NEVER CAGE YOUR GUESTS

Downstairs, most people had changed except for me. I slipped a mint in my mouth. I always carry them. Mother tapped my hand and I handed her one too.

'Right gang, are we ready for a little safari?' Marsha looked overly excited in that strained way that seemed to colour everything she did. She and Lord Elzevir had stationed themselves at opposite sides of the pink parlour, each of them clutching a glass. Lord Elzevir was beginning to look increasingly morose as the alcohol took its toll. His face was florid and a thin line of sweat left a sheen on his top lip.

'I want to show them the gatehouse first,' he slurred.

'What? We don't have time for that now, darling.' Marsha made it sound almost like a plea. 'You can do the tour tomorrow morning. There'll be much more time then, dear.'

Throughout all this, Dupin had edged his way along the perch and was carefully lifting the edge of Lord Elzevir's toupee again. He was being a little bolder now, pulling the back up much higher.

I looked down at my feet and saw Bridget's cat had a small sheepskin-style coat on.

Bridget eyed me suspiciously as if I might be some form of threat to the cat. I smiled, and that seemed to make it worse. Mirabelle was, of course, sitting next to her and gave me an unexpected smile in return that was even more unnerving.

Mother purposefully and very deliberately looked away. Mirabelle's eyes fell.

'Be warned! Zavvy will want to show you *everything*. He's got a full tour. There's hours of the stuff. Cannons, trebuchet, and we've even got our own ducking stool.'

'Yes,' Lord Elzevir slurred. 'For any of you wayward little witches.'

As he staggered to his feet, the monkey quickly snatched off the fake hair piece and put it on his own head. The animal began to stumble along his perch in perfect mimicry of Lord Elzevir.

'What the Devil . . .' Lord Elzevir's face was puce now. He slapped his hand on his bald head and began feeling around it. He swung round to see the monkey dancing.

Dupin paused, the wig still on his head. He made a low sound. 'Uh-oh.' Then smiled at us all.

'Bloody buggering animal! Marsha, do something!'

She laughed.

'Come here, you little—'

The monkey paraded up and down in the gingery-brown wig.

Lord Elzevir lunged at the monkey and clattered into a suit of armour. He looked at the rocking helmet accusingly as if it might have someone inside.

'Come on now, Dupin darling,' Marsha said smoothly. 'Give His Lordship his little wiggy back. There's a good boy.'

Dupin looked crestfallen but slowly held out the small pile of very ruffled hair.

Lord Elzevir snatched the hairpiece and smacked it down clumsily on his head. It sat at a strange skew-whiff angle with tufts sticking up in peaks. 'That monkey must go!'

He turned to the rest of us. 'Right, you witches, we've got drinks in the great hall.' He made an effort to smooth down the wig while glowering at the monkey.

'Lead on, Macduff,' Bridget said cheerily and picked up the bald cat, who seemed fascinated by the wig.

'Who?'

I studied Aunt Charlotte for a moment. 'Is there anyone you do know, Aunt Charlotte?'

'Lots of people, darling. But I'm not sure you've met them.'

We filed out and assembled in the Great Hallway, a process that somehow had the feel of a fire drill rather than a cocktail party. The monkey screamed and applauded our departure.

'I should ring its bloody neck,' Lord Elzevir grumbled.

At the end of the entrance hall, Mother immediately slumped into one of the large, dark wood thrones which made her look suitably tyrannical. She was openly giving Mirabelle barbed looks now, but Mirabelle resolutely refused to meet Mother's gaze. Bridget seemed to be loving the whole experience. It had noticeably elevated her sense of self-importance and she was relishing every moment.

She stood rigidly holding her bald cat, gently rocking him and cooing. 'Dingerling, my little Dingerling. Oh, darling, you look a little hot.'

'Disgusting,' Aunt Charlotte mumbled.

Bridget began removing the small woolly coat from the animal in the rough, practical way a fierce nanny might whip off a baby's clothes. She glanced over at Lord Elzevir, whose dishevelled toupee still sat at a bizarre angle. 'Would this be of any use, Your Lordship?' She held out the fleecy little cat jacket. 'I mean, that won't keep your head very warm, will it?'

He didn't respond.

Mirabelle watched the cat and Bridget both carefully, and it crossed my mind that there was a touch of jealousy in that look.

Aunt Charlotte stood close by looking appalled in tweed. She'd put on so many layers of jumpers, cardigans and scarves that she looked as if she'd dressed in two or three different people's outfits at the same time.

'Zavvy wanted drinks served here. He thinks it will be more baronial.' She didn't seem to blanch at the word. There was no embarrassment. It was clearly second nature now to refer to their elevated status.

She grabbed a glass of Prosecco and drank half of it, her eyes closed as if she was drinking in a new calmness. When she held the glass back out in front of her, I could see the lights flickering on the surface as her hands jittered anxiously.

Lord Elzevir was swaying worryingly close to another suit of armour. 'Lucy's going to help serve the drinks since you've sent Mrs White over to Verity's.'

'What?'

'Lucy's going to—'

'You didn't tell me the tart was going to be serving. Where is she?'

'Another glass of Prosecco, Your Ladyship, or have you had enough?' The young girl had calmed down significantly and had a sour little voice now. Lucy Morello stood by the side of Marsha holding out a silver tray glittering with glasses, her eyes defiantly reflecting the bright pins of light. Marsha took a moment to inspect her as if she was deciding which way the evening should go. Finally, she petulantly took a glass. 'Thank you, Lucy.' It was the kind of gratitude you might reserve for a thief forced to return your goods. Only, from the looks passing between Lucy and Lord Elzevir, it didn't appear that the girl had any intention of giving back anything she'd stolen.

Marsha twirled the glass in her hand, watching the bubbles burst on the surface of the liquid.

A brash-sounding electronic doorbell imitated the chimes of Big Ben before a grainy image appeared on a small screen by the door.

Four faces were peering uncomfortably into a camera. The first leaned forward, a frizzy halo of hair caught in the light. 'Hi, yeah . . . Hi. We don't seem to be able to get in. The—'

'Portcullis.' An older man leaned into the centre of the picture and spoke authoritatively.

'Yes, yes, that's right. Thank you, Gerald. The portcullis is down. Both of them are.'

Mrs Abaddon stepped out of the shadows and glided silently towards the intercom. She pushed a button and spoke with a calm, collected voice that suggested this was not the first time she'd had to deal with barred guests. 'Thank you, Mr MacDonald.'

'Ron, please. Call me Ron.' I took a moment to acknowledge the fact that Mr Ronald MacDonald actually did have a large amount of frizzy hair framing his face. That, however, was where the similarity ended. From what I could see on the small image, he was wearing a high-necked wing collar, a large cravat and a cape that seemed to be fastened at the front by a large pentagram brooch. It was a decidedly disturbing look. He wouldn't have sold many burgers to kids dressed like that. Unless it was Hallowe'en.

Mrs Abaddon pushed another button but nothing happened. She frowned and pushed it again.

'Please wait a moment while I attempt to find the remote control, Mr MacDonald.' Mrs Abaddon turned to Lord Elzevir, who looked suitably mystified. 'Sir, I believe Mr Ronald MacDonald cannot gain entry as the portcullis is down.' She spoke these words without a flicker of emotion. 'Both gates are, sir. The intercom button isn't working, again.'

Lord Elzevir began patting down his trousers with one hand and searching through his pockets while keeping a tight hold of the glass with the other. 'Bloody, buggering remote control. It's never where I left it. This is you, Marsha. Your bloody Greengage man. Those gates haven't worked from day one. They never bloody go up.'

'Like a few other things I could mention.' Marsha stood with her arms folded and raised her eyebrow first at Lord Elzevir then at the girl serving the drinks.

'For God's sake, where the bloody hell is the remote, woman?'

'I don't know. Look, I'm sorry . . . I . . .' Marsha's tone seemed to have shifted distinctly. Her arms dropped and her shoulders sank. She looked around us, the anxiety rippling through her face.

'Oh, this is just so typical of you. How can you forget where you've put things so often?' Lord Elzevir's slack jowls shuddered beneath his chin.

'I just forget things. It's—'

'All the bloody time! This is why I tell you not to touch things. You're wanting a bloody bank card of your own. Well, you just tell me what you'd do with that? Lose it, that's what. Same as you did with my wallet.' His eyes bulged.

'It's just the remote that's lost.'

'You're always moving it, that's why. You're useless. I don't understand why lover boy couldn't have given us more than one remote.'

She shoved her hands in her pockets as if summoning some courage. This last comment seemed to have provided some spur. 'Because, dear, you told him you were master of your own castle and only you should be controlling it. Remember? You said you didn't want any old riff-raff being allowed in, especially if you weren't here. So we only needed one.'

A weak voice from the screen called out, 'We've made it through the first gate.' It was beginning to sound like a TV game show. 'But the second one isn't coming up. Oh . . . Oh . . . I think the first one is coming back down.'

The faces had disappeared with just the eerie view of an empty driveway on the screen now.

'How the hell has that happened?'

'I have no idea, Zavvy. Let's just go down there and sort it out, for God's sake.' Marsha slammed her glass down on a small, antique side table then fixed her gaze on the maid. 'I'm sure Lucy will have no objections to serving people through the bars. She's quite used to visiting people like that.'

The maid's eyes widened in fury and she turned away muttering through clenched teeth, 'I might even add something a little special to *your* drink.'

'Hi. Hello there! This is Jocasta,' a brittle voice called out from the intercom.

Lord Elzevir glanced at Marsha. 'Why you had to invite Ron's wife I don't know.'

'Why wouldn't I?'

'Because she's a practicing witch, that's why. What's she going to eat, eye of newt and wing of bat?'

'She's a vegetarian.'

'Can anybody hear us? We're caught in between the two portcullises, in the gatehouse.'

'Portculli,' the older man's voice interrupted again.

'Thank you, Gerald. Portculli.'

Bridget cleared her throat. 'Dingerling needs a little ting-a-ling.' She bent down and carefully attached the lead to the cat's collar and started walking with it across the room. 'Dingerling shouldn't be made to wait, should you, darling? Come along, Mirabelle.'

Everyone looked across the room to where Mirabelle was standing, looking strangely disconnected. She frowned a little. Bridget lifted her eyebrows and gave Mirabelle a frigid look of impatience. Mirabelle followed without a word.

'What *is* going on with her?' Aunt Charlotte whispered too loudly to me.

I shrugged as if I didn't care, but there was something disturbing about this new Mirabelle, something in this new dynamic that was off-balance.

'Quite right,' Marsha nodded, still with that strained look about her, 'let's just take the party down there!'

'Can you hurry up, please,' the disembodied voice called. 'It's freezing and it's belting it down out here.'

Mother took out her phone. 'I'll check the weather.'

'Oh, yes. Just one thing.' Marsha was pulling on a coat. 'We're having superfast broadband fitted in the village.'

'How nice,' Mother complimented.

Marsha grabbed a handful of umbrellas from a stand and opened the door. She looked out doubtfully and put the umbrellas back. The wind flooded the hallway, leaves circling and rain splattering the stone. She put her handbag over her shoulder and started to walk out into the courtyard.

'There'll just be a short interruption to service while they power down the exchange.'

Mother, Aunt Charlotte and I looked at one another. 'All of it?' Mother asked.

Marsha turned to us. 'Essential work, they told Joseph, to allow for the upgrade. It'll only be for a day.' She smiled. 'I'm sure you don't have anything that urgent. You're in the countryside now, ladies!' She said it with a flourish and pulled up her large hood.

I quickly took out my mobile. Nothing. No signal. No Wi-Fi.

'It's only a day,' Mother said quietly, looking at her own phone.

'And what could possibly go wrong in one day, eh?' Aunt Charlotte replied archly.

The three of us looked out at the torrential rain filling the black sky before looking back at each other.

CHAPTER 10: TO CAPTURE THE CASTLE

I stepped out into the cold grit and dazzle of the rain blowing into my face. Torches cast only moments of light into the darkness. The wind had a harsh, ragged edge to it, whining round the courtyard.

'I shall lock up here, Your Ladyship, before I make my way down to Miss Verity's house,' Mrs Abaddon said.

'Yes, thank you.' Marsha began walking. She had an absent look about her, as if something else was distracting her.

We hurried down to the gatehouse across the slippery stones. The air was fast with rain, drumming relentlessly across our hunched backs. Our bodies curled round like leaves battered by the wind. Threads of water made their way down my neck and under my collar. It certainly wasn't the night for a safari of any description.

I looked over at Mother. She seemed small, almost fragile, huddled into her swathes of scarves. She gave me a hurried glance but turned away. We're not good at dark and stormy nights anymore.

The outline of the castle was blurred against the troubled sky. The flag whipped like a damp rag on the wind. It was an empty, weak moon shrouded in cloud but the torches kept burning, pulled in all directions by the gale, sending shadows running up the walls. Lord Elzevir seemed oblivious to his wig flapping perilously in the wind. He was watching me with those vulture-like eyes. He was drunk, yet there was still an astute sharpness in his look. Nothing escaped this man. Everything was fair game to be lined up and shot at.

Lord Elzevir pointed at the tortured flames that remained lit. 'Gas!'

'Yes, it's the sausage rolls!' Aunt Charlotte called back.

He squinted at Aunt Charlotte then downed the glass of watery fizz and strode on ahead.

Lucy Morello scampered along behind, her mouth half-open and eyes pinched into small slits. She had more than a passing resemblance to a rodent, all hurried and agile. Even in the bitter wind and rain she still managed to carry the large silver salver laden with tall Champagne flutes. Small beads of rain ran down the sides of the glasses, glittering in the torch-light. It pooled on the bright metal of the tray.

'Bloody hell, she's fast!' Aunt Charlotte nodded at the girl as she neared the gatehouse. 'She didn't even spill a drop.'

'Don't worry. We'll have you out in a jiffy,' Marsha called to the expectant faces behind the bars of the gatehouse. 'There's a manual override in the room above the gatehouse.'

The four caged guests watched us stonily through the bars. In the torchlight, disguised by shadows, they didn't look at all like four innocent villagers on their way to the neighbours' for drinks. Imprisoned, the bars instantly cast them in a much darker light.

And then I saw the tall, thin scaffold at the side.

I pointed towards it. 'What the hell is that?'

Marsha swung round to look at me, a stray curl falling from beneath her large, fur-rimmed hat. Her water-blue eyes shone out in the darkness.

'It's an old gallows,' she smiled smoothly

My mouth cracked open.

'Of course it's not!' She shook her head lazily and laughed. 'It's Joseph's scaffold platform. Some of the beams were rotten and we're having some renovations done, aren't we, dear?'

Lord Elzevir made no effort to respond.

'Verity's a marvel with design. She came up with this design and Joseph just whizzes around all over the place, mending and painting. See, he put the wheels on it Verity suggested. Isn't that clever?'

Lord Elzevir was grumbling his way along. 'Joseph this. Joseph that. He's here more than I am, the bloody plum.'

He swayed towards a small arched doorway at the side of the gate. I could make out the first couple of damp stone steps shining silver with rain, curling round and up into the darkness of the small tower. He struggled to find his footing.

'Be careful, sir,' Lucy called. There was genuine concern on her face, but as she turned to Marsha it quickly melted into spite.

'Mrs Abaddon, please escort His Lordship and then, if you wouldn't mind, use the side gate to go down to Miss Verity's. She'll be expecting you to assist Mrs White. Thank you.'

Mrs Abaddon nodded to Marsha and she too disappeared up the steps with much surer steps.

'So you've finally decided to grant us admission then, Your Majesty.' The face of a young, angular looking woman was framed by the bars. A large steel pentagram hung down her chest, similar to the one Mr MacDonald was wearing. She spoke in fast, angry breaths. 'We are utterly soaked. I can't believe—'

'It's raining, Jocasta,' Marsha sighed heavily. 'It's always raining. That's why it's called Greystone.'

'Well, no. Actually, I think you'll find, Marsha—'

'Oh, Gerald, darling.' Marsha leaned towards the bars. 'We don't need another history lesson now.'

It was the older man we'd seen earlier and he was looking a little deflated now. He'd seemed very grey on the intercom panel and I'd assumed that was because it was a black-and-white screen. But seeing him in the flesh, he was just as monochrome.

'I'm sure you and your wife can discuss such exciting matters later,' Marsha added snidely.

An equally grey woman stepped forward. 'I think you should listen to him.' Gerald nodded appreciatively as she continued, 'As a prominent member of the Archaeologists' Rural Society Executive—'

'Ah, yes,' Marsha smiled, 'the ARSE. I think we've heard quite enough about the ARSE, thank you.'

'—Gerald is a highly respected conservationist of some of rural England's most historic buildings. If it hadn't been for him and myself leading the charge, this castle would have been utterly destroyed.'

'Don't we know it,' Marsha murmured.

'Harriet is quite correct.' Gerald gave a sanctimonious smile. 'We have single-handedly prevented some of the most egregious so-called upgrades planned here. Sadly, not the remote-controlled portculli, though. Which I think we can see are an utter disaster.'

'This is ridiculous.' Jocasta's face sharpened. She scraped a swag of black hair back. It had a very unnatural blue green shine to it. It was clearly dyed, and very recently by the look of the inky stain on her skin framing her face. 'When are you going to get us out of here?'

Marsha turned to Mother and me. A reluctant smile leaked out across her face. 'Let me introduce you properly to our prisoners.' She held her hand out towards the gate. 'Jocasta and Ron are our resident pagans, as you can see from their lovely capes. Gerald and Harriet, as you've heard, are the moral guardians of our history. And these,' she said, gesturing to us, 'are my old book club chums, the Smart Women.'

The faces stared back impatiently at us through the bars.

Bridget was lowering herself down onto the large cannon by the side of the portcullis.

'Be careful it doesn't go off,' Aunt Charlotte laughed.

'No. It's a Civil War—'

Marsha shook her head. 'Yes, yes, Harriet. Thank you.'

'Bloody thing goes off every night,' Ron muttered and drew the black cape around him.

'It's—'

'The Midnight Gun.' Marsha sounded weary, as if she'd been called upon to explain this many times before. 'Elzevir likes it.'

A low, guttural wave of thunder rose up from the village. The sound spread like a warning. I looked through the bars and could see Mrs Abaddon walking into the darkness down towards the road as Marsha had instructed.

'Perhaps our prisoners, sorry, guests would like some drinks, Lucy.' Marsha looked at the girl expectantly. 'You can serve them through the bars, dear. It won't be a novelty, I'm sure.'

'Marsha, really!' Lord Elzevir had reappeared from the small entrance at the side of the gate.

'Why is the gate still down?' Marsha asked. There was a slight shift in her voice, almost imperceptible.

Nobody spoke when they anticipated this man was about to. It was as if he owned that moment, that space to speak, and everyone knew it.

'I couldn't find the override.' He swayed and staggered with the weight of the drink sloshing around inside of him. His ballast was unstable, but he refused to sink, even though it was already very clear that a lot of people would be happy to stand by and watch him drown. 'Don't question me again. And you can leave Lucy alone. It's not her fault.'

'I'm sorry, are we missing something here?' Harriet leaned forward towards the bars.

'No, Harriet—'

'Oh Zavvy, they should know about your altruism, surely?' Marsha bent towards the four caged faces. A defiant little spark flashed across her eyes. 'Young Lucy here has a brother in Dartmoor prison, don't you, dear? Just over the moors. Very handy working here, you see. She can pop by and see her felon family any time she likes.' Every word was rich with spite.

'For God's sake, Marsha.' Lord Elzevir glared at her.

'What? Did I say something wrong?' Marsha adopted a sudden expression of innocence. 'And no luck with the gate either, Zavvy?' She seemed to switch between so many different versions of herself that it was bewildering. It was like looking at a patchwork quilt of a woman.

The torchlight burned in Lucy's eyes. It wasn't just anger in her face when she looked at Marsha. It was disdain. There was a brazen assurance to her. She barely moved, but little tremors of anger jittered the ends of her wet hair. She held out the tray towards the bars and each of the four people carefully took a glass and slotted it through.

'Thank you,' Gerald said quietly. 'Wait.' He peered at me and then Mother. 'Did you say the Smarts? The murder women?'

'We are not the murder women!' Mother was appalled, again.

'We just happen to have been around a lot of murders,' I added for clarification. It didn't seem to help. Their gaze travelled across each of us in turn. I'm very used to this supermarket shelf treatment, as if we're an array of magazines each appealing to a slightly different readership. The word 'murder' does tend to spark immediate intrigue.

'We prefer the "Smart Women". Let me give you a card.' Mother started searching through her handbag.

Marsha laid her hand on Mother's arm. 'I'm sorry, dear, but we don't allow advertising. We have strict rules about promos. Now, Zavvy, what's happening with this gate?'

'Don't you worry about that, Your Ladyship.' A new voice came from the other side of the gatehouse.

The sound of this arrival somehow seemed to ignite Marsha. Her face suddenly became very animated. 'Oh, thank goodness! Joseph, you came! We seem to have imprisoned our guests. Can you rescue us?' She looked genuinely thrilled for the first time since we'd arrived.

But in stark contrast, Lord Elzevir was suddenly very sober. His face was stony. There was a new stillness to him, a cold fury. The expression on his face was very far from excitement. In fact, it looked almost murderous.

CHAPTER 11: HOW TO ESCAPE FROM JAIL

I couldn't make out the man's features, but his silhouette was sturdy in a farmyard sort of way — or how I imagined that might look.

'Righto. Your Ladyship needs to use the manual override button.'

'Already tried it,' Lord Elzevir slurred. The cold, sober face had faded quickly. He'd reverted to being unsteady and drunk again.

'Ah, right. It can be tricky. If you let me in through the side door, I'll come and do it.'

Lord Elzevir spluttered. 'I'm not letting that bast—'

'I'll let you in, don't worry.' Marsha was already disappearing into the small side entrance. The door on the outside wall soon opened and the man she'd called Joseph disappeared inside. Within moments the first portcullis began to rise. A juddering and clanking began again, and the gate on our side then began to lift. It moved at an unnaturally modern pace for such an ancient large gate.

'Thank goodness for Joseph,' Marsha smiled.

'Bloody plum, knows more about my house than I do,' Lord Elzevir murmured and started to walk under the lifting portcullis. 'Sniffing round here all the time.'

'I'd wait until it's completely lifted,' Gerald suggested. 'These old gates can be temperamental. Wouldn't want any accidents to happen now, would you?'

'Might be a blessing for some.' Lord Elzevir staggered past the assembled guests, who looked cold and bedraggled, clutching their glasses.

'Joseph! Joseph, come and meet my guests. You saved the day, as usual.' Marsha's effusiveness was embarrassing, not least of all to the young man who entered the small area between the two gates.

'It's really not that difficult when you have the trick of it.' Joseph spoke with a soft Devon accent. He pulled his hand nervously over his thatch of brown hair. 'It's just an override. I think some water might have got in the electrics though. I can come and take a look at that.'

'I bet he can.' Aunt Charlotte eyed him suggestively.

Joseph looked at us with concern. 'You're still doing the wandering around teatime thing then? The rain's coming down and Lee reckons the roads are out across the moor, from here to the main road. Everything's flooded. Can't even get his tractor out. Came up here to warn you all.'

'What?' Mirabelle's face was suddenly very animated.

'There are flood warnings in place. Happens regular up here,' he explained to us.

Marsha sighed. 'We'll see how we go. Let's get to Verity's and we can work from there. It was her idea and I know she's very keen to do it. It would be a huge shame not to.'

No one seemed keen to move from our small spot in the gatehouse. It was cold and cramped but at least we weren't being rained on. The wind teased round us again.

Lord Elzevir was shaking his glass as if he couldn't understand why it was empty. Lucy moved quickly to his side and swapped the glass for a full one. A look passed between them and I noticed Marsha watching them closely. Marsha immediately slipped her arm through Joseph's, who looked suitably embarrassed. For a moment, Marsha's eyes softened and seemed to shine amber in the torchlight as she looked up at him.

'At least you set us free.' Her voice had mellowed to almost a hum. 'This place can be an impenetrable fortress sometimes.'

There was a rough edge to him, a troubled air to him. He seemed tired. His chin had a blue tinge where the stubble was growing through and there was a small nick from a blunt razor on the curve of his jaw. Wisps of silver flecked his hair. His eyebrows were thick and hung over the brow bone as if he was trying to hide his dark eyes. This man wasn't as young as his silhouette had first suggested.

'Should be pretty easy to fix.'

'Shame you can't say the same about my wife, eh?' Lord Elzevir's voice had that harsh rasp of a drinker after hours, rough with liquor and smoke. I know that sound very well. I glanced over at the spectre of my father lingering aimlessly in the shadows. Yes, I know that sound.

Jocasta laughed viciously and Marsha swung round to stare at her.

'Oh, that's funny, is it, Jocasta?' Something in Marsha had flared. The two women locked eyes. 'Well, don't go thinking your secrets are safe around here, Hermione bloody Grainger.'

'Who?' Aunt Charlotte leaned in eagerly.

'I don't know what you mean, I'm sure. I have no secrets.' Jocasta swirled her long cape and began to walk towards the gate onto the drive.

'Oh, I think you do,' Marsha called. 'Ah! Speak of the Devil and he's sure to arrive. Reverend Vert, how lovely of you to join us.'

Framed by the large spikes of the lifted gate stood a tall, slender man. His silhouette was slightly bent as if he was already apologising for his arrival. 'Good evening, Lady Marsha, Lord Elzevir. I hope I'm not too late.' He was wearing all black, the only visible parts of him his pale face and the white strip of dog collar below. He could almost have been a spirit drifting there so serenely in the darkness.

'Not at all, Vicar.' Marsha gestured for Lucy to serve him a drink, which the maid sullenly offered. 'We've had a few technical faults, but Joseph came to the rescue.'

'Thank you,' the vicar nodded to Lucy. 'Ah, Joseph to the rescue again, eh? You really are making yourself indispensable, aren't you?' As he stepped forward into the glow there seemed to be almost the flicker of something darker in the vicar's face. His features were thin, in a hungry way, wrapped in concern. His eyes were birdlike and keen.

He had the plain, blank appearance of a man who was regularly called upon to arrange his face into an array of appropriate expressions — compassion, forgiveness, understanding, judgement.

Marsha let her attention drift back to Joseph, who stood awkwardly in the centre of the gatehouse, his hands looking clumsy on the delicate Champagne glass.

'Only this morning, Verity was telling me all about the new improvements.' The vicar spoke in staccato words, crisp and nervous.

'Was she?' Lord Elzevir seemed to come alive for a moment.

Marsha checked her watch. 'I consult her on everything. She's wonderful. She has a real eye for design. The new facade Joseph's painting was all her work. Listen, shouldn't we be getting to her? She'll start to worry.'

'You, Greengage.' Lord Elzevir's words blurred into one. 'When you going to be finished? When you moving that scaffold?'

Joseph Greengage flushed. 'Sorry, sir. I'll have it gone by tomorrow. It's on wheels.'

'I don't care if it can bloody fly. Just shift it.'

'Who are we waiting for?' Marsha asked.

'Scarlett?' Joseph spoke quickly, before looking away.

Marsha's eyes narrowed.

'Oh, she doesn't want to come to something like this.' Harriet turned to me. 'Scarlett's our daughter. You know youngsters. She's at home on that YouTube.'

Joseph resolutely stared at the ground.

Marsha squeezed his arm. 'We were just talking about all the work Joseph's done here, Vicar. And all the work there's left to be done. It's costing a fortune, but then it's always worth paying for good work, isn't it Joseph?'

Joseph shifted uncomfortably.

'Now, Vicar.' Marsha smiled. 'Let me introduce you to these ladies from my old book club.' She introduced us efficiently.

As we stepped out into the driving rain, I saw Marsha stumble unnecessarily into Joseph, who was forced to hold her up. He glanced at me quickly, and I gave him a sympathetic smile before looking away.

'It's not far to the vicarage,' Marsha called back through the rain. 'Lucy, run on ahead and make sure Verity is ready for us.'

Lucy gave Marsha a barbed little look, then turned to Lord Elzevir, who simply nodded. The girl put the tray down on a small ledge and pulled up her hood. She ran stealthily over the slippery pebbles, disappearing into the rain.

Away from the torchlight, the darkness was blinding. I placed my feet carefully, without any feeling of security. The road was uneven and the edges rough, blurring out into ditches that I couldn't properly see. Beyond the immediate vicinity of the castle, the village seemed to be completely unlit. I could make out some distant lights down the road that we'd driven up earlier, but beyond that, out into the moors was a black sea that my imagination quickly drew into a darker world.

The rain took my breath away. We walked on, heads bent, eyes tightened against the battering wind. The air itself seemed alive and wild.

Marsha was calling some instructions but I could hear very little. The occasional phrase swept back about some other guests who would meet us at their houses and that 'Lee wasn't coming. In another one of his moods.' I remembered her talking earlier about Lee Colman, the farmer. As we'd driven in, we'd seen a farm at the outer edge of the village and I wondered now if that was his. In this weather, it didn't surprise me that he wasn't going to trudge all the way up to the higher part of the village. But Marsha had inferred it might not just be the weather that was holding him back.

Lord Elzevir staggered along up ahead, oblivious, still clutching the empty Champagne glass. He seemed more drunk than ever.

I could see the vague outline of the church spire silhouetted against the pale moon. The rain was blown in waves through the air.

'Not far now.' Marsha moved lithely across the lane. Dodging the deeper puddles adeptly, completely unaffected by the driving rain, it was as if she was merely dancing with her own shadow that flitted along on the wet road. We, however, looked much clumsier, slipping and staggering in the dark waters and running mud.

Mother swore as she slipped heavily through piles of damp leaves. 'This is ridiculous.'

Finally, we stood in the circle of light at the front door of the vicarage, bedraggled and windswept. We were as unprepared to enter a drinks party as it was possible to be and that was never going to sit well with Mother. She stared, her wet hair wrapped in strange patterns around her head by the wind. Small trickles of black mascara traced in rivulets down her face. She was not going to let anyone forget this. But then, no one was going to forget this weekend in a hurry.

CHAPTER 12: THE VICARAGE

'So, this is your home?' Aunt Charlotte was wiping the rain back from her face as quickly as it fell. She blinked against the droplets falling into her eyes.

Reverend Vert didn't answer Aunt Charlotte immediately, and when he did, he looked away. 'I'm afraid not. Lord Elzevir purchased the property for his sister to convalesce after her . . . accident.'

'She fell from a horse,' Marsha said solemnly. 'One of Elzevir's, unfortunately. And we've told you before, Reverend, she needs to be close by and in comfort. A vicar doesn't need to live in a vicarage.'

Jocasta laughed bitterly. 'No, that's why it's called the Vicarage.'

'It is no concern of yours.' Lord Elzevir staggered into a large stone pot at the side of the door. 'Verity is very happy here and I'm sure—'

'Patrick . . . Reverend Vert, that is—' a faint blush spread through Jocasta's bone white face — 'is living in a caravan at the back of the church! This house has had vicars and, before that, priests living in it for hundreds of years. That's not a good look for Greystone's vicar, is it, when there's a massive vicarage right here?'

'Hello, Jocasta.' The door had opened to reveal a ten-der-faced woman with a warm, lively smile.

'Verity,' Jocasta winced. 'Lovely to see you. I was just—'

'Don't worry, Jocasta. You're quite right. Every day I see Reverend Vert struggling.' She turned and looked at the vicar with soft eyes. 'I'm so sorry, Vicar. I do hope it's not too awful. I really will fix things soon.' She was leaning noticeably to the side and I followed her arm down to a thick walking cane.

'Oh Verity, I'm so sorry!' Jocasta stepped forward. 'I didn't mean—'

'What?' Lord Elzevir swayed beneath the porch light. 'I won't hear any more of it. You need to be here Verity, with me and Marsha taking care of you. We're right here, to eat with you, look after you, take you where you need to go. Who else would take you for your check-ups? Are you going to do that, Vicar? Why don't you sleep in your massive church?'

'He can't,' Jocasta sneered. 'There's a hole in the roof and you won't help the fund to pay for it.'

'Too bloody right.' Lord Elzevir rocked again. 'Church has enough money. I don't send a collection plate around the village every Sunday. Anyway, I'm sure he can find a comfortable bed somewhere. Right, Jocasta?'

Her nostrils flared.

'The vicarage is Verity's and that's that.'

'Please, just come, come in.' Verity waved her thin hand. 'Elzevir, my dear, you and Marsha are too kind to me, but let's talk it through some other time. Please don't worry, and everyone—' Verity smiled round us all — 'let's get you all in out of the rain. Come on, now. Let's get you warm, dry and with a drink in your hands! We've got Greystone punch!'

'Sounds like it hurts,' Aunt Charlotte laughed.

'Only in the morning.' Verity stood aside and we filed into the welcoming hallway.

I returned her smile as I passed. She had an eloquent face, graceful and calm.

'Where the hell is Mrs Abaddon? Why are you answering the door?' Lord Elzevir blustered.

'Elzevir, I wanted to greet my guests. I'm quite capable of opening a door!'

Neat little tables, with vases of fresh flowers perched on them, nestled against the soft cream walls. Unlike the portraits we'd seen up at the castle, the paintings here had faces as kind and welcoming as their host.

'Verity, my darling, how are you?' Marsha embraced the frail woman with such exuberance that for a moment I thought they might both end up on the floor. 'We've brought friends! Everyone's here.'

Verity smiled round all the faces, but then her face fell a little. 'Lee?'

Marsha shook her head quickly and glanced at Lord Elzevir. He hadn't noticed and was busily trying to shove flowers back into a vase he'd knocked over.

'You know how it is,' Marsha said.

Verity's shoulders fell and she nodded. She forced a smile. 'This is going to be a lot of fun, isn't it?'

We nodded silently, rain dripping from us down onto the dark stone floor. I looked at Mother trying hard to maintain her composure. In fact, all of us looked like a dejected, solemn mess, rather than guests at a party.

Verity pulled the sides of her mouth down apologetically. 'It probably doesn't feel like much fun at the moment though, does it?' She limped forward along the hallway, her stick tapping rhythmically on the hard floor with every step. 'You must excuse our weather, but if we didn't do anything when it rained, we'd be prisoners in our own homes most of the year. It can get a bit wild up here on the moor! But let's see if we can turn it around a bit, eh?' She paused and smiled. 'Lucy will take your coats. Thank you so much, Lucy dear.'

Lucy Morello was already stationed at the bottom of the stairs. She seemed to get around this village with alarming speed. She gave Verity a smile that softened her face, making her look very different to the girl she'd appeared to be when we saw her at the castle. There was none of that hard edge to her, and all the steel had gone from her eyes.

As we walked quietly down the long corridor and into the room, I saw Verity slot her arm through Lord Elzevir's, and he gently placed his other hand under her elbow in support. But from the drowsy state he was in now, it looked as if it was him who needed help walking.

'Now, Elzevir, have you been behaving?' Verity had a subtle grace to her that brought an easy atmosphere to the room.

'Don't you worry about me, Verity. How are you coping? Is this wise?'

She shook her head and laughed. 'I can host a few people for drinks. Now, you stop worrying about me, darling, and let's get on and have a nice evening. We'll talk in the morning when you're . . . less tired.'

He patted her arm gently. 'All right, but I want to make sure you're happy.'

'You're a darling and I'm completely fine.'

The housekeeper, Mrs Abaddon, had stationed herself at the far end of the corridor, which opened out into a comfortable, well-used sitting room. She too smiled as Verity approached on the arm of Lord Elzevir. 'Your Lordship,' she nodded with a thorough, competent look that inspired immediate confidence. 'Mrs White has laid on some canapes and there is punch, which Lucy will serve when everyone has gathered.'

'Thank you, Mrs Abaddon. Please do make sure you've eaten as well and ask Mrs White to join us. That's very kind of you.' Verity ambled slowly towards the large comfortable armchair. She sighed and lowered herself down. Her hand went to her knee and rubbed.

'I'm afraid Mrs White is very strict about coming out of the kitchen. She likes to eat there,' Mrs Abaddon apologised.

Verity grimaced a little, whether it was from the awkwardness of this last statement or her obviously painful leg, I was unclear. 'Now, ladies. I'm so sorry to greet you from my chair. I do hope you will excuse me.'

'Of course, of course!' Mother gushed and made her way quickly over to where Verity was sitting. 'I'm Pandora Smart.'

'Oh yes! Ursula's mother.' Verity nodded.

Mother managed to maintain her smile through gritted teeth. She pursed her lips until they turned white at the edges and shot me *The Look* as if it was somehow my fault.

'And you must be the lovely Ursula that I've heard so much about.' Verity held her hand out to me.

I looked at her, bemused. 'My wonderful sister-in-law, Marsha, told me all about you. Such a clever, beautiful young woman. It's a pleasure to meet you.'

I could feel the heat coming off Mother's annoyance as I edged my way past her.

'Lovely to meet you,' I said quietly.

'I'm Bridget.' I felt a swift push to my side. 'And this is Dingerling.'

Verity's face wrinkled a little as she saw the cat, but she managed to rescue it. 'How . . . lovely. And . . .?' She peered past the leering face of Bridget, who was standing just a little too close.

'I'm Mirabelle.'

'She's with me,' Bridget added and looked at Mother.

Aunt Charlotte lunged for Verity's outstretched hand. 'Charlotte.' She attempted to curtsy and fell into the large vase of dried flowers on a side table. Verity didn't seem to notice — or was too polite to mention it.

'Now, please do help yourselves to food. For goodness' sake, eat! Lovely Mrs White has put on some marvellous canapes that demand to be eaten.'

Over on the long, polished dining table was a neatly set-out selection of platters with intricate little morsels and a whole raft of Champagne flutes filled and sparkling under the glow of the chandelier.

Gerald and Harriet Bradshaw were already loading plates up high into pyramids of food and balancing glasses in their hands. Jocasta's husband, Ron, was similarly indulging, but his wife lingered in a corner, wrapped in her long black cape that still glittered with rain drops. Her smooth hair was damp and lank against her face now and she glowered across the room towards Joseph Greengage and the vicar.

'This really is very lovely, Verity,' the vicar said smoothly. 'Thank you.'

It didn't really feel like that. Tense or awkward, perhaps. But not lovely.

Joseph nodded along.

'It's an absolute pleasure, Vicar. I'd love to have more visitors but . . .'

The doorbell rang.

'Your wish is my command,' the vicar smiled.

Verity started to move to the edge of the chair, but the vicar, Marsha and Lord Elzevir held up their hands. 'No, I'll go!' Marsha said.

'It's alright, Marsha, my love,' Verity smiled. 'Lucy has been indispensable, she really has.'

I looked down along the length of the corridor, where Lucy was standing holding a large crystal bowl filled with a dark red liquid that sloshed around it.

'I . . .' She looked towards the door and then back to the bowl she held so precariously.

Without speaking, Marsha walked swiftly down the hall towards her. I couldn't see very well because Marsha's back obscured most of it, but the next thing I heard was the glass bowl striking the stone floor. The noise splintered out with the great shards of glass. The floor glittered with shattered pieces among the dark liquid pools on the stone. It had spread all over the hallway.

A perfect hole of silence opened up in the room. I saw Lucy's mouth hanging in disbelief and her eyes eventually travelled up to meet Marsha's. 'Why the hell did you do that?'

'Oh God. Oh God,' Marsha stammered. She looked back towards us and at the fury unfolding on Lord Elzevir's face. 'I didn't mean it. I don't understand, I barely touched you. It was an accident. I was going to open the door.'

'Of course! Of course!' Verity held out her hands. 'Mrs Abaddon, the door please.'

She nodded and walked efficiently across the hallway, avoiding the spillage.

'Marsha, please don't worry.'

Marsha was already bent down, picking up great blades of the crystal.

'Get up, for Christ's sake.' Lord Elzevir's voice was harsh. 'Act like a bloody lady for once. You embarrass me wherever we go. You sad, pathetic—'

'Elzevir, enough!' Verity didn't raise her voice. 'Lucy, please clean this up.'

'But—'

'Please, Lucy. I'd like us all to enjoy the rest of the evening.'

Lucy waited for a moment. 'Very well, madam. Since it's you.' She gave Marsha a stinging look.

'These people are worse than us,' Aunt Charlotte said in a low voice at my ear.

I nodded slowly. Our group had retreated, gathering in a small corner of the room away from the villagers and their hostilities. This wasn't our fight. We had enough of our own without wading in here, but my thoughts were already working on a quick exit after breakfast tomorrow, devising various reasons why we had to get back early. Mother's not a swift mover in the morning, but from the look on her face, I assumed she wasn't going to make any objections to a quick departure.

In the midst of all the chaos in the hallway, Mrs Abaddon was opening the door to an unsuspecting arrival.

She welcomed a large man in a long purple coat that swirled out from him on the wind.

Mother smirked. 'It's only bloody Dumbledore.'

'Who?' Aunt Charlotte was still rearranging the disrupted vase of dried flowers, which now looked more like a haystack.

'Gerald and I have visited all the Harry Potter historical locations,' Harriet Bradshaw announced matter-of-factly and popped a vol-au-vent into her mouth.

The man who had entered glanced at Lucy and the mess on the floor, although it didn't seem so bad now. He frowned before drifting into the room as if he'd been pushed in on wheels, his over-sized coat flaring out in a great purple circle around him. His hair shone greasy black against the lights; his beard was so immaculately clipped it could have been drawn on in pen. And as he drew closer, that looked like it was a distinct possibility. He'd clearly done something very unnatural to his eyebrows.

He announced himself with a flourish. 'Tony Voyeur at your service. The man who sees everything!'

There was something vaguely distasteful about this statement, and Aunt Charlotte took it upon herself to make sure he knew it. 'Mr Voyeur, the man who sees everything? Really?'

His face gathered in on itself and he abandoned his bow mid dip.

'Madam, I have appeared on stage with both Penn and Teller, I don't mind saying. And Paul Daniels was in awe of my finger work—'

'I'll bet he was,' Aunt Charlotte murmured.

He leaned forward and stared at us. 'With the cards, madam. With the cards. I'm not known as the Seer of Greystone—'

'No?'

'—for nothing.' He looked down worriedly at his leg, where the bald cat was circling him and padding at him with its claws out. 'Who does this familiar belong to? Jocasta, darling, is this your succubus?'

She gave him a cool look.

Bridget shuffled over primly and picked up the cat. 'Dingerling is mine, thank you very much, and he doesn't suck anything.'

Tony Voyeur attempted a smile that looked more like a grimace as he drifted dramatically towards Verity. Lord Elzevir and Marsha were still in heated whispers in the opposite corner. Lucy continued to clear the mess in the hallway.

Although most of it was gone now, she still had a sour look of resentment on her face.

I stood quietly and watched all their little dramas unfold with an increasing sense of unease.

* * *

We didn't stay much longer at Verity's house after that. The party had already begun to separate out into various factions. Whether they were warring or not wasn't obvious yet, but the residents of Greystone clearly had more history than one of Gerald Bradshaw's Sealed Knot re-enactments, and not all of it was good.

CHAPTER 13: THE HOUSE OF MAGIC

As we opened the door to the street, the wind sheered across us as if a train had suddenly sped past a station platform. The fierce, sharp air took my breath away. Long, thin bars of rain shone as they caught in the small pool of light. It was a sea of sound washing down the muddy, small road, rushing in a great cascade. Flurries of leaves rolled through the air and piled around the entrance in wet heaps. The wind buffeted us back at the door.

'It's biblical out there.' Mirabelle had been very quiet until now and she spoke hesitantly. She glanced at Mother and then quickly at the vicar. 'Sorry.'

He smiled. 'No need. You're quite right. It really is something.' With his thin face and round eyes caught in the light at that moment, it struck me that there was something vaguely reptilian about this man.

Mother looked down at the mud sliding past the door. 'Can't you part the sea or something?'

''Fraid not, ladies. Come on, let's be brave.'

The tip of Verity's cane was tapping down the hallway behind us.

'Woah!' Lord Elzevir was holding out his arms. 'Where do you think you're going?'

'On a safari supper party, I believe.'

'No chance, Verity. Look at this. You can't go out in that. You'll be over in seconds.'

'Dear brother, when you can stand upright without swaying you can lecture me on how stable I am on my pins.' She was already pulling on a large, padded coat while leaning against the bannister. Lucy Morello had paused and put the dustpan and brush to the side. She was diligently helping Verity to negotiate the cane and the coat.

'Marsha, speak to her.' Lord Elzevir turned savagely to his wife.

Marsha sighed heavily. 'She needs a little fun. We can help her. There's enough of us. This has taken weeks of organising and she really wants to come.'

'Ridiculous,' was his only response.

I glanced at Mother, who didn't look entirely pleased to be heading out. Aunt Charlotte just shrugged.

The brutal wind drove the rain past the open door. As we filed out with our heads bowed, it caught each one of us as if it was trying to drag us down the street. A distant beat across the moor was clearly thunder. An occasional light blinked in the darkness, presumably houses, but none of their outlines were visible anymore. As we walked down the small path, I could barely even make out the shape of the castle or the church now. Beyond the light from the house, I couldn't see my feet on the road, which was now no more than a thick slurry of leaves and mud. I looked out at the black rain.

The magician theatrically wrapped his coat around himself in a swirl of material, drawing it up in a great scoop through the air.

'My house is just here!' he called. 'Over on the left.'

We followed in weary procession, separated out down the unlit street. I could hardly see who was with us anymore in the dark road. Voices drifted in and out of the torrential rain and the low whistle of the wind. It was a feral night, the unwelcoming kind that's not the sort for noticing the small things.

Mother was near me and casting occasional vicious looks at Mirabelle and Bridget. The cat looked appropriately evil in the darkness. Aunt Charlotte was just behind being stoic with a no-nonsense stride. But the others, the villagers, they were all blending into a mess of broken conversations that were snatched away on the wind and snapshots of faces lost in the dark. This was a harsh, disorientating world we had stumbled into.

The magician man was certainly there, just up ahead, looking like a pantomime villain experiencing a down period in his career that was slightly more prolonged than he'd have liked.

Lord Elzevir swayed in and out of view and slipped repeatedly as he tried to grab at Verity's arm to steady her.

'Zavvy, stop! You'll have her over.' I saw Marsha push his hand away. She turned to Lord Elzevir with sudden anxiety and he gave her a look that promised recriminations.

The vicar was a tall, dour shadow striding down the street, his hands tucked behind his back and nodding to Jocasta and Ron as he passed. The pagans seemed extremely disgruntled in their damp velvet capes. In fact, everyone looked decidedly miserable, even the keen village historians. From what I could make out, the staff — Mrs White, the cook who we'd never seen, Mrs Abaddon and Lucy Morello — were all still at Verity's and there was no plan for them to join us. But it seemed like I'd miscounted. Someone was missing already, I was sure. At that point, I neither minded nor cared. There was no need to. I just wanted to get this over with. But the thought did start to play at the edges of my mind, that if someone had asked me after all this was over who was present at which points, I wouldn't have been able to answer with any degree of certainty.

Marsha and Lord Elzevir were still viciously whispering to each other, and I felt sure I heard her say, 'It's your fault. He felt uncomfortable.'

But by the time we got to Tony Voyeur's house, I couldn't have cared less who was still with us. It was only a five-minute walk, but the wind was raw and my clothes were heavy with rain.

As everyone filed into the house, I stood momentarily in the small entrance hall, pausing to enjoy the respite from the rain. I slipped my hand inside my coat to feel the reassurance of the Bible and looked round guiltily for the vicar. He'd already gone in and was down the hall in what looked like a sitting room, helping himself to a large glass of red wine and cleaning the rain from his glasses. He looked like the kind of vicar who was never without his dog collar. He probably even wore it to bed. As he smeared his glasses round the inside of his jacket, I saw the suspicious little grains of his eyes darting round the room. He looked nervous. But then everyone seemed to look a little on edge, even then.

I moved down the hallway and into the cluttered sitting room. There were certainly plenty of distractions in this house. Every surface was cluttered with a strange array of bric-a-brac — a crystal ball on a plinth, next to a miniature coffin with a coin slot that said 'Funeral Fund'. A skull was positioned alongside a plastic dagger that looked like a toy, a Ouija board had been set on a low table with an empty can of beer and an ashtray left in the centre of it. The whole room had a pub-closing-time smell about it, a cold, dank air that had soaked up years of this man's neglectful life. This was the smell of too many days spent in dirty clothes with sour breath, the smell of loneliness and a man who had stopped caring. It was a shabby space that was no less cramped beyond the hallway. Mismatched furniture occupied most of the floor space, and old sofas were littered with limp cushions and threadbare throws, one of which bristled then moved when Dingerling came prowling in. It was only when it opened its eyes that it was obviously another cat peering from the mess of tatty blankets.

'Come in!' Tony flapped his hands. 'Come in! Welcome one and all.' He said it as if he was about to put on a show.

He was.

He opened out his vast coat to reveal a T-shirt with the words 'Magic in my wand', stretched across his belly. The word magic had faded. Everything about him inspired a sad, cheap, end-of-the-pier feeling.

A poster on the wall behind him read 'Tony Voyeur — the Man Who Sees Everything!' Another, in the corner declared, 'Voyeur — he sees what other men don't.' And then there was a very artful one with a tiny Tony pictured inside the head of a woman, with the tag line below, 'Tony Voyeur — he'll get inside you.'

I looked at him and frowned.

He quickly produced a plastic bunch of flowers in his hand and leaned over towards Jocasta. 'For the lady they all love to love.' He winked, and I felt myself flinch involuntarily.

Jocasta simply arched an eyebrow and left the flowers in his hand.

'Ah, I see.' Tony wiped the sweat from his top lip and smiled. 'Only if they've come from a graveyard.'

A quick spark of anger lit up her face but she said nothing. She looked nervously at the vicar, who presumably didn't like the graves being denuded of dying bouquets, even by the pagans.

'Perhaps Lady Black would like flowers from an adoring man instead.' He held them towards Marsha, who looked equally unimpressed.

'I don't take flowers from any man except my husband.'

'That's not what I've heard,' Mrs Bradshaw muttered into her glass of wine.

'Harriet, dear.' Gerald looked worried. 'That's not like you. Don't descend to their level.'

'I'm only thinking of Scarlett,' she whispered before she caught me looking at them. She squeezed out a smile and they both turned away.

'I'll take them.' Aunt Charlotte grabbed the bouquet quickly in a tight fist, a little too swiftly for Tony Voyeur to be able to unhook the long piece of fishing wire that seemed to attach the flowers to somewhere in his T-shirt.

'Wait, wait! For goodness sake.' Tony Voyeur's head bent down lower as he was pulled to the side. 'Wait, I've got to—'

She tugged again and the neck of the T-shirt pulled down to reveal pallid rolls of flesh and the other end of the wire snaking across his chest.

As she pulled harder, a look of pain came over the magician, and the T-shirt pulled further down to reveal that the end of the wire was very clearly fastened to a nipple ring. He saw my shock. 'It's an extremely useful part of a modern magician's secrets,' he winced.

'And we all know how good you are at keeping secrets!' Lord Elzevir slurred.

A flush of anger rose through Tony Voyeur's cheeks. 'Some people just have to trample on other people's success. I know it was you who told the Magic Circle.'

The room paused.

Aunt Charlotte looked stunned, still holding the flowers attached by the wire to Tony's nipple ring, which was being stretched to what must have been a very painful length. She stared intently at his chest and frowned, then gave it another tug. He gasped.

Aunt Charlotte raised her eyebrows. 'Seems I've been caught peeking behind the curtain again.' She dropped the flowers.

No one cared to examine this statement.

Carefully, and what seemed to be painfully, Tony managed to unhook the wire from himself. He wiped the thin wisps of hair back across his head and cleared his throat as if to shake off the embarrassment.

'One more trick, I think!' he announced to an underwhelmed room. He put his hand in his trouser pocket and, with some difficulty and wriggling, proceeded to pull out a coin and place it on the smeary glass coffee table, covering it with his hand. He then put his other hand awkwardly underneath the table and looked round the room with a disturbing smile. As he stood up, he held out the hand that had been beneath the table, which now had the coin in it. All his flourishes gave it the flavour of a cheap little trick that had lost its shine many years ago.

He gave a lacklustre sigh. 'I can feel a lot of negative energy in the room tonight.' His eyes widened as if something had just occurred to him. He stared around us all with the disturbing look of a man who was about to do something we might not all find appropriate. His voice descended to a worrying whisper. 'I fear we must commune with those greater than us.' He paused and gave a sudden jolt before throwing his head back and attempting to roll his eyes up into his head. He looked like he might be about to lose consciousness. 'I can sense that the pull of the cosmic afterlife is very strong tonight.'

Lord Elzevir let out a laugh. 'All right, Ali Bongo, why don't you make me disappear in a puff of smoke?'

Tony lowered his eyes and stared at him as if he might actually be attempting to do just that. 'The spirits are with us!'

I glanced over at Dad's shadow lingering in a cluttered corner. I frowned and nodded questioningly over towards the magician. Dad shook his head slowly. No. This man couldn't see him.

'I am the Seer of Greystone! Speak to me, oh ghosts of the dead.'

I raised my eyebrows at Dad and folded my arms.

'By the power of Greystone—'

'Doesn't he mean Greyskull?' Aunt Charlotte murmured.

Tony continued to shake and twitch in a similar fashion to Mother when her eBay bid is in the last few minutes.

'Sorry, Aunt Charlotte?' I whispered.

'Greyskull.' She took another bite of a sausage roll she'd found. It didn't seem to have come from the sparse buffet table though. 'It's in *He-Man*.'

I looked at Aunt Charlotte. Now didn't seem like the time to start asking how she knew all about *He-Man* but had no idea who anybody else was.

Tony continued to jitter like a cornered shoplifter. 'I command ye spirits . . .'

'Are there spirits on offer?' Mother asked sourly. 'Because this wine is battery acid.'

Tony dropped his hands and his eyes met Mother's. 'Madam, I am attempting to enter a state of mesmeric trance so that I might communicate with the spirit world. This is natural magic in all its infinite power.' He sighed. 'There's beer.' He pointed to a large bucket full of cans, next to which were a pile of mismatched paper cups with pictures of Spider-Man and *Frozen* characters on them. One said, 'Happy 5th birthday.' He shrugged. 'I used to do kids' parties.'

'Do you have children, Tony?' Harriet Bradshaw said, looking more closely at a wall with an array of disturbing drawings on A4 lined paper. There were a series of crayon and felt tip scribbles.

'No.' He looked at the wall of drawings. 'I did these.'

'Oh.'

Another silence descended.

Lord Elzevir ended it by falling into the sideboard, where a multitude of small animal skulls, china dolls and a miniature guillotine fell to the floor.

'What the bloody hell is this?' he mumbled. 'It's like Jonathan Creek's car boot sale.'

'Do not insult the gods!' Tony said wide-eyed.

'Bloody charlatan,' Lord Elzevir muttered. He picked up a doll and the head instantly rolled off. 'I don't know why we have to suffer this fraud. Deserves everything he gets.'

Verity leaned heavily on her walking stick and placed a hand on Lord Elzevir's arm. 'Please, Elzevir, let's have a good evening.' She smiled softly as if it might smooth out his abrasive edge.

'Is that right, *Lord* Elzevir? I'm the fraud, am I?' Tony shook his head and began to turn away. 'At least I didn't have to buy my title.'

'What title's that then, "Disgraced Magician"?' Lord Elzevir seethed. 'Not beyond selling yourself were you, you cheap little trick? Why don't you tell them what the *Magic Circle* said when they expelled you? "A complete betrayal of the—"'

'Zavvy,' Marsha scowled.

Tony paused before murmuring through clenched teeth, 'I know what you did, you vicious bastard.'

Aunt Charlotte cast me an anxious look and then glanced at Mother, who was still pulling distasteful faces at the wine.

Lord Elzevir looked evasive. 'I'm sure I don't know what you're talking about.'

'For God's sake, Zavvy.' Marsha closed her eyes. She glanced to the side. 'Sorry, Vicar.'

'It's quite all right, Marsha. I'm used to profanity and the taking of the Lord's name in vain in this village.' He glanced across at the pagans before his eyes came to rest on a large upside-down crucifix and a pentagram that someone had made out of lollipop sticks, some of which still had little pieces of Chupa Chups wrappers attached.

Lord Elzevir threw the doll's head down on the floor. 'Not above a bit of sin yourself though, eh, Reverend?'

The vicar looked at him with cold, polished eyes.

'I'll say one thing for the church, though,' Lord Elzevir slurred. 'They've got better props than this shambles.'

'*Lord* Elzevir!' Tony cast his coat back defiantly. 'They are not props. They are sacred objects.' He picked up the doll's head and began smoothing down its hair. 'These drawings may look inconsequential—'

'Or shit.' Mother sipped on the wine before looking derisively at Mirabelle.

'—But they are trance drawings done while I was possessed of the spirit.'

Bridget picked up Dingerling, who was clawing at the old cat I'd initially mistaken for a cushion. 'We don't need to know about that sort of thing, do we, Dingerling? And you need to get your cat treated for fleas.'

She thrust Dingerling at Mirabelle, who looked appalled but said nothing. Mirabelle's acceptance of this treatment was becoming increasingly annoying. It had so many levels of frustration, not just that she wasn't biting back but that it was the sort of treatment Mirabelle had always metered out to me, and she was making me almost yearn for those golden days. She'd been neutered.

'Has Dingerling got fleas?' Bridget demanded of her.

I laughed. 'It's hairless!'

Bridget eyed me suspiciously. 'Aren't you the little perceptive one today?'

Tony stepped further into the room and spread his arms. 'Let peace descend.'

I edged my way into the corner next to a small, cluttered bookcase. Titles such as *Hypnotism for Dummies* sat alongside *A Manual of Sorcery* and *Teach Yourself Voodoo*. At the bottom was a battered shoebox with the words 'Ghost Hunting Kit' scrawled on it in Sharpie. I resisted the temptation to open it.

Marsha was beginning to look very unsettled. 'Look, Tony can we just get to the cold soup and move on.'

'It's gazpacho.'

'Tony, I don't care if it's llama milk, get it served. We're on a schedule.'

He paused to stare at Marsha and then at Lord Elzevir. It didn't seem like the cold soup was the only problem here. As he passed Lord Elzevir, he muttered something under his breath that sounded remarkably like 'snitches get stitches'. But I could have misheard.

It was very clear by this point that everyone was eager to escape, even if it did mean venturing back out into the flailing wind and rain. Somehow it seemed more welcoming.

The dirty, cold air breathed out at us as soon as the door opened as if it was a warning, pushing us back inside. Just who it was aimed at was unclear, but really we should have worked it out already.

CHAPTER 14: INACCURATE HISTORIES

The road was a black river of dirt. Mud and leaves gathered in the darkness at its edges, and a film of oil had formed on its surface, catching in the house lights. The water slipped along, carrying the slurry down in a quick rushing sound that merged with the noise of the frantic rain. My hair was dragged back and I gasped with the shock of another swell of icy rain.

I looked across at Mother, burying herself further into her scarf. She glanced back, wary this time. Anxiety was kindling fast among us now as we stared out into that bitter night. Aunt Charlotte held my elbow. She quickly shot a look at the rest of the party standing ahead. But she said nothing. No one did. There was no need. This was clearly a village that harboured a lot of ill will, and none of us wanted any part of that.

Bridget was the first to follow the disparate group of villagers, dragging Mirabelle by the hand as if she was on a leash as well as the cat. The pagans' cloaks lifted like rooks' wings as they stepped into the blast of rain. For a moment, I half expected them to lift up into the black night and fly off. They did vanish quickly, dissolving into the darkness.

Marsha negotiated Verity through the stream running down the road, her cane tapping warily through the river of leaves and rain. Lord Elzevir was no help at all as he stumbled and turned just before losing his footing. He half fell into a large bush at the end of the path.

'Bloody silly idea,' he mumbled.

'Oh, Elzevir.' Verity smiled. 'Come on. It's fun. Remember when we were little and used to run in the rain down at the stables?'

He glanced down at her stick and a sadness crossed his face. He forced a smile and nodded.

We walked dutifully and quietly through the darkness and onto the next house. This was becoming a very sombre pilgrimage, but we'd passed the point of questioning any of it.

The Bradshaws lived in the Cottage, next door to the pagans in the Lodge. It was impossible to see anything beyond the small pool of light coming from Marsha's torch. I couldn't even tell who was with us anymore. But it seemed like there were fewer of us.

We could only just make out the thin path leading up from the gate. The house was suspended in the dark as if it wasn't even anchored to the ground.

There was a single lantern by the side of the door, casting an acid light on the grey stones. On first inspection, this was no typical cottage. Two crossed swords hung above the oak door in warning and the small window to the side had thick, black bars across it. It had the appearance of a house ready for an impending attack.

'Home, sweet home.' Gerald Bradshaw's voice had an ironic edge to it. He opened the door with an expectant face, as if he'd primed something to go off as it swung back.

Inside, there was nothing but a morbid hallway. Black wrought-iron sconces dripped pools of candlewax on the floor below, and candlelight flickered across the dark stone. Chains were strung above doorways. They seemed to have taken great pains to cultivate a sort of Victorian prison mood board.

As I stepped into the long, shadowed hallway the air was steeped in dust. It seemed strange that someone would leave so many candles burning with no one in the house. Then I remembered they'd mentioned a daughter. Scarlett?

We all entered warily. The house was damp in an ingrained way that suggested it had never known warmth. This was a starved house, and although there were carefully placed historical artefacts everywhere, a scant air of neglect resonated through it all.

It was so musty it reminded me of all those grim school trips to run-down museums.

Bridget pulled insistently on Mirabelle's arm again and she immediately responded like a mistreated dog.

'Scarlett?' Harriet Bradshaw took off her long coat and hung it over the arm of a suit of armour in the hallway. She peered up the stairs as if she expected to see a face. We all did, but there was no response. 'That's odd, Gerald. Didn't she say she had some studying to do?'

He shrugged as if her disappearance was not unusual.

'Probably with that plum.' Lord Elzevir laughed bitterly. 'He slunk off early, didn't he?'

He was right. Joseph Greengage wasn't there anymore.

Gerald sighed heavily. 'Let's go to the parlour.' He led us on through the dank hallway, past antique soldiers' helmets and muskets.

Mother raised an eyebrow. 'Expecting a war?'

'Always,' Gerald nodded and marched through the door.

Harriet gave a thin smile. 'He's not serious. We're just local historians, that's all.'

'Trouble-makers,' Lord Elzevir grunted and wiped the back of his hand across his mouth as if he was trying to get rid of the taste of the words.

'Come on you, let's remember to have that fun, eh?' Verity took his arm and smiled at him. He paused but couldn't help smiling back. Her cane clipped on the cold stone with a natural, easy rhythm that somehow seemed to restore the balance.

Lord Elzevir glanced back at Marsha, his rat-black eyes shining in the half-light. 'Bloody silly idea this, Marsha.'

101

'Not now. Not tonight, Zavvy.' She said it like a plea.

Aunt Charlotte gave me a sideways glance and shrugged.

We entered the room tentatively. The evening had been primed for something, and whatever it was felt very close to firing now. We were being manoeuvred around on this strange trail. There was an irritable air, something itching at the edges of every conversation and look. And Lord Elzevir was not intending to let any peace invade any time soon.

He fell against the door frame and grabbed for one of the thick mugs of ale on the side. Verity steadied herself on her cane. Lord Elzevir carried on grumbling. 'Sticking their noses in people's business.'

'It's not *business*, Lord Elzevir.' Gerald looked over the rim of his mug. 'It's history — the history of this village that we will fight to the death to preserve, as centuries of Bradshaws have done. You're not the first to try to destroy it, and you'll not be the last. But none of you will ever succeed. Not until I'm six feet under.'

'I know people who can arrange that.'

'Are you threatening me?' Gerald pulled back his head. 'Did everyone hear that?'

Harriet was in-between them now, holding out both arms, looking like a middle-aged woman who'd been crucified in an M&S twin set. 'Let's keep the peace, tonight.' She stared at Gerald meaningfully. 'Just tonight, that's all you've got to manage. Then it'll be over. It'll be done.'

It seemed like a strange set of words to use. They couldn't possibly be talking about moving away from the village, given the vehement display of loyalty they'd exhibited.

Gerald paused for a moment to consider her words. He downed his mug of ale and opened the door to another room, which from the steam and vegetable smell clouding out from it, must have been the kitchen.

'You'll all have pie, I take it?' he mumbled. 'It's a medieval recipe.'

'Some peasant food. Wouldn't be surprised if four and twenty black birds were baked in it.'

'Sooner bake you in it, Elzevir, you bastard,' Gerald muttered with a final look of disdain.

The evening had begun to unspool very quickly now.

An embarrassed quiet spread through the room. We were all clustered in the centre as if something dangerous might be lurking at the edges.

Marsha helped Verity with her coat and found her a chair that she fell into gratefully. Her legs were splashed all the way to the knee with mud. No one had taken their shoes off, but the stone floor looked well-used and both Harriet and Gerald had kept their thick boots on. Perhaps it was somehow more authentic. I looked around. It wasn't a welcoming room that greeted us.

A large iron cage was hung in the far corner and it seemed to gently sway with the draught from the windows. Small candles had been placed beneath it on a pewter plate, sending shadows clawing up the stone walls.

'That's a strange ornament.' I smiled and nodded over towards it.

'Oh yes, that's one of Greystone's treasures.' Harriet's face grew quite animated. 'We keep it here to preserve it. It's a gibbet.'

'I'm sorry?' I frowned.

'A gibbet. They used to string people up in them and leave them to rot. The birds would peck—'

'Stop!' I'd shouted the word, although I hadn't meant to. The room seemed to pause. I could feel Mother looking at me. All of them were, judging me. I closed my eyes and the image flashed up again, as familiar as pain — Dad. The bird pecking at him.

I opened my eyes. He was there, waiting behind that gibbet — looking as guilty as the souls it once housed.

I turned my back to him and instantly saw Mother watching me.

Aunt Charlotte walked towards the gibbet.

'Don't touch it! It might be precious,' I said.

'Worthless!' Lord Elzevir swilled down the ale. 'Like all the rest of the old bric-a-brac they collect.'

'Well, you'd know about collecting old things, wouldn't you?' It was a new, young voice at the door to the sitting room. The girl held her head at a provocative angle. The first image of her against the darkness was a shock of blonde hair and sharp, pointed boots. She cast a long, slim shadow that seemed to cut the room in half. She looked round us all with expectant eyes, the kind of eyes that saw possibilities.

'Ah, Scarlett! There you are.' Harriet made her way over to the girl. 'Where've you been? Your father and I have been worried.'

'You haven't. You're cross that I wasn't here for your dinner.' She spoke with a surgical voice, each word very carefully cut.

'Look at the weather!'

'I can't. We're sealed in this tomb. You never open the curtains.'

Scarlett was right. The whole house had the atmosphere of a place in heavy mourning. The dark flowers on the curtains didn't look like they'd seen sunlight for years.

'Scarlett.' Harriet shook her head. 'You know we have to keep our precious pieces out of the light.'

'You make us sound like vampires, Mother.' The girl's voice was keen, with a sharp edge. She had cultivated a dismissive, sullen expression.

'I only came home because of the lightning,' Scarlett continued. 'Hit something in the village. The Peacocks were out running around in the rain like frightened little birds. They said it hit the exchange.' As the girl moved further into the room, an agitated air spread. 'Ron.' She nodded at him as he turned the beer glass nervously in his hands.

'Scarlett.'

'Where's Jocasta?'

I looked around. I'd only just realised she wasn't there but I had no idea when she'd left. From what we'd been told, she didn't live too far away. Perhaps she'd got fed up of the weather, but why would her husband Ron still be here?

Scarlett let a long smile seep out. 'Lost your wife again, eh?' She tutted twice, slowly. 'Very careless.'

The air leaked out of him as if he was deflating. He looked away.

She walked towards the table of drinks, prowling the room, her eyes flicking from face to face.

'She's right,' Harriet said frowning into her phone, 'I've got nothing.'

'New friends, Marsha?' There was an instant tension between them.

Marsha made a nonchalant noise.

'Shame there's no new men for you.'

'That's enough,' Harriet said. She had the resigned voice of a woman who'd lost control of her daughter years ago. 'Gerald, try the phone in the kitchen.'

'What?' he shouted through. He sounded flustered, the way Mother does whenever she visits the kitchen.

'The phone,' Harriet called. 'The Peacocks say it's down.'

Gerald peered round the corner of the door, his face looking mildly steamed. He was holding a large serving spoon in one hand and the telephone in the other. He shrugged and whipped the tea towel over his shoulder as if he was heading back into battle.

Tony took the first plate of pie that was handed out of the kitchen.

'Don't look so worried, ladies. Dartmoor gets a lot of heavy weather.' Harriet tried to sound reassuring. 'We're used to it up here.'

'Pie?' Gerald glowered at Lord Elzevir.

'I'm not eating that.' Lord Elzevir struggled to stand still.

'I've not poisoned it,' Gerald muttered and turned away back to the kitchen.

The room fell into a heavy silence, the rain pattering against the glass like nervous fingers drumming on a table. We ate our pie in quiet anxiety, an occasional attempt at small talk dripping into the silence, then falling away.

Eventually, Lord Elzevir made a strangled sound of frustration. 'Can't we just leave? The bloody vicar's gone, and if it's all right by God then . . .'

I looked around. The vicar had gone. The party was obviously as popular with the locals as it was with our group. By now, the fascination for their neighbourly disputes and gossip had worn as thin as our clothes felt in the freezing rain. The evening was quickly turning into a confusion of people dipping in and out of the dark while we visited damp village houses. The guests were starting to fall into the background of their local feuds and tiffs.

Mirabelle and Bridget hadn't moved from the small sofa.

'What's going on with those two?' I said quietly to Aunt Charlotte, who was carefully pouring from her hipflask into the beer mug. I nodded over towards Mirabelle and Bridget.

She looked up and sighed. 'Not much, as far as I know.'

'Come on, Mirabelle never goes this long without talking to Mother.'

Aunt Charlotte looked at Mother. She turned her eyes back to the hipflask. 'You'll have to ask Mirabelle. Some secret. I don't know.'

'Secret? What secret? Mirabelle doesn't have any secrets from Mother.' I bent and looked up into Aunt Charlotte's face. 'Does she? You can't tell me she's that much of an enigma.'

Aunt Charlotte frowned at me. 'It's got nothing to do with code-breaking. Why on Earth would you think that? Silly girl.' She drank heavily from the mug.

'That's an enigma machine, Aunt Charlotte.'

'Call her what you want, but I can't help with what's going on.' Her mouth yawned open and she downed the rest of the drink.

The room had quickly splintered into small factions now, intently whispering and watching one another through the suspicious gloom.

Harriet Bradshaw was deep in muffled conversation with her sulking daughter; Lord Elzevir was slumped over the back of the chair that Verity was sitting in; his sister still seemed quite breezy and was smiling at Marsha, who brought them both more drinks; and Ron was talking animatedly to Tony the magician, who pulled out a large spotted handkerchief. A bundle of ten-pound notes fell out of its folds. He laughed nervously and quickly scooped them up.

'Win on the gee-gees?' Ron nodded towards the money.

'Yeah, something like that,' Tony said self-consciously. 'Just a job I did for someone local.' He seemed to look over the room towards someone, but it was impossible to tell who in the dim light and no one acknowledged him. He hurriedly shoved the money back into his jacket.

'So, how are you enjoying our little soiree?'

I hadn't noticed Harriet slip in beside me. Scarlett wasn't with her anymore. In fact, she wasn't in the room now and I couldn't say at what point she'd left.

'Oh, it's lovely, thank you,' I lied.

'You must ignore our little spats. Just village life, you know.' She forced a smile. 'Gerald and I have worked tirelessly to secure the historical importance of this village. Some people,' and she nodded indiscreetly across at Lord Elzevir, 'will stop at nothing to destroy centuries of archaeological importance. You should come with us tomorrow — we're metal detectorists. We've got a meeting. You can find all sorts. It's great fun. We found all those coins.'

She nodded over to a large bottle filled with loose change. 'None particularly valuable but a good little horde, shields, bits of armour, all sorts. Oh, and a couple of shopping trolleys. There's always shopping trolleys. You know, Gerald and I have been digging all over Greystone. We found a small, abandoned cemetery round the back of the church. Going down towards the stream there's a little overgrown grave we both love, and then down towards the outer edges of the village there's an old millstone, and we found a boot in a ditch only the other day. Then there's . . .'

I nodded and my thoughts glazed over. I stared into the middle distance until my eyes started to hate me for not blinking. I knew if I'd looked over at Dad right then we'd have shared a knowing smile and an eye roll, one of those moments when we both knew what the other was thinking. So I didn't look. I don't give him that anymore.

'Hello there!'

Gerald had come in from the other side of me as if he and his wife co-ordinated their tactics and formed a kind of pincer attack of boredom. He smiled and I imagined him actually enjoying torturing someone to death with boredom, his face leering over the delicious last moments of their victim begging for mercy. 'No more local history! I beg of you . . . I . . .'

'And I said to Harriet, "Harriet, should we have the medieval pie or the mead?" Because, you see . . .' He paused. 'I'm not boring you, am I, miss?'

I took a moment to understand what he'd said then too late I stuttered, 'No! No! Not at all.' It didn't sound convincing.

Their daughter never reappeared and I didn't blame her. She'd presumably had a lifetime of *ye olde flagons* found in the ground, broad swords, coins and torturous weapons of boredom. The Bradshaws were worse than any thumbscrews.

By the time we were invited to drink up, the queue for the exit had already formed.

'On to the last house!' Marsha sang.

'Thank God.' Lord Elzevir was so farcically drunk now that it was becoming the distraction of the evening to see how much longer he could stay standing. Verity took his arm. It was hard to tell who was holding who steady.

'Now, do we have everyone? Where's Ron?' Marsha looked around.

'Went home. Probably to try and find his wife.' Tony seemed to enjoy saying that.

As we stepped out of the house, the wind was fast and instantly snatched the hair across my face. This was no longer the twee little village I'd imagined but a disturbing world where everything seemed slightly tilted in the wrong direction. I gave in and finally looked for Dad, but I couldn't see him in the fast, dark night.

I had lost my compass.

CHAPTER 15: LAST RITES

A general fatigue was spreading, and I could see I wasn't the only member of our group relieved to hear we were about to visit our last house. Branches and leaves littered the dark road. As we stood looking out into the dank street, a grim, lacklustre spirit spread through the party.

I saw some lights flickering in the house opposite. It wasn't one we'd visited. As we came through the gate out onto the road, I saw two figures stumble sideways through the open door of the house. Moments later a light came on upstairs and was interrupted by a shadow passing through it. Two shadows that moved together.

'We need to get to the last house.' Marsha had adopted a disaffected, almost defeated mood now. The gleaming hostess was crumbling. 'Come on, you.' She grabbed Lord Elzevir's arm but he pulled away.

'Get off me,' he growled and stumbled into our group. There was a raw animosity now between Lord Elzevir and Marsha. The bickering had simply been a prelude to this unguarded, vicious truth. It was as if we were being given a glimpse into their home late at night when the mask of acceptability had slipped, the alcohol had finally worn them down and the full-scale argument was let off the leash.

'Stupid bitch. Always have been.'

'Elzevir!' Verity said. 'Please.'

Marsha looked to the floor. All the charming confidence dissolved once more and yet another version of Marsha surfaced. It was clear to see that beneath that veneer of well-groomed control was a self-conscious woman being eroded by her own husband. This man had a lot more power than I'd assumed. He was no foolish drunk. He had complete control, particularly over Marsha.

The wind shook the bare branches above.

'Oh, this is cold for my Dingerling, isn't it?' Bridget wrapped the cat inside her coat, its wrinkled pink skin in the dim light giving the impression that it was some part of Bridget we were getting a glimpse of through the gaps in the coat. 'Is that scarf spare?' She looked at Mirabelle, who was wrapping a large woollen scarf up high around her neck.

'Well . . .' Mirabelle's hand paused on the scarf.

Bridget looked expectantly at Mirabelle.

Mirabelle began to slowly unravel the scarf from round her neck.

'Oh, how kind of you, Mirabelle! Isn't that kind, Dingerling?' Bridget took the scarf before Mirabelle had fully unwound it. Mirabelle flinched as the end of it dragged across her neck. 'There we are Dingerling.'

'This is unbelievable,' Mother said sharply. 'I really—'

Aunt Charlotte shook her head slowly at Mother. 'Let's just get on with it.'

'For God's sake.' Lord Elzevir pushed through the group. 'This is bloody ridiculous. Marsha, you've dragged me, my poor sister and these sad, depressed-looking women—'

'Who?' Aunt Charlotte leaned forward as if she couldn't hear.

Mother gave everyone *The Look*.

'We won't make it back for midnight,' he sneered at Marsha.

'I can't help all the delays with *your* stupid gate. We were meant to be there by now.'

'Elzevir,' Verity spoke softly. 'Elzevir, it's been fun. An adventure. We don't need to stay long. They're expecting us.'

He paused and let out a sigh. Small droplets of rain rolled down the side of his face. 'Very well. One last house. But . . . ' He staggered a little, as if he'd just remembered to, and held up his finger too close to Marsha's face. She pulled up her large fur hood, shielding herself. She didn't flinch, but I could see her fingers fiddling at the edge of the material.

'This is a tragic mess of an evening, woman.' Lord Elzevir's eyes slimmed. 'We will discuss this in the morning.'

There was a new sense of menace now that felt all too authentic. I looked into Marsha's face and she drew herself up, trying to manufacture some form of courage. But she wasn't brave. She was scared, in a very deep, entrenched way that spoke of too many nights like this.

The tendons down Lord Elzevir's neck were taught, standing proud of the skin, his eyes wide and unblinking. 'You'll pay for this.' His voice was low, guttural. 'You won't humiliate me again. *You'll see.*' There was a deep malice here.

Mother frowned and dropped her head to the side. I was willing her not to speak, but when she did, I was glad. 'I think you should stop there.'

Slowly, Elzevir turned his head towards her, his body still positioned aggressively towards Marsha. 'Oh.' He feigned an intrigued little look. 'You do, do you?'

Instinctively, I moved towards Mother and felt Aunt Charlotte do the same.

'Because I don't give a shit what you or your band of freeloading—'

'Elzevir, that's enough,' Verity said.

He took a deep breath and closed his eyes, calming himself.

A droplet passed down over the curve of Marsha's face. It could so easily have been the rain. But it wasn't. She wiped it away quickly. 'Come on then, everyone,' she sniffed and drew on a smile. It seemed like an automatic act, one she was very used to. 'On to the next house! Last one.' She pulled on her gloves and began walking towards the gate.

I saw the Bradshaws look at each other knowingly. This wasn't the first time they'd had an insight like this. But they both stayed silent. The magician Tony lingered awkwardly in the doorway drawing his long coat around him. It was embarrassment on all their faces, not anger, not concern. They just looked away as if wishing themselves elsewhere.

We walked in a silent, broken line down the lane, the wind pushing at our backs insistently. I shoved my hands deeper into my pockets and felt the dimpled leather grain of Dad's Bible. My thoughts stirred at the thought of a single mouthful of that brandy. I looked to the side of the road. There was no path, just a high line of hedgerow. But Dad was there, drifting along beside our miserable little party. I tried to look angry, dismissive even, but the night was becoming too disconcerting for any more angst. I needed calm. I needed kinship and comfort. I needed him. Something was percolating here and it wasn't good.

I paused and looked back. Tony the magician walked up alongside me. 'Come along, dear girl. Don't want the spirits of Dartmoor to see you out here.'

In the distance, near where I thought the church was, I could see small lights drifting in and out of the darkness. There was a strange blue tinge to them. 'What's that?'

Tony raised an eyebrow. 'Corpse candles, dear. The dead carry them. This is the corpse path up to the church.' He nodded and walked on ahead.

Dad's eyes seemed to cleave the darkness and cut straight into the centre of me. I missed him. That was the real truth. I could feel the rush of tears building, my throat blocking, sealing everything into my chest until it felt like there was no room left inside me and it would all burst out.

Why? I only mouthed the word but Mother was there.

'Why what?' she said suspiciously. She looked over at the empty air. Dad looked straight back at her as if he wanted her to see him. But she didn't. Her eyes searched the darkness but slipped over the outline of him.

She never really had that much time for looking at him when he was alive, so why I thought she'd see him now was anyone's guess.

'Let's get this over with,' she said firmly and marched on ahead.

I looked at Dad as his head fell, his eyes looking up from under the hanging fringe.

* * *

The Peacocks' house was no less forbidding than the others we'd visited. As we neared the door, I saw lights come on across the road and past an old broken gate.

'Lee Colman's place,' Harriet nodded. 'He won't be joining us tonight. Thank God.'

'Harriet, there's been enough confrontation for one night. Don't look for more.'

'Sorry, Gerald, dear. I was just pointing out that we don't need anyone else spoiling our evening.'

'Oh, Harriet, I don't think Lee would spoil anything.' Verity was beside her, looking quite exhausted now.

Harriet leaned towards me, conspiratorially. 'Lord Elzevir has served an eviction notice. Been Colmans in that farm for centuries. I don't know what Lee will do, to be honest. It does worry me.' It clearly didn't. This was just more gossip.

'Elzevir wasn't too keen on him and Verity being together,' Marsha said quietly, her eyes fixed on Lord Elzevir's swaying back.

The door to the house opened and two blank-looking women peered out as if they'd been woken in the middle of a stormy night by a group of strangers hammering at their door.

'Is this the right place? Are we meant to be next door?' Bridget leaned over the small fence to the side and peered at the adjoining cottage that had its outside light on, but the rest of the house looked to be in darkness. The curtains were all still open.

Marsha shook her head. 'No, that's Mrs White's cottage, the cook.'

'She was going to clear up and then head home, I think.' Verity nodded towards the house. 'I hope she's not working too hard. She's been wonderful. I'm so grateful, Marsha, thank you. I couldn't have done this without all your help.'

'It's a pleasure, darling.' Marsha smiled at her.

'None of this shambles is a *pleasure*!' Lord Elzevir blurted and fell to the side. 'Are we coming in or not, Millicent?'

The two women at the door were unmoved. 'Of course, come in.' One of them smiled with too many teeth. Along with the high-necked white blouse and deathly pallor, there was definitely something of the vampiric about her. The other woman looked equally undead.

'Please, enter.' The door swung back to reveal a small, cave-like entrance with dark panelling and a pewter-grey floor. The whole effect was reminiscent of a graveyard. 'We bear you no ill will.' This last statement was directed firmly at Lord Elzevir.

His eyebrows flickered up a little but then his eyes closed over and he swayed again. 'Couldn't care less. Just so long as there are drinks.'

Harriet leaned over to me and Mother again, with her conspiratorial look. 'Cassandra and Millicent own an interior design shop in an old hay barn. The Goth Loft. They sell all sorts of . . . well, Gothic-style furnishings. Lord and Lady Black purchased a lot from them last year and are refusing to pay for them. The landlord's chasing the rent on the barn and now they can't afford it.'

Mother frowned. 'You're remarkably well-informed about your fellow village inmates.'

'Harriet is our resident spy for the WI,' Tony laughed. I'd almost forgotten he was there.

'It's not spying,' she said sharply. 'It's community spirit.' She sealed up her mouth like a neat little envelope.

'There's only one spirit that's going to salvage this.' Lord Elzevir barged through and staggered again. This time he fell heavily into Verity's side. Her stick dropped, sending her instantly to the ground. 'Oh Christ!' Suddenly he seemed a lot more sober. 'Jesus, I'm sorry, Verity.'

She groaned and patted the floor with panicked hands.

'Verity!' Marsha crouched down quickly and put her hands on Verity's shoulders.

I could hear Verity taking long, slow breaths as if she was trying to calm herself. Her legs looked buckled under her and seemed to splay out at unnatural angles to her body.

'I've got you,' Marsha said quietly. 'You're OK.'

Lord Elzevir looked more distressed than anyone else. He was on his hands and knees, staring in disbelief at Verity. 'I'm so sorry. I can't . . . I'm sorry. I . . .'

Verity put a hand on his arm to calm him. 'It's OK,' she said with a smile. 'It's not the first time I've fallen.' She looked round us all. 'Bit unsteady on the old pins.'

'Move aside. I'm first-aid trained,' Gerald said firmly. 'Let me help to lift you.'

The Peacocks stood motionless at their front door, utterly unconcerned.

'You clumsy man,' Bridget said, clutching the cat even closer.

Lord Elzevir glanced at her in confusion.

'That's where drinking too much gets you, Dingerling.' Bridget adopted her most judgemental face.

'Wait, wait.' Marsha held up her hands.

Gerald paused, ready to lift her.

'Take it slowly.' Marsha's voice was soft. 'Does anything hurt? Do you think anything is broken?' Verity started to shake her head. 'Seriously, Verity, none of your "keep calm and carry on". We need to know if you've broken anything. If we need to take you to hospital.'

'That won't be possible,' one of the Peacocks said. 'Mr Colman came over earlier to inform us the roads have flooded. They're impassable even in the tractor.'

Mirabelle flinched. 'You're kidding me. No phones, roads flooded . . .' She stared round us all. 'This can't be happening. I . . . I can't do this again. I can't be here. I can't.' She was shaking so hard the raindrops were spraying out from her hair.

'Mirabelle?' Mother leaned in closer.

'Leave her to me,' Bridget said sternly. 'You had your chance.'

Mother drew back her head. 'What the hell do you mean by that?'

Lord Elzevir was struggling to his feet, the knees of his trousers wet and torn, mud smeared down his face. 'Shut up, you bloody—'

'No, Zavvy!' Marsha was almost shouting. 'You've done enough. I'm going to take Verity home with Gerald and Tony. You're going to look after our guests and see that they're taken care of.' She'd made it sound very much like we were to be disposed of.

'Marsha . . .'

Marsha turned her eyes to the rest of us. 'I'm very sorry for all this. I will make sure Verity is comfortable. Tony? Gerald? Is that all right? Would you mind helping?'

'Not at all!' Gerald began lifting Verity with her arm over his shoulder. 'Get on the other side, Tony.'

'There's really no need,' Verity said in embarrassment. 'I can . . .' She winced as her weight started to fall onto her leg. 'My stick, please.'

Lord Elzevir grabbed it and folded Verity's hand over the top. 'I'm so sorry, darling.' It was the first genuine thing he'd said since we'd met him. 'I'm—'

She put her hand on top of his reassuringly. 'It's not a problem. You know I fall and I get back up again.' She said each word positively.

'Here we go, dearie.' Gerald took a deep breath. 'Tony?'

The magician swept back his long coat, and I almost thought he was about to try and levitate her to her feet. Instead, he put her other arm over his shoulder and nodded to Gerald.

They pulled her up onto her feet and I saw the vivid pain crease her face. She momentarily closed her eyes but didn't make a sound. She was quick to smile. Lord Elzevir looked more stricken than her.

'It's OK,' Verity reassured him as she stood strung between Ron and Tony, her hair dripping with rain.

Lord Elzevir narrowed his eyes. 'This is your fault,' he roared at Marsha. 'Your insistence on—'

She sighed heavily. 'I don't care. I'm going to take Verity home and make sure she's safe and comfortable. I'll see you at home later.'

They began to edge towards the gate, Verity hung loosely between the two men. Marsha was slightly behind, and as they reached the gate, she turned and walked quickly back towards Lord Elzevir. 'Verity just reminded me to tell you not to forget the portcullis comes down at midnight. You'll have to be inside before then, Elzevir. I'm not sure I can make it back before then, and if I do, I'll be out like a light after this evening. Don't wake me.'

She turned to us and lowered her voice. 'The portcullis always comes down at midnight. Someone has to be in before then as it can only be raised from inside since *he* lost the controller. It lowers with the Midnight Gun.'

She leaned in closer. 'Actually, a stroke of genius from Verity. She got Joe Greengage to set it like that when Elzevir kept coming back at all hours. Keeps old Cinderella on the straight and narrow.' She smiled nervously. 'You ladies should stay though. Don't let us stop you having fun with the Peacocks.'

We all looked doubtfully at the unmoving Peacocks. Marsha turned and walked quickly back to Verity and the two men as they negotiated the gate.

'Wait!' Harriet called. 'I'll come with you. She looked at me and Mother warily. 'I've got one of my heads coming on and Gerald can't stay long. We need to get home. It's the detectorists' meeting tomorrow morning.' She cast us one last apologetic smile and scurried after them.

Slowly we looked over at the Peacocks and Lord Elzevir.

CHAPTER 16: THE MIDNIGHT GUN

'I can't believe they're just going to leave us here.' Bridget looked astonished — which she never is, she just likes people to think she is. 'And with *him*!' She nodded unsubtly at Lord Elzevir. 'This is ridiculous.'

'Says the woman with a shaved cat,' Lord Elzevir slurred.

Bridget clutched the animal closer and lowered her voice. 'He's not shaved. He's naturally smooth!' She was shaking. 'Dingerling is freezing, wet and hungry. He's not at all impressed with this evening.'

'I don't give a damn what Gollum thinks!'

'Who?'

'Be quiet, Charlotte,' Mother sighed. 'We just need to get inside before we drown.'

'It'll be fine, Bridget.' Mirabelle was letting a little of the old frustration seep out.

'Oh, fine! Fine is it? I'm sure you're the best judge of fine.' Bridget gave a sarcastic little sneer. 'That man just knocked over his infirm sister. Imagine what he could do to us.'

We stood around awkwardly, our heads slung low, trying not to look at Lord Elzevir. He was already heading into the Peacocks' house and the two women stood to the side, their eyes fixed on him.

We followed, a mournful little procession now, and about as far away from a safari as I could have imagined.

Inside the house, it was disturbingly reminiscent of a chapel of rest, even down to the intricate bits of lace scattered across every side table and bookcase, and the overpowering smell of lilies.

'Poison! Poison everywhere!' Bridget gasped.

'OK, Bridget enough of the crazed eyes,' Mother said out of the side of her mouth.

She was right, Bridget's eyes were darting all over the hallway as if she'd just been thrown into a laser quest tournament in a funeral parlour. 'You don't understand. They're poison! Poison!'

Mother grimaced at the Peacocks. 'We have a little history with deadly substances. It occasionally causes some of us *issues*. Nothing for you to worry about.'

The Peacocks didn't seem disturbed at all. Their unmoving faces looked like they might just have emerged silently from some Victorian photographs of the dead.

'Lilies are poisonous to cats!' Bridget stood firm.

'But sadly not irritating women.' Lord Elzevir staggered into another room without being invited. 'Where the bloody hell is the drink?'

The Peacocks looked at each other with the same sly confirmation people use in a film when they've decided they're definitely going to carry out their nefarious plan. They floated into the sitting room, and I couldn't help looking down to check if their feet were touching the ground.

It was no less undead in this room. The situation wasn't assisted by the fact that all the large oil paintings on the walls were of—

'Cats!' Bridget whispered in awe.

Not just cats, but clothed cats. Some had Elizabethan ruffs, some were in Charles II wigs. The one closest to me had what looked like a long moustache painted on it. I looked at the engraved plaque on the bottom. The simple word 'Vlad' was on it.

'I knew it!' Bridget recoiled. 'Cat killers. I can smell them a mile off.'

'What do they smell of?' Aunt Charlotte enquired.

Bridget leaned closer and hissed, 'Evil.'

Aunt Charlotte recoiled.

'Bridget,' Mirabelle said softly. 'It's all OK.'

I looked at the Peacocks with their teeth gleaming in the low light and I wondered if that really was the case.

'These are all our pets,' one of them explained. No one cared to ask where they were now.

Lord Elzevir stumbled into one of the small tables and a little casket rocked to and fro. We all watched in horrified silence and he grabbed it with both hands to hold it still. He sniffed. 'I need a drink. What have you got except for virgin's blood?'

'We are not virgins,' one of them declared in an eerie voice.

No one spoke for a moment.

Lord Elzevir staggered again and I feared for another small reliquary.

One of the women had moved closer to Bridget and held out a long hand. She peered into Bridget's arms and in the dim light had the remarkable look of a malevolent nun. Bridget was suitably alarmed.

'A bald one!' the woman announced and grinned. 'I've never had a bald one.'

Bridget looked like she was about to be hit by a train and didn't know which way to run. I made a note of the image.

'Where's the drink?' Lord Elzevir demanded.

They both smiled, but their eyes never left Bridget's arms. 'We brewed some nettle cordial. It's taken years to perfect the recipe.' One of them stood up suddenly and we all held our breath. 'Would you like some?' Her eyes were round.

'For God's sake.' He stumbled over a stuffed rat on the floor.

'Careful, now. That was Attila's favourite,' one of them said fondly.

'Right, that's it. The end.' Lord Elzevir barged past us and headed towards the hall. 'I've had enough of this circus. Find your own way back. You can't miss it. Big fucking castle up the road.' He flung back the door and swayed into both sides of the frame before falling out into the hall.

His voice was lost as I heard him open the door to the rain, but the unmistakeable tone was that of a man swearing heavily.

'Come on then,' Mother sighed. 'Let's finish this thing. Bring on the nettle juice.'

The two women were gliding over to one of the many small tables and started pouring something that looked pharmaceutical into old crystal glasses. There wasn't any smoke drifting up but there should have been. Why Bridget didn't choose now to start shouting about poison, I do not know.

'Really? We're staying here?'

'Yes, really, Ursula. Since when do we not see something through to the end?'

'Well, let's think, Mother. There was the book club weekend at the Slaughter House, that was cut abruptly short by multiple murders. Then there was the Isle of Death holiday excursion — truncated by another four killings.'

'There's no need to split hairs.'

'Please—' Bridget covered the cat's ears — 'he's suffered enough.'

'I'm sorry, Mother.' I lowered my voice. 'I just think we should call it a night. We've done more than enough, surely. We've been abandoned in *Night of the Living Dead*.'

'Ursula's right,' Mirabelle whispered. I looked at her in astonishment. 'We should leave. There's none of the villagers left.'

Mother sighed and turned towards the Peacocks, who were holding out the dark green concoctions with 'Drink me' faces. 'I'm so sorry, but we really must g—'

'Leaving so soon?' one of them drawled.

We were already on our feet.

'Yes, sorry.' Aunt Charlotte eyed the poisonous-looking brew.

'What about our Stingers?' They held out the fierce-looking cocktails.

'We're fine, thank you.' Mother gave one of her 'leaving the party now' smiles. Never before had it been more welcome.

The Peacocks followed us to the door silently.

'Thank you so much,' I called as Mother blustered me out into the rain.

'Don't look back,' Aunt Charlotte warned.

I did.

The Peacocks were already closing the door. Their rigid faces remained unmoved, caught in a final moment of moonlight. The green drinks glowed venomously.

They didn't speak as they slowly sealed themselves in, and the last thing I saw, lingering in the darkness, was the line of their bone-white teeth.

I stood for a moment looking at the closed door and I could have sworn I heard stifled laughter coming from inside.

We wearily turned away. All of us were bent low by the constant rain on our heads, our clothes heavy and damp.

Bridget drew in a long breath. 'Come along, Mirabelle. Home time. Dingerling has had a narrow escape.'

Mother watched them suspiciously. She wasn't going to let this go on for much longer. Aunt Charlotte looked away quickly. I was sure she knew more than she was saying.

But who can say what Aunt Charlotte knows?

* * *

The road back was slick and treacherous, the rain rolling down over the fields and through hedgerows. There was an agitated feeling about us now as we headed along the lane. We only had our mobile phone lights and they didn't seem to break through the darkness at all. We were swimming blindly in the dark. Even the sky was hidden. There were no stars or moonlight. The road was barely visible in front of us.

We passed house lights dotted through the darkness but we had no idea whose they were anymore. It was a disorientating world now without anyone with us from the village. The map had gone. It wasn't in my pocket. Perhaps I'd left it at one of the houses, although I had no idea which one. I could barely remember the order of houses we'd been in, much less the ones we hadn't. Who lived where and who had been at each section of the party had all merged into one.

As the road turned and began to rise, the water came down in a dirty stream, covering our shoes.

'Some dinner party,' Aunt Charlotte murmured to me.

I made a sound in agreement but kept my head bent low from the rain.

'I don't know if my Dingerling will ever recover,' Bridget said, shaking her head in dismay.

'I'm sure he'll survive,' Mother said sharply. She angled her face to avoid the rain but it ran round her cheeks and down her neck.

Bridget gave a light little laugh. 'And you know all about that don't you? How to look after something or someone?'

Mother's face fell into a confused frown. Mirabelle looked at her with doubtful, fragile eyes. Bridget gave me a sly glance but said nothing.

* * *

The last part of the road was almost impassable. The rain was driving into us, the wind pushing us away. About halfway along, a terrific sound broke the air. I seemed to feel it first before I heard it, as if it rose up from the ground. Its deep low thunder lingered in my ears and resonated in the air.

'What the hell was that?' Mother turned to us all.

'Incoming!' Aunt Charlotte suddenly fell into a low, crouched pose.

I looked down at her and frowned. 'What are you doing, Aunt Charlotte?'

'Enemy fire. Get down.' She tugged on the bottom of my coat.

'As dramatic as usual,' Bridget sniffed. 'It's the Midnight Gun. You were told.' She marched on into the darkness with a stiff pace.

Aunt Charlotte unfurled herself slowly. 'Well, always best to have a drill.' We watched her wipe the dirt down her skirt. 'Just in case, you know.'

'The cannon?' Mirabelle looked round us all.

I nodded and watched her carefully. She had a nervous, ragged edge to her all the time as if she was trying too hard to please.

I held onto Aunt Charlotte's arm and she smiled at me. 'What a night, eh, dear?' she said warmly. 'Witches, magicians, cannon fire and drunken lords in the iron maiden. They certainly know how to party in Greystone.'

As we scaled the hill, I saw the vicarage with its lights on and imagined them all in the warmth, out of the rain and discussing the incident with Lord Elzevir.

The church spire was partially lit behind the house. Rain circled in the shaft of dim light. And those strange, blue-white lights drifted around below it. Corpse candles, the magician had called them. Making this the Corpse Path. It wasn't a calming thought.

We climbed the short drive up to the castle, and in the flickering fire light of the torches, I could see the portcullis was down.

'Wasn't the bloody fool meant to get in before the Midnight Gun so he could raise that thing?' Mother said.

'We can't stay out here all night!' Aunt Charlotte looked around. 'Where the hell has he gone?'

We walked up closer to the great closed bars. Both sets of gates were down. Mother wiped the rain from her face. 'Probably dead in some ditch.'

He wasn't.

He was dead on the floor of the gatehouse.

CHAPTER 17: A LORDLY DISH

He lay there, feeble on the hard stone floor. In the darkness, he looked like no more than a shadow cast on the ground. As we moved silently closer, disbelief formed in each of us. I began to make out his face turned to the side. I could only see part of it, frozen in a look of anguish. With every dead person I've seen, it is the face I've always looked to first.

A dark stain was spreading from his head into the puddle of water. His wig had slipped slightly to the side and a section of it was sticking up. It was a pitiful image. The torches cast a burnt light over everything in the darkness, their reflections flickering restlessly on the pools of rain that had formed among the cobbles.

I looked through the bars. It was such a desolate scene — Lord Elzevir a small, abandoned outline in the shadows of his portcullis, just lying there on the dark, flint wet stones, cold and unforgiving. It had the unreal nature of a stage set, the final scene, everything perfectly placed — the blood, the body motionless behind bars, the lights faded. My mind shot back to us all standing in the sitting room only a few hours ago, our reflections on those dark windows poised and ready to begin.

We stared bewildered through the black bars of the portcullis.

'Not again,' Aunt Charlotte sighed. 'Get up, man.'

'I don't think he's acting this time.' I could hear the sound of my own voice hollowed out.

'Lord Elzevir,' Mother said hesitantly, then with more insistence. 'Lord Elzevir!' She held the gates and rattled at them as if we were the ones trapped.

'This is ridiculous,' Bridget said. 'It's not funny.'

We pressed our faces up against the bars. There was something distasteful in our appalled awe. Death is private, a moment only the cherished few should witness. I barely knew this man. It felt wrong to look at this, as if I'd made myself part of it, elbowing my way into a picture I did not belong in.

'Is he really dead?' Mirabelle said carefully.

No one spoke. I thought of his prank, his body rigid on the floor, the fake blood seeping through his pale coat. It was similar to this, no doubt about it. But there was something very different.

'Lord Elzevir, if this is some sort of joke . . .' Mother's voice trailed off.

'Your Lordship, one fake death is enough for any evening. Two just looks needy!' Aunt Charlotte shouted.

Lord Elzevir's legs seemed to have collapsed under him. Part of the picture didn't look human anymore. The man he was had instantly gone and left nothing but a pile of clothes and flesh. His hands lay flat to the stones, a gentleness about them, as though his last act was to feel the earth beneath him.

Everything pulled in tight to the centre of me, some need to protect sparked. My muscles hardened and gripped my bones. I was rigid, the breath trapped inside me, held in until my head sparkled with lights. I let go of the bars but I could still feel the cold imprint of them.

All of me froze instinctively as though catching sight of a predator, and unable to move, I waited, completely still, watching as it stalked past. I know Death's scent very well when it passes now.

My hands bunched into fists, the fingernails driving hard into the palms. My jawline bulged out at the sides as my teeth drilled into each other. My legs began to feel heavy. I let my eyes wander to the side and caught sight of the shape of Dad in the flickering light. Sadness was heavy on his shoulders. But this time he held my gaze as if he was holding me up.

'Get the bloody gate open.' Mother looked around the walls.

'Lord Elzevir,' Aunt Charlotte called through the bars. 'Lord Elzevir, are you dead?' She peered through the bars at him as if he was an animal. 'Or is this another farce, man?'

'If this is a joke,' Mother called, 'I will sue for therapy bills.'

Panic was starting to blow through our group.

'What do you mean, Mother, "if this is a joke"? He's clearly dead!'

Mother looked at me, anger and panic gnawing at the edges of her. 'He's done it once, he can do it again.'

'Look at him, all of you. Of course he's dead or near as damn it. It looks completely different.'

'Perhaps we should ring the intercom.' Bridget leaned her head over to the side and looked through the bars. 'Lady Black will definitely want to see her dead husband, that's for sure.'

She clutched the cat close to her before pushing the button on the grey box. It was a weak buzz, one that seemed utterly inappropriate for such a place — for such a moment. She tried again, and we listened to the rain dashing the cobbles. She leaned closer to the intercom. 'Lady Black, if you can hear me, your husband is dead, we think for real this time, and we can't get the portcullis up.'

'We don't know he's dead.' Mirabelle peered at him with an anguished look. 'We need to get to him. Check if he's alive.'

'That's what I'm doing!' Bridget pushed the button again. Somehow the insistent little buzz seemed to be creating even more anxiety.

'Wait, won't she be at Verity's? She took her back there.' I held onto the bars and looked closely at the sprawled body.

I half expected him to jump up with a supercilious grin on his face and laugh at us for our foolishness, just as he'd done with the iron maiden. But he didn't. He was dead. I was sure of it. Dead people are different. They don't look like people anymore but a kind of near-perfect imitation. There is something other, something instantly different about a dead face. It has an uninhabited shell-like nature, an immediate emptiness.

Lord Elzevir was one of those deserted bodies.

'There's no answer.' Bridget looked expectantly at us, as if it was our turn to try something.

'Maybe Ursula's right and she's still at Verity's.' Mother frowned and wiped the rain from her eyes. 'We have to get the gate up.'

'Why is the gate down?'

Mother gave an exasperated little sigh. 'Marsha told us, it's that bloody midnight gun!'

'But if—'

Mother held up her hand. 'We just need to act. Not think. Not go over and over the scenarios. We need to get this gate up and check he isn't still alive.'

I was sure he wasn't. I looked at Dad. He shook his head slowly.

'He's dead,' I said quietly.

Mother looked over to the empty wet wall behind me, then back at me. She frowned. 'We still need to get the gate up. We need to check him and we need to find Marsha. She might be in danger.'

'That looks very doubtful now, doesn't it?' Bridget said archly.

'We don't know what happened here. We shouldn't speculate,' Mirabelle said quietly.

Bridget drew back her head. 'Oh, shouldn't we? Well, thank you for telling me what I should and shouldn't be doing. I appreciate that, coming from you.'

The rain was being driven into us by the brittle wind, slanting across our faces. It typed with fast efficient fingers on the stone cobbles. There was a shrill little sound in my ears, half there, half not. A desperate, tuneless note of something trapped inside my head. I touched my face, wet with rain. I reached for Mother's arm to steady myself. I'm not good with death, not good with looking at it, which isn't useful for someone who is confronted with it so often.

Dad's spirit watched me with hooded eyes. In that moment, I didn't want him to go away. As I stood with the rain puddling in my shoes, it was him I looked to.

Mother watched me. 'Ursula?' Her voice was clipped, as if she didn't want too many words to come out. The rain was frantic in our faces but neither of us moved. She didn't flinch. She let the droplets roll down over her cheeks unchecked. One lingered on the end of her chin and I watched it hanging there.

'Ursula.' She peered closer. 'Right, we need to get you inside. Bridget, try the buzzer again.'

Bridget held the cat close under her coat and pushed the button again. There was still no response.

'She must be asleep,' Mirabelle said quietly.

'Or dead,' Aunt Charlotte added. The idea had been in all our heads but no one else had felt the need to set it free.

'Unless she killed him.' Mirabelle didn't look at us but just stared at the motionless body.

'We need to get the gate up.'

'What about the side door?' Aunt Charlotte ran over to it. She pushed hard. 'No handle. It's tight shut. There's no getting in there.'

'Yes, Charlotte.' Mother was a clenched fist of frustration. 'It's built to keep out armies, not just random dinner guests.'

Aunt Charlotte's face clustered as if she was focusing every cell in her body on this. Finally, she said with an air of revelation, 'The plum man . . .' She left the words hanging in the air.

'What?' Mother paused. 'You mean Greengage?' Sometimes Mother is on her sister's wavelength.

Aunt Charlotte nodded once.

Bridget pushed the button again with a sharp, frustrated jab. It sounded into the darkness. Still no one responded, and I looked at the crumpled-up form of Lord Elzevir on the floor. 'We need to go for help.' My words were short and broken. Mother put her hand under my elbow.

I stared at the ink stain spreading out into the black water. That was it. That's all he left.

'We need to find Joseph Greengage and get these gates lifted. He seems to know most about them.' My eyes blurred with tears. I blinked and let them fall, disguised among the rain drops. 'We're never going to lift it, and Marsha either isn't here or hasn't heard.'

'Or . . .' Mother began.

'Let's not speculate.' I tried to inject some efficiency into my voice, but it still trembled. 'All we know is Lord Elzevir is probably dead and we need help.'

'Or he's pretending to be dead, in which case we'll have to kill him anyway,' Aunt Charlotte said determinedly.

'I vote we go to Verity's first,' Mirabelle said slowly. 'They'll know what to do. Mrs Abaddon might still be there, or the maid. Marsha might be there. I don't think we can just turn up at the Greengage man's house.'

'Why ever not?' Bridget blustered. 'We need assistance and we know he can give it.'

'I just—'

Bridget leaned closer. 'Are you questioning me, Mirabelle?'

Mirabelle seemed to retreat into herself and Bridget locked eyes with her until she finally looked away.

'We could always split up,' Aunt Charlotte offered.

We all stared at her in disbelief.

Mother folded her arms. 'Because that always works so well for us.'

'What's that?' I peered into Lord Elzevir's cage.

'What's what?' Aunt Charlotte followed my eyeline. They all did.

'There.' I pointed to a small, black ball on the floor beside Lord Elzevir's head.

'It's a cannonball,' Mother said slowly.

'Not a very big one,' Bridget sniffed. She was right. It was not much bigger than a grapefruit but a lot deadlier.

I leaned my head to the side. 'Big enough.'

We continued to stare at it as if we expected it to do something.

'Well, at least we know what killed him.' Bridget began walking down the long slippery path away from the light.

'The Midnight Gun!' Aunt Charlotte gave me a wide-eyed look and started to follow. 'Now all we need to do is find out who and why, fix the phones, get the roads cleared and we can leave without any more problems.' She strode off into the rain, which was still coming down as if it didn't know how to stop. Even Dad was staring after her in surprise.

I gave him one more quick look and he nodded for me to follow them. I walked into the rain, and I could feel the hot glare of Mother's eyes on my back.

CHAPTER 18: TELLING VERITY

We hammered with a rude insistence on the door. There was no need. Simply knocking would have brought about the same result after midnight in this quiet place. But there seemed to be a need in us to announce the urgency — to attempt to somehow prepare them.

It didn't. It never could have. Nothing would.

After some time, Mrs Abaddon answered the door. She was still clothed and didn't look like she'd been to bed yet. She didn't get the chance to open the door fully before Aunt Charlotte was ploughing past into the house.

'There's been a terrible accident,' she said bluntly.

'We don't know what's happened for sure.' Bridget frowned.

Lucy Morello emerged from another door downstairs. She was in her pyjamas, a strange, little-girl Disney outfit that she'd presumably worn in some attempt to make her look Lolita-like. It seemed so out of place in the moment.

'Accident?' From the sound of her voice she hadn't been asleep; a pair of AirPods were just visible under her hair.

Verity also emerged into the hallway, bleary eyed, her cane tapping heavily on the stones. She winced with every step, and as she turned to Mrs Abaddon, I could see at the bottom edge of her night gown that the livid bruise from her fall was already beginning to form down the back of her leg. She gave an enquiring look, but Mrs Abaddon frowned and shook her head.

Verity turned to us. 'Hello, ladies. How are you? How may we help?' She tapped towards us, not seeming to pick up on the urgency of the situation. 'How was the Peacocks?'

It was Mother who stepped forward first. 'We need to talk to you. Do you know where Marsha is?'

'Yes.' Verity's eyes were widened, as if taking us in for the first time. 'She's up at the castle. Mrs Abaddon walked up there with her.'

'Aye, that's right,' Mrs Abaddon confirmed. 'I just got back 'bout ten minutes ago. I've been down in the kitchens clearing away.'

'Did you see anything? Is Marsha in the castle alone?' Bridget put the cat down and clipped on its lead.

'What's going on?' Lucy Morello took out her AirPods. 'Why are you asking all this? You said there's been an accident.'

Eyes suddenly sharpened, Verity's darting between us. 'What's happened? *Please.*'

Bridget sighed as if the burden to tell them was hers. 'I'm afraid we have some possible bad news. We think Lord Elzevir might . . . he might be very badly hurt or, well, possibly . . . dead.'

Lucy Morello's face gathered into a frown. 'Again?' She shook her head. 'It'll be one of his little tricks.'

'I'm afraid it didn't really look like that . . . this time,' I said quietly.

'What do you mean?' Verity asked.

Mother stepped forward. 'He really did look as though he was dead, or very near to it.'

The room slowed. The next sound was the cane clattering on the stone as it fell. The dull sound of Verity's body followed it.

'Miss!' Mrs Abaddon was there, crouching down beside her.

I stepped towards them to help but Mrs Abaddon held out her hand to keep us back.

'No! No, that's not true. No!' Lucy's scream was low and grainy as if her voice couldn't accommodate all the pain rushing out of her at once. Her cry faded into nothing but a dry rasp. 'It's one of his tricks. It's a prank.'

'I don't think so,' I said gently.

'He did look very dead. More dead than before, anyway,' Aunt Charlotte added for unnecessary clarity. 'He looked pretty dead last time though, I suppose.'

'Aunt Charlotte,' I whispered, 'that's enough I think.' I nodded towards Verity on the floor.

'He can't be dead. He's never dead,' Lucy screamed. 'It's just a silly game he plays. There's no harm. Just a game!' Her mouth was wide and the spit spread in strings between her lips. She dropped to her knees and the small, white AirPods rolled out of her hand. No one ran to comfort her. We all stood in the hallway, our feet surrounded by little pools of water. Not moving. Not speaking.

* * *

Verity was motionless in the chair, her walking stick leaning beside her. She clutched her arms around herself as if she was holding herself in. She sat silent, wild-eyed, her gaze unmoving as if in that moment she could actually see her brother there on the floor in front of us.

Lucy Morello had a different reaction — still howling like she'd been scalded by the news. A desperate, rabid self-pity that had none of the dignity Verity was struggling to maintain.

'He can't be dead! He can't. It must be a trick. We need to get help!' Lucy was shaking, wringing her hands. 'I need to go up there. He needs me. I need to go now!'

Mrs Abaddon frowned. 'He don't need you. He needs his wife. He needs his family.' She turned to us. 'What exactly has happened? Lord Black does have a tendency to perform *stunts*, as you've seen. Perhaps . . .'

I shook my head.

'Where is he now?' Mrs Abaddon asked the questions with a calm professionalism that put nobody at their ease.

'I'm the one he loves! Me.' Lucy wrapped her arms around herself and swayed gently, rocking. She didn't look at Verity. 'I'm going up there now!'

'Yes, we need to get up there! Someone needs to help him.' Verity measured each breath as if trying very hard to control herself. 'Where is he now? What exactly has happened to him?'

'It looked like a cannonball,' I said weakly. 'A small cannonball. It was there by the side of him. He was stuck. He's between the portcullis gates.' I paused and watched a tear fall heavily down her face. 'It looked like it was his head. I'm so sorry. I don't know what else to say.'

'But you haven't been able to check him closely?' Mrs Abaddon asked.

'No,' Mother answered.

'I'm fairly sure it's not a trick this time,' Aunt Charlotte added.

Lucy wailed out again. 'But you can't be sure!'

Verity was ringing her hands so tightly the knuckles gleamed white through the skin. 'Right, well . . . We need to get help.' Her voice barely lifted above a whisper.

'It might be too late for that,' Bridget replied coldly.

Verity looked up into her face and squeezed her hands together. 'We need to help him somehow. We need to get back there and get the gate up. Marsha is in the castle. Mrs Abaddon took her up there just before midnight. Mrs Abaddon was back just after the sound of the Midnight Gun though. Marsha said she didn't need her to stay and she should come straight back here to be with me. He can't have been injured for long.' She looked at us hopefully.

'That's right, miss. The gate was up and no sign of him when I left Lady Black.'

'He could still be . . . We need to get some help up there. Anyone.' Verity was fighting to remain calm, her face grey and drawn, a note of desperation seeping into her voice. 'Joseph! We must go for Joseph. He knows the gate. And . . . and . . . The Bradshaws! They're trained in first aid for their battle re-enactments. If anyone knows what to do with cannon fire, they will.'

'I'll get Joseph, miss,' Mrs Abaddon said. She looked composed and efficient, which should have been comforting but felt a little forced. Right at that moment though, I was just grateful she'd stepped forward so quickly. 'I'll take Joseph straight there. If anyone knows that gate it's him.' She was making for the door as she spoke. 'Someone go for the Bradshaws and we'll see you up there.' Her eyes settled on Lucy, who was still jolting with tears. 'You go for them Bradshaws, girl. Go now! And don't waste a minute.' Mrs Abaddon left with a face of grim determination.

'We have to find Marsha,' Verity said, her voice wavering. 'She might be in danger.'

'Who cares?' Lucy stood and held out her arms. 'It was me he loved. Me he wanted to be with. We were going to get married.'

'Very quick use of the past tense there,' Bridget observed.

'And who are you? You who came storming into our lives and told me the man I love might be dead! It's most likely another prank, can't you see that? And you've come here worrying us all half to death.'

'Look.' I walked towards her carefully with my hands spread out. 'We saw him on the floor. He wasn't moving and he's got a serious head injury. We came to get help. We just need to get help up there as quickly as possible.'

Lucy screwed up her face as if the words were distasteful to her. 'It's just a stunt. Just his fun—'

'Lucy,' Verity said softly. 'It's not their fault. They've come to help. Please, just go and get the Bradshaws. Now. Ladies, perhaps you could try and find Marsha. I'll come and . . .' She tried to stand but the pain cut quickly through her face.

'You need to stay here, dear.' Aunt Charlotte nodded and moved towards her. She took Verity's arm and guided her gently back into the chair. 'You can't go back out into the night. It's too dangerous. You're injured too. We'll do everything we can.'

'I can't leave him! I can't just leave him. I need to . . .' The tears fell easily now. 'I need to be with him. I need to see him. He can't be on his own. He hates being on his own.'

Mother moved to Verity's other side. 'We need you to stay here. I'm sorry. But we have to act quickly and we need to keep you safe.'

'I need—'

'I know.' Mother placed her hand on Verity's arm. 'We need you to stay here though — for your brother's sake.'

Verity stared with big tear-filled eyes. 'Please help him,' she whispered into Mother's face. 'Please.'

Mother nodded and pulled a blanket over Verity's legs. 'We'll be back very soon. I promise.'

CHAPTER 19: BLACKBALLED

The rain was unforgiving. It didn't care whether he was alive or dead. By the time we made it back up to the castle, we were drenched and Joseph Greengage was already there with Mrs Abaddon.

The Bradshaws were there too, their faces set with confused horror. Lucy Morello had already sunk to her knees and was sobbing relentlessly with her head in her hands. 'Please, Elzevir, just get up. The trick's over. Don't do this again.' It looked like there'd been no lull in her dramatic reaction.

Joseph Greengage was repeatedly pushing the button, shouting, 'Lift the gate!' into the intercom.

'Is that it?' Mother frowned. 'Can't you do something else?'

He shook his head. 'Not really, madam. You can't lift the gates from this side and you can't get up above the gatehouse to the mechanism. The door's locked with a huge wooden beam across the inside that you have to lift out. You need to come from the castle side, otherwise anyone would be able to get in. I can try and break the door . . .'

His voice trailed off as we watched the gate lift quickly, the clanking mechanism turning and grinding. There was still no response on the intercom.

The wind breathed round the stone walls, low as if it came from the belly of the castle. The only other sound was Lucy's grief.

The body was still. The cannonball innocently sitting alongside him.

The gate had lifted with that fast disregard for its history, as it had before, and Joseph ran towards the still shape of Lord Elzevir. He bent and felt Lord Elzevir's neck. Joseph turned to look at us.

'He's dead.'

Lucy let her head fall back. She looked up to the bottomless sky and issued a sound that carried across the darkness, so sharp it cleaved the air. The rain seemed to part around us, pausing mid-air to listen.

The nausea was rising like a sour tide in me. The breath had stalled in my chest. I felt winded. Everything about me seemed to be dragged down to the ground. Dad was drifting at the edge of the scene. I watched his sad face, caught in memories of another bleak moment. Our own bleak moment. He was there again, dying on my lap. The final breath escaping from him.

I looked at Mother. Was it the same for her? Did every death spark memories of his death? Or was her husband long buried to her, along with his infidelity? Can the dead still hurt us? In my experience, much more than the living.

My thoughts flitted to Verity, waiting patiently at home, praying, wishing desperate thoughts. What promises would she have made to keep her brother alive? 'I'll never lie. I'll never be cruel again if he can live.' Perhaps she'd give more. 'I'll not walk again. I'll keep all the pain. Just let him live.'

I looked around our bedraggled, solemn little group. I reached for Mother's hand. It felt cold and damp against my skin as her fingers slipped between mine. Aunt Charlotte placed a heavy arm across my shoulder and I felt her breathe deeply. The three of us held onto each other and, for a moment, we were all back in the same place. I looked at Dad. Death can create the strongest bond.

Mirabelle stood separate from us, watching. She seemed to grow more distant from us with every day, as if the tide were carrying her away and she wasn't swimming anymore. She was just letting it take her.

Bridget was already moving towards the body, her cat clutched under her arm like a wrinkled pink bag. She scanned the body and the area around it. 'Touch nothing,' she said firmly.

Mother, Aunt Charlotte and I let go of each other's hands slowly.

'I can't understand this,' Harriet Bradshaw was saying in disbelief. 'We've only just seen him alive. How could this happen?'

'Well, it's not rocket science, is it?' Bridget snapped. 'He's been shot by a cannon.' She pointed needlessly to the small cannonball and then to the blood that still drained out of Lord Elzevir's head. 'That ridiculous Midnight Gun of his.'

'No.' Gerald Bradshaw stepped forward. 'That can't be the case.' All eyes settled on him immediately. He cleared his throat as if he was about to deliver a lecture. His hand rested on one of the cannons. 'This has not been fired. Nor any of the others. None of them have. Not for a long time.'

'How can you be sure?' Aunt Charlotte looked confused.

'Because, dear lady, they do not work. They are purely for decorative purposes.' He gave a smug little smile which seemed very inappropriate given the circumstances. When he saw our disapproving faces, his smile quickly dried up. 'They are replicas of Civil War—'

'Wait,' I frowned. 'I heard the Midnight Gun go off. We all did. When we were walking up the hill.'

'It's a pre-programmed sound,' Joseph said distractedly, still staring at the body. 'Lord Black liked the idea of it.'

'I was here dropping Lady Black off at about ten to twelve,' Mrs Abaddon added. 'It could have been five to, I suppose. I heard the gun go off as I was walking back. I must have just missed Lord Black but I certainly didn't hear any screaming or shouting or anything like that.'

'So we can assume he was killed at midnight and the pre-recorded gun fire masked the sound of his death.' Mirabelle looked cautiously at us for confirmation.

'Perhaps,' Mother said doubtfully. 'But we don't really—'

'He left us at roughly quarter to, maybe ten to twelve. It's about a ten-minute walk. We found him at five past twelve.' I was working through it slowly.

Aunt Charlotte was staring in disbelief at the lord's body. 'So if the cannon didn't fire, then someone threw it at him or hit him with it?'

'Don't be so ridiculous, Charlotte.' Mother shook her head.

'It's possible, I suppose.' Joseph leaned closer to Lord Elzevir's head but kept his body back as if protecting himself. 'You'd have to use quite some force, but hitting someone on the head with that would definitely give them a wallop.'

'Looks like it was more than a *wallop*,' Bridget said, peering closer at his head.

I moved nearer, careful to avoid any pooling blood. I cautiously bent and looked at the broken head of Lord Elzevir.

It was a pitiful sight. His face twisted into a look of confusion and pain. His skin had already taken on a waxy sheen, as if the life had just evaporated from it. His open eyes were hollowed out and empty. There was nothing behind them anymore. Where had he gone? I glanced at Dad again.

Lord Elzevir might have died alone or he might have looked into the eyes of his killer, the last thing he saw. Had the image of his murderer passed across the surface of his eyes just before the blow was delivered? Did something of them still linger there?

His face was unmarked though. If someone had thrown this cannonball at him, would it have hit him like this? I studied his head more closely. The spread of the damage to him seemed to centre on a point directly on the top of his skull. Judging from the mess of splintered bone and the blood-matted mix of real and fake hair, the cannonball had dropped on him or he'd bent down for someone to throw it at his head, which seemed unlikely.

I looked up. Above us, a glass panel was set in the thick stone roof like a small window.

I pointed at it. 'What's that?'

Gerald filled out his chest in readiness. 'That,' he said knowledgeably, 'is the murder hole.'

We all looked up at the roof then down at the body directly below.

'Well, it seems to have lived up to its name,' Aunt Charlotte commented.

'Aha, so, the murderer has dropped the cannonball on Lord Elzevir's head through that little window.' Bridget looked so smug I began to hope the window might open again.

'No,' Joseph said. 'That's not a window.'

We all looked again at the piece of glass over a hole. It certainly looked like one.

'It's a piece of thick reinforced glass. Did it myself a while ago. Set it in with concrete. There's no opening that. It won't shift. I can go up and take a look though.' He walked towards the small door on the castle side of the gatehouse that he'd used earlier.

'Why on Earth would anyone do that?' Mirabelle asked slowly.

'Because, dear lady, that is a thirteenth-century murder hole which Lord and Lady Black wanted to simply fill in. They said it was just a hole in the ceiling that needed fixing. But it's a huge part of the heritage of this castle and this village. Murder holes are very important historical pieces of architecture that need protecting from vandals such as . . .' Gerald trailed off.

'Such as Lord Black?' Mother offered.

'You won't need to bother about him destroying your precious castle now, will you?' Bridget let her eyes come to rest on Gerald's.

There was a thudding above and we looked up to see Joseph jumping on the glass window. It held firm. He bent down, clearly shaking his head.

'This is not for us to be trying to solve. The police will have to do that,' Harriet said.

I held up my phone. 'Still no signal.'

'We should check if Marsha is OK.' Mother sounded almost defeated. 'We need to give her the news.'

'Why the hell isn't she here?' Lucy cried. 'She obviously lifted the portcullis just now.'

Joseph appeared from the small doorway to the side of the portcullis. 'The gates closed two minutes before midnight, according to the timer. It was all meant to lock and be alarmed at midnight.'

Lucy Morello wailed again.

'But it closed at 11.58. Before the midnight gun,' Aunt Charlotte said in wonder.

Mother gave her *The Look*. 'Yes, thank you, Morse.'

'Who?'

Mother ignored her. 'I thought they were timed to come down at midnight.'

'They are,' Joseph said. 'But someone made them come down just before that.'

Lucy Morello cried out again.

'Must have been after I was here,' Mrs Abaddon said. 'That gate was open when I left Her Ladyship.'

'The gate must have come down as soon as he'd arrived. The murderer wouldn't have had time to hit him, drop the ball and get out. The gates come down very quickly. You couldn't get out from this point once they started to fall. The killer couldn't have thrown the ball through the bars, they're too narrow. Joseph looked at each of us in confusion. 'Lord Elzevir was locked in here with the gates down, and the ball is in here with him. But the murderer is not in here with him.'

'Why bother to bring the gates down two minutes before they would have done anyway?' I murmured.

'So they could be sure he was trapped in here and standing in the right place,' Bridget answered decisively. 'There was only time for Lord Elzevir to walk in. The gates came

143

down quickly and the cannonball hit him on the head.' She looked very pleased with herself standing over his corpse.

'Maybe we should discuss this up in the castle.' Mrs Abaddon glanced at the pale face of Lucy. 'We shouldn't be doing this here. With his body and everything. Not respectful. We need to go inside and find Lady Black and check that *she's* safe.'

Mother looked round the group. 'Someone will have to tell her that her husband's dead.'

'I'm not going anywhere near that murdering bitch,' Lucy screamed.

'Now, Missy, there's no suggestion—'

'There's every suggestion, Mrs Abaddon. She was the only one here when he was killed. She's the only one on that side of the gate with the ability to override the timer and bring the gate down.'

'Unless someone had Lord Elzevir's remote,' I added.

Mrs Abaddon didn't seem to have heard me and was still focusing on Lucy. 'Now, now, girly. No use carrying on. His Lordship is dead and that's an end to it.'

Lucy Morello cried out and ran on ahead.

'She's always been such a silly girl.' Harriet shook her head dismissively. She didn't have the look of someone walking away from a murder victim.

Mrs Abaddon seemed to be deciding whether to speak. 'Quite a few of them silly girls in this village though, ain't there?'

'I'm sure I don't know what you mean, Mrs Abaddon.'

'Joseph there does. He weren't alone when I went to fetch him. He was with your Scarlett.' She said it quietly but clear enough for me to hear. She knew we could all hear.

Harriet flushed and shook her head.

We stepped out into the rain, our heads bowed solemnly, our thoughts travelling towards the black outline of the castle and the closed door ahead.

CHAPTER 20: THE OPENING OF ALL HEARTS

Mrs Abaddon had a large key for the front door on a ring that hung on her side. She unlocked the main door and we walked into the hallway.

Standing at the top of the stairs, Marsha looked like she had only just woken up. Or at least that's what she wanted us to think. She called down to us, bleary eyed and confused. 'Hello? Who's there?'

I don't know if I was just suspicious of everyone at that point, but it sounded a little contrived.

She took a step down the large stone stairs. There was a dim light coming from somewhere behind her that cast her in silhouette, blurring out her features. It was hard to see any expression on her face. She paused and pulled her long, dark-red dressing gown around herself. It was big enough to hide every part of her except her hands, feet and head. It struck me as very 'un-Marsha' to wear such a shapeless, unfashionable item.

'What are you all doing here?' she said.

'You let us in.' Harriet frowned.

'What?'

'You just lifted the portcullis, didn't you?'

'Yes, but I thought it was Elzevir and he'd missed the Midnight Gun again. I was a little irritated, so I came down, pushed the button and just went back upstairs.' She looked around us. 'He's always doing it. What's—'

'Your Ladyship,' Mrs Abaddon began, 'I'm afraid there's been an accident.'

'What do you mean, "an accident"?'

'You'd better come and sit down,' Aunt Charlotte said quietly. I don't know why people insist on saying that in times of crisis. No one, in my experience of breaking the news that someone is dead, has ever just quietly gone and sat down to wait to be told.

In any event, there was no time for that. Lucy Morello unleashed a blistering noise and started towards the stairs. 'You bitch! You murdering, fucking bitch. I knew you'd never let him go.'

'What? Where's Elzevir?'

Without warning or sound, Aunt Charlotte moved quickly from the side of me. Before my eyes could really comprehend what they were seeing, Aunt Charlotte shouted, 'Clear!'

She threw herself towards Lucy, grabbed her waist from behind and rugby-tackled her. Lucy Morello was a slight woman, and as Aunt Charlotte gripped her, she lifted slightly from the ground. Bewilderment unfolded on her face. She didn't fight it, but almost like a car hitting her, she let the force take her with astonished awe. No one moved. We just watched.

At the bottom of the grand sweep of stone stairs was a large suit of armour. It was the only thing available for Lucy Morello to reach for. Her arms spread in front of her as her head was flung back. With Aunt Charlotte firmly embedded in her back, Lucy Morello clung to the suit of armour as if there might actually be a real person inside of it. As the two women began their descent, the armour began to topple in a cascade of noisy metal. They landed firmly on top of it, Lucy face down sandwiched between the armour and Aunt Charlotte.

The helmet detached and slowly rolled off to the side, and for a moment both Lucy Morello and Aunt Charlotte remained still, breathing heavily. Aunt Charlotte made no effort to disengage and remained on top of Lucy's back, pinning her into the armour.

'What the hell do you think you're doing?' Lucy gasped, unable to move.

'I've got her!' Aunt Charlotte announced efficiently and decisively. 'She's neutralised.'

A horrified silence was broken by Mother. 'For God's sake, Charlotte. Get off the woman!'

Aunt Charlotte looked confused as if it hadn't occurred to her that she shouldn't rugby-tackle a grieving woman into a suit of armour. She turned her head towards Mother and frowned. 'She's dangerous!'

Lucy struggled.

'Oh my God,' Gerald breathed. 'That's thirteenth-century!'

'How dare you!'

'The armour, Aunt Charlotte. He means the armour.' I ran towards them and grabbed her. 'You need to get up. Come on.' I bent and looked into the young woman's face. 'It's all going to be all right, Miss Morello. Don't worry.'

'Get the stupid old bag off me! Now!'

'There's no need to be personal.' Aunt Charlotte began to slowly move.

Dingerling jumped out of Bridget's arms and padded silently over to the helmet, sniffed, then urinated into it before walking away.

Harriet and Gerald both released a plaintive sound at the same time.

As Aunt Charlotte began to slowly lumber to her feet, the armour started to fall apart. First an arm fell to the side, then the metal gauntlet clattered to the stones.

'Would someone like to tell me what on Earth is going on here?' Marsha was still standing at the top of the stairs with her dressing gown gathered around her. 'Where is my husband? If this is another prank and you've decided to play along—'

Joseph bowed his head. 'It's no prank, Your Ladyship.'

147

Aunt Charlotte, who was now on all fours, turned to look at Marsha. 'We think that he might be a bit . . .'

'Well?' Marsha snapped. 'A bit what?' She stared at Aunt Charlotte who was still on her knees.

'A bit . . . dead.'

Nothing about Marsha moved. Then she blinked slowly as if she hadn't understood.

'You are well aware that my husband finds these stunts amusing. I do not, and especially not at this time of night.'

'Charlotte's right,' Mother confirmed. 'I'm afraid this time your husband really is dead.'

Marsha looked doubtful. Her eyes came to rest on Lucy Morello, who lay sobbing on the floor.

'Mrs Abaddon, you would not be embroiled in some trick of his. Is this true?'

'Yes, Your Ladyship,' she nodded gravely.

'I . . . I don't . . .' Marsha was slowly shaking her head, her faced pulled into a frown.

'For God's sake, get up Charlotte.' Mother squeezed the words through the side of her mouth. She grabbed Aunt Charlotte's arm and pulled.

Marsha looked steadily at Aunt Charlotte. 'How can he be a *bit* dead?' Her voice was flat.

'He's not,' Aunt Charlotte said.

'He's not?' Marsha's eyes widened.

'No. He's just dead. All of him. Not just a bit.'

We watched Aunt Charlotte lumbering to her feet and the suit of armour noisily falling into separate pieces as the weight started to lift. Lucy didn't move.

'I have no idea what any of you are talking about.' Marsha started to walk down the stairs. A coldness had started to take hold of her face. Her eyes were sharp, carefully landing on first one then another of us. It felt very much like she was analysing us in turn, watching our reactions.

The Bradshaws scurried towards Lucy and lifted her roughly. Harriet pushed the disorientated girl to the side, before standing back in dismay. They both looked down on the broken jigsaw of armour parts and shook their heads. Harriet picked up the helmet and looked into its face. They both seemed very preoccupied, given that we'd just announced a man's death to his wife.

But for that matter, Marsha herself seemed remarkably unperturbed. She drifted down the stairs, eyes fixed ahead as though mesmerised, her long, red gown pouring down the stairs behind her. Lucy lifted her head and watched her descend with hard, resentful eyes. But Marsha was, for the first time that evening, every inch Lady Black, and this was her castle now. In that moment, she was subtly transformed. This was all hers, no one else's.

Our eyes followed her smooth procession.

She turned back to face us.

'Well, where is he?'

CHAPTER 21: THE WIDOW

Marsha knew she was being watched. She was watching us. Her eyes drifted over each of us in turn, assessing who was for or against her.

Lucy's gaze hadn't moved from Marsha once. She was shaking. Every part of her was tensed until the tendons stood proud on her neck. The skin beneath her eyes was swollen and had a purple tinge to it. A thick line of tears seemed permanently settled at the bottom lid of each eye.

'So, where is he?' Marsha repeated.

Mirabelle cleared her throat. She'd said very little so far, but now she adopted a solemn, almost patronising voice like a vicar greeting the bereaved. 'Lord Elzevir is at the entrance gate. We had to leave him there for when the police arrive. It would have been very sudden.'

'Don't you even care what happened to him?' Lucy raged.

'Unlike you, I'm not about to start weeping and wailing. I am not a hypocrite.'

They locked eyes.

'He was divorcing you. He knew what you'd been up to with Joseph, you adulterer.'

Joseph jerked his head back and frowned.

'Whatever I am, this is my house now.' Marsha stood defiantly. 'And I wouldn't use *that* word if I were you.'

'We were in love! You were just sleeping with the handyman out of boredom.'

'Hey!' Joseph said.

'I'm not going to hear any more of this!' Lucy strode towards the door before stopping as something occurred to her. 'You know what, you were the only person here when he died. You were the only person who could have brought that portcullis down.' Her voice was trembling. 'You killed him, you poisonous cow. You think you're so clever. I know you did it. You won't see a penny of his money and this won't be your house for much longer. I'll make sure of it.'

She swung back round to the door and pushed the Bradshaws out of the way.

Harriet was still holding the helmet as cautiously as if it had someone's head still in it. 'Careful!' she said.

Lucy glared at her before smashing the helmet out of her hands. Harriet looked suitably horrified as it clattered to the ground and a thin trail of cat urine trickled out.

Aunt Charlotte leaned in close to me. 'She's right, you know,' she said stony faced. 'Forfeiture rule.'

I frowned.

'Can't inherit a person's estate if you're criminally responsible for someone's death.' Aunt Charlotte was nodding. 'I remember the lawyer telling your mother that when George died.'

I stared at her. Mother was on the other side of her and could hear everything. She sighed.

'I'm just saying, Pandora,' Aunt Charlotte continued, unaware all the room was now watching her, 'no one can inherit the estate of someone they've murdered.'

'I'd like to see my husband now,' was all Marsha said.

'We left him where we found him, between the two portcullis gates,' Mirabelle said softly.

'I see. And you're sure he's dead? This is not just another of his lame stunts?'

'He's dead, Your Ladyship.' Mrs Abaddon nodded solemnly.

'A cannonball seems to have hit him on the head,' I added.

I couldn't help thinking that in some way the tables had turned. Instead of us carefully imparting the news, Marsha was extracting it from us cautiously and meticulously.

'We can't get an ambulance or the police up here yet,' Joseph said hesitantly. 'The village is still flooded, Your Ladyship. And the last time I checked, the phones weren't working and nor was the internet.'

I pulled out my phone and checked. I nodded to her.

'So that must mean there's a killer on the loose in the village, yes?' Marsha spoke deliberately and purposefully, maintaining absolute control.

We paused and the only noise was the sound of Harriet picking up the helmet and raising the visor.

'Is anyone on their own?' Marsha said steadily.

'Well, we should get after Lucy,' Mrs Abaddon announced. 'And then there's Verity too.'

'Wait, you left her on her own?' Marsha sounded agitated. This was the first real emotion she had shown since the announcement of her husband's murder. 'Does she know?'

Mrs Abaddon nodded once.

'And you left her? When her brother's just been murdered?'

Now she said it out loud, it did seem callous, if not dangerous.

'Right, we need to get organised.' Marsha undid the voluminous dressing gown and let it fall into the chair behind her.

She was fully dressed underneath.

* * *

The bitter cold air greeted us. There was no pause in the rain. Water streamed down the courtyard towards the gatehouse and Lord Elzevir's body. We stepped out tentatively into the darkness and instantly bent our heads, shielding our faces.

I glanced at Marsha. She still seemed determined, almost businesslike. But I've spent enough time mired in the various outpourings of other people's grief to know that the shock of death can make people act in the most extraordinary ways. There is an ocean of sadness out there on the internet, where every form of grief exists. Grief is custom-made, a perfect couture experience. I've spent so much time lost among the non-dead that at times it's been hard to live.

Lady Marsha Black didn't look like a single one of those people, and I'd definitely never seen a woman quite so determined to approach the body of her dead husband. This was someone seizing control and safeguarding her new-found power. As she approached him, it looked like a victory march. Joseph held out an arm to her, but she ignored him, striding past. When we caught up with her at the gate-house, every part of Marsha seemed collected, restrained. She walked under the portcullis and stood over the body of her husband.

She looked down at him with steely eyes, analysing him as if she was making sure he was dead. Her head leaned over to one side, almost in confusion, as if she didn't quite understand. She squinted, but no tears came from her eyes. Her eyebrow raised a little and she shook her head. He could just have committed another of his indiscretions. It was the picture of someone utterly unmoved. As I watched her in those few seconds, she seemed to me to have such an eloquent face and looked at him so ponderously that she could almost have been described as serene. But who can say how each of us will respond when Death brushes past us? Perhaps she was just grateful it hadn't moved onto her. Perhaps she was just in shock. But she seemed too controlled.

The rest of us edged tentatively round her and the body, as though we were fearful it might all have been some form of prank like the iron maiden incident and he would just leap up with a grin. Maybe that's what it was, a badly enacted stunt that had gone terribly wrong and malfunctioned in some way.

I flattened myself against the damp stone wall creating as much distance between me and the body as possible. I kept my eyes on his face.

He seemed smaller, more tragic, like an animal dead by the side of the road. Worthless. Would that please his killer? Was that part of the intention?

There wasn't much more blood than when we first saw him. I'd imagined a stream of it, watered down by the rain and running into the village, but it had just pooled around him in a small, dark puddle. The cannonball looked small as well, like a child's toy. But it was big enough. It had done its job perfectly.

'And you say both portcullis gates were down?' Marsha still stood over her husband's body, taking in every detail. There was no sadness there. No tears. She looked with a forensic eye.

Joseph nodded. 'Yes, Your Ladyship.'

She gave Lord Elzevir a final look, her eyes narrowing as if she was determined to remember her husband as he was at that moment. Then she forged out into the heavy night, fearless and determined. She didn't look back once. We followed silently.

Halfway down the drive, Marsha looked round at us. 'Come on! I need to get to Verity now.' Her voice cracked with an emotion she'd not shown before. She turned to Mrs Abaddon. 'She'd said she wanted you and Lucy to stay the night there. She was very clear about that.'

'I had to get Joseph, and we couldn't wake you, Your Ladyship. We had to get that gate up, and Miss Verity said she would be perfectly fine.'

'What about Mrs White?'

'Gone home, Your Ladyship.'

'For God's sake! You were all down there because she needed you to be there. She'd made that very clear from the beginning that it was the only way she could do all this. I only agreed for you to walk me home because Lucy and Mrs White were with her and you promised to go straight back.'

She turned to us and, for the first time, looked anguished. 'I should never have come back here at all. Verity insisted I should be here for Elzevir in case he got back after midnight and was locked out, but I really needed to be with *her*. Don't you see?' A note of desperation was starting to surface.

She set off with renewed purpose into the dark rain. She did not look back again.

CHAPTER 22: THE SISTER

As we drew nearer to the vicarage, Joseph announced, 'I need to go home. I need to check on . . .'

Harriet and Gerald both raised their eyebrows. He glanced at them before setting off down the lane at pace. No one questioned him or tried to stop him.

When we arrived at Verity's, Marsha hammered insistently on the door of the vicarage. There was a silence, and the thought scurried in that whoever had killed Lord Elzevir might have also had his wider family in mind as well.

A shadow quickly appeared at the glass in the door. When it opened, it took a few seconds for my eyes to adjust. Before anyone else could move, Marsha had flown forward. I couldn't see what she was doing as her body blocked my view, but as she moved to the side, I could see that the two women were holding hands tightly. They locked eyes as if they were silently speaking to each other. Both with anguished looks. Then Verity held Marsha unbreakably tight.

'Oh Verity, dear Verity,' Marsha whispered into the side of her head.

'I can't believe he's gone.' Verity said the words carefully as if each one made it more real.

'I'm so sorry, my darling. I'm so sorry.' Marsha spoke tenderly. She kissed the side of her head before slipping her hand from under Verity's and wrapping her arm around her.

'Hello?'

We swung round to look back into the night.

'Who's that? Who's out there?' Bridget called. 'Show yourself.'

There was a moment before a figure in a cape stepped out of the rain.

'What on Earth is going on?' Jocasta MacDonald moved into the porch light, and I could see that she was wet and looking very dishevelled.

No one answered.

She looked from face to face until her eyes landed on Verity and Marsha.

'Marsha? Verity? What's happening here? What are you doing?'

'We might ask the same of you, witch.' Harriet Bradshaw gave her a judgemental look.

'I . . . What do you mean?'

'She means, what are you doing out on such a dark and stormy night? Where have you been?' Bridget stood stiffly, holding the cat.

'Where have I been?' Jocasta repeated.

'I know exactly where she's been,' Mrs Abaddon sniffed. 'Churchyard.'

'I'm sure I don't—'

'Tell them what you were doing there.'

Jocasta stared furiously at her. 'Watching the ghosts.' She raised an eyebrow at Marsha and Verity, who slowly let go of one another.

'My husband is dead,' Marsha said.

'What?'

'Murdered.'

Jocasta's lips parted slightly.

'So perhaps this is no time for your brevity,' Marsha added.

'I . . . What? I don't understand.'

'What's not to understand? He's been bludgeoned to death by a cannonball.'

It struck me what an interesting choice of words this was. And I wasn't the only one of us to be intrigued. Mother was watching Marsha very closely.

'I'm so sorry,' Jocasta whispered.

'Might be best for you to come clean, dear.' Mirabelle gave Bridget a swift glance as if checking it was all right for her to speak.

Bridget nodded. 'Mirabelle is quite right. If there's a dangerous killer on the loose, we need to be sure of everyone's whereabouts.' Bridget placed a reassuring hand on Mirabelle's arm. Mirabelle didn't look very reassured — more wary.

'A dangerous killer?' Jocasta repeated. She looked around our faces. 'I need to . . . I need to get to him.' She paused, suddenly adopting a flat voice. 'I need to go home. My husband will be wondering where I am.'

'I doubt that, dear,' Gerald said archly. 'I imagine he's got a very good idea where you are.'

The tension seemed to almost vibrate in the air.

'I'm not staying here to listen to this.' Jocasta spoke vehemently in hurried breaths. 'Goodnight, and I'm sorry for your loss, Marsha. Although, I suspect you're not.' She turned and let her cape flare up behind her. Then she was gone, back into the night.

'Let's get you sat down,' Marsha said wearily. She spread her arm across Verity's shoulder and guided her through into the sitting room. The door was closed very purposefully.

We stood in the hall for a few moments, suspended in an awkward moment where we knew we should leave them alone with their grief but had no idea how to.

'Gerald and I need to go home,' Harriet announced.

He gave her a questioning look which slowly unfurled into understanding. 'Yes, yes. Quite right. Our daughter, Scarlett, you know.' They backed out of the door with thick smiles painted on.

'I'll make some tea,' Mrs Abaddon said and disappeared through another door without waiting for a response.

We waited, Bridget stroking her cat and shaking her head. The rest of us stood in stunned disbelief.

'How are we involved in this?' Aunt Charlotte sighed.

'We are not involved.' Mother widened her eyes. 'We just happen to be here.'

'We happen to be in a lot of places we shouldn't,' I murmured.

'And who's fault is that?'

'Well, not mine, Mother. You were the one wanting to come and play with the lady of the manor.'

'I wasn't even invited!'

Bridget laughed.

Thankfully the doorbell rang before Mother had a chance to respond. We looked at each other.

'Oh, for goodness' sake, I'll answer it.' And Bridget opened the door to a very wet and agitated Lucy Morello.

'I had nowhere else to go,' she said.

'And where have you been?'

'Nowhere. Just wandering, lost in the rain.'

Bridget gave her a suspicious look. 'How very *Wuthering Heights* of you.'

The door to the sitting room opened and Marsha emerged, her eyes swollen with tears.

Lucy looked at her with a surly face.

'I want you to sleep here tonight, Miss Morello.' Marsha didn't look at her when she spoke.

'With pleasure,' the girl snapped.

'You can sleep in the upstairs room, as you were instructed to previously. Verity will sleep in her bedroom downstairs.'

'But—'

'Just do as you're told.' Mrs Abaddon had reappeared from the kitchen with a distinct lack of any tea.

Marsha continued. 'Mrs Abaddon, I'd like you to accompany me back to the castle.' She cast her eye over our group, stranded in the middle of the hallway. She spoke softly, already adopting the manner of someone in a house of mourning. 'And you too, ladies.' She glanced back towards the sitting room, where Verity sat motionless. 'Verity has insisted I come back with you to the castle and make sure everyone is as comfortable as possible and everyone has a bed tonight. If that is all right with you ladies.'

We nodded in unison.

* * *

We walked back to the castle in cold silence. There was a very long way to go until morning. This night still seemed frighteningly long.

CHAPTER 23: AFTER DEATH

Most people associate death with peace, silence, rest. I do not. It's a scream inside your head that never dissolves. You crave silence from your thoughts every waking second — every sleeping second.

The bed was church pew hard. There was a sparseness to everything here, even the air felt mean and cold. I wrapped the thin, unfamiliar covers around me pretending there was some comfort in them. There was only one way I was going to find sleep in this dank place. I levered myself up on my elbows and reached for Dad's Bible. I took out my hipflask and only fell into a dead sleep when most of it was gone.

It felt like I'd barely touched sleep when the first sound woke me.

A scratch. Muffled as if it was under something. Or behind something. My eyes flickered open. The moonlight spread a cold, grey light across the room.

Scratch.

This time louder. My eyes travelled quickly along the walls.

The sound came again and more repetitively. It echoed as if it was inside the stones themselves, rising up from

161

beneath the ground, inside the walls, moving round the perimeter of the room. Stalking me.

Scratch. Scratch, scratch.

It came again, a much longer and deeper sound as though something was being scraped along the thick stone.

No, not scraped. Dragged. In that one word, my thoughts had given the sound movement. A frightening action. I pushed myself up onto my elbows. There was nothing in the room. That's what I told myself. I tasted the bitter saliva pool behind my teeth. I instinctively pulled my arms around myself and gripped tight.

The noise made a busy path along the inside of the wall now, unaware or dismissive of its new audience. It was grating along the other side of the wall, opposite to me.

I took a deep, cold breath that shocked my throat. Then I moved — slowly at first. Swinging my legs round and standing. As my feet touched the rough carpet, I felt the overwhelming need to run. To get out of the open centre of the room. I was too exposed here. I had to get to the edge. I ran with soft steps.

I tripped on an uneven lip of the carpet and landed on my knees near the door. My head glanced along the edge of a small side table and I instantly felt a shard of pain. As if in response, there was a sudden dead thud from behind the wall and then silence. A sigh.

I waited.

Whatever was there paused. Could I hear drawn out breaths? Or was that me?

'Dad?' I whispered.

It was the last thing I heard.

* * *

The light cut a thin, sharp line along my eyelids. I paused before flickering into consciousness. As they opened, a shock of blue-white light flared round the circles of my eyes like a gas ring lighting up. I pinched them shut but the glare remained. The darkness of dreams had gone.

I was still on the floor, the rough imprint of the carpet against my cheek. I could taste the sour remains of the brandy, the faint ginger scent lifted up on my breath. In one sigh, I let my eyes slowly drift open.

I hadn't got as far as closing the curtains last night. I seldom do, even though dawn always punishes me. I waited a moment. The day was still at that tipping point where nothing would be real until I moved. An insipid light washed over my eyes. Specks of white floated across and I felt the first shivers of pain surface in my head.

Carefully, I felt my temple and the crusted trail of blood down the side of my face. I began to sit up as if my body weighed me down. As my eyes adjusted, I could see a precarious light slipping over the high tower. The day already felt tentative.

Thoughts started to trickle through the gaps. There was a dead man down there. Framed by his own black pool of blood. Crumpled and small, as if someone had screwed him up like rubbish. I rubbed at my forehead briskly trying to scrub away the image. But it was too late, the thought had already congealed. My brain felt swollen up against my skull, trying to push the pictures out through the front.

I stood up and walked to the window, the world warped by the thick bottle-bottom glass slick with winter grime. Curves of light hung under the low clouds. Grey layers of rain were still being driven over the far-off moors. There was no sun waiting on the edge, just a line of cold light behind the rain.

I looked down into the courtyard. The grim daylight picked out the slippery cobbles, water trickling in crooked streams all meeting down there at the gatehouse. There were cracks in some of the windows and ivy spooling its way up the walls.

My eyes drifted back to the gatehouse and last night. Both portcullis gates had been down. The cannonball sat on the floor beside him. But it couldn't have got through those small gaps in the gate without damage. There was no damage to the gate. Lord Elzevir would have been blown backwards. But the injury was to the very top of his head. In any event, we'd been told the cannon had not even fired. The gates came down so fast. No one could have been in there with him, hit him and got out as the gates were falling. Why would anyone hit him, then come out and purposefully close the gates? Why not just wait for the Midnight Gun? They would have come down anyway at twelve o'clock. Someone took the trouble to bring them down two minutes before that.

The only thing above him was that murder hole and that was conclusively sealed. Nothing could have moved that and it had been concreted in for some time.

Marsha was very obviously, perhaps purposefully, the only one here. All the staff were elsewhere. It was impossible to remember who had dispersed and at what point from our strange travelling dinner party. But we'd had enough time to work out all wasn't well in His Lordship's marriage. And Marsha told him to be home before midnight or the portcullis would come down. Everything pointed to who and why. Just not how.

I watched my breath leave circles of fog on the window that slowly pulled in and dissolved. Shadows of clouds drifted in black stains across the hills. The light had a different edge here, a veiled quality. It should have been a very prim and perfect village, all 'More tea vicar?' and Sunday services, but this village had an anxious nature and had watched us all with a distrustful eye from the very beginning.

Something moved behind me. I turned. There was a subtle change, a ripple in the air. I could sense something in the room with me. Life? Death?

'Dad?'

'Don't be so ridiculous.' Mother had opened the door with her usual inability to knock. 'Get ready. We're meeting downstairs.'

'I . . .'

She held up her hand. 'Not today, Ursula. Lock up your crazy and get changed into something you didn't sleep in.' She started to turn away and then paused. 'And brush your teeth.'

CHAPTER 24: AN ASTRAL HOLE

I only noticed the dry mud splattered up the sides of my jeans when I was approaching them all. Mother watched me with her 'What have you been up to?' face. Her eyes instantly landed on my dirty, slept-in clothes.

I looked around the rest of them. Aunt Charlotte was slumped in the large, pink chair looking as though she was becoming part of it. Mirabelle and Bridget sat rigidly on the sofa with Dingerling perched between them. The cat wasn't much more than two black eyes against the flesh-coloured cushions.

Mrs Abaddon had materialised and was setting out coffee cups on the sideboard where the Champagne glasses had sat in rows just a few hours ago. The iron maiden still stood open in the corner by the long picture windows, a silent reminder that no one was going to be leaping out of there this morning. The spikes were clean of blood. Had Mrs Abaddon spent time scrubbing away the fake blood when Lord Elzevir's real blood had just been spilled?

Standing by the side of the contraption, staring out across the windswept gardens, was Marsha. Rain was still dappling her reflection in the windows and rolling down. But there were no tears on Marsha's face. She was immaculate in the kind of jeans that were clearly expensive and a black cashmere jumper, a stylish nod to her new-found widowhood. The rows of pearls were an even bigger nod to her new-found wealth. She held a cup of coffee but made no movements to drink it. She looked so perfectly posed, as if she was about to have her picture taken — *Lady Black in mourning*.

The red-furred monkey, Dupin, sat crunching on some nuts with a look of evident delight. He'd just been given some marvellous treat. His busy little eyes glimmered as he looked around us all. He made a sound that seemed like he was laughing at us.

'Would you like some coffee, ladies?' Marsha's voice cracked on just the right note. She turned. 'Mrs Abaddon, is Lucy here yet?'

'She's still with Miss Verity. Lucy's making out she's been hit hard. Taking on screaming and crying like that when it's Miss Verity's brother! Just isn't right.'

'And my husband.'

We all paused.

'I'll take some coffee,' Mother interrupted as if she couldn't help herself. I looked at her bloodshot eyes. She had that pinched look of regret for how much brandy she'd had the night before.

'Tea for me,' Aunt Charlotte chimed. 'Tea for breakfast. Coffee later.'

'Then straight onto the scotch,' Bridget sneered.

'How very dare you?'

'Not now, Charlotte,' Mother sighed. 'There's been a death. I'm going to need my coffee first.'

Marsha turned her mouth down and looked back at the gardens brushing us all away.

Dupin gave her a strange little grin and then carried on eating.

The electronic doorbell sounded out of tune. Being at someone else's house when there's a death is difficult enough to negotiate, but when you suspect the owner might be the murderer there's a whole extra layer of excruciating tension that makes even the most normal of occurrences seem awkward.

Mrs Abaddon set down the cup. 'A moment, please, ladies. I will serve coffee after I've answered the door.'

Marsha turned to us with her first look of genuine concern. 'See? This is what happens when staff fail to turn up. Lucy Morello should be here to serve coffees. Mrs Abaddon always opens the door.'

It seemed like such an unnecessary, fatuous comment to make for a grieving widow. But grief can make even the smallest of things take on dramatic levels of importance. When Dad died, nothing could interrupt my rearranging of the books on my shelves as if somehow it might re-order events until the story read differently. The strange fiction growing from the order of the words would somehow make it all a mistake and he would still be alive. But then no words in any book could ever change that. He was dead. Amen. And when I fell into his Bible, it wasn't words I was looking for anymore.

But there was no mistake here. Lord Elzevir was dead, and Marsha seemingly had no wish to rearrange any of that. A new self-possession had already settled in and she was more contained, more serene. More controlled. We'd all seen first-hand how he'd treated her, so why should we expect grief or even, perhaps, remorse from her?

'Mr Ronald MacDonald,' Mrs Abaddon announced without a trace of irony.

Faces twitched. The morning was already slipping back into that surreal world we'd encountered last night.

Ron didn't wait to see if anyone was laughing. He barged into the room with the look of someone who had an earth-shattering announcement to make.

'There's . . . There's a . . . Someone's dead!'

'We know.' Marsha sounded almost bored. 'My husband. In the gatehouse. With the cannonball.'

The man's face contorted into a strange look of astonishment. 'I was actually on my way to tell you that Jocasta didn't come home last night. I think she might be dead.'

Everyone waited for someone else to speak.

Mother was first, of course. 'Isn't that a bit of a leap? Just because she didn't come home doesn't—'

'I can't feel her anymore. She's not in my astral hole.'

'I should hope not!' Aunt Charlotte looked appalled.

'Mr MacDonald—' Bridget grabbed the cat and began viciously stroking it — 'you're asking us to believe your wife is dead because you cannot feel her in your—'

'We have had a spiritual link going back over centuries.'

Bridget paused her hand on the cat. 'What? Over—'

'Now is not the time to start explaining the other astral planes. She's missing!'

'Have you tried the church?' Marsha smiled

The monkey laughed and flipped over on his perch.

'We're pagans. We don't . . .' his voice faded.

'It's just that Verity mentioned the reason your wife and the vicar disappeared at the same time last night. That they were having . . . a little astral communication themselves.' Marsha looked pleased with herself.

'Well done for not mentioning anyone's hole,' Aunt Charlotte said as an aside.

'This is ridiculous!' Ron stuttered. 'I came here to tell you my wife might be in danger and first of all I'm confronted with a dead body . . .'

'Oh, I do apologise for leaving my murdered husband at the gate.'

'I'm sorry. Look, I'm just worried. If he's . . . he's dead, then Jocasta might very well be in extreme danger.'

'He's right,' Mirabelle said quietly, 'we should mount a search party.' It was the first time I'd heard her speak this morning and her voice sounded weak and raw. The skin around her eyes was noticeably swollen.

Bridget stared intently at the side of Mirabelle's head as if she'd somehow spoken without permission.

'She's right!' I jumped in. I quickly glanced at Mother, who looked at the floor. 'I mean, if someone's dead—'

'There's no "if" about it. He's dead.' Bridget seemed to enjoy saying that.

I paused. 'And someone's missing, we do need to get up a search party for this gentleman's wife. She can't have gone far. If we can't get out of the village then nor can she.'

'And nor can the killer,' Aunt Charlotte added.

All eyes travelled to Marsha.

'And why would I kill Jocasta?' Marsha asked. She'd noticeably not asked that about her husband.

No one answered.

* * *

We decided a pack mentality was the best approach and that a search party had to involve all of us. It wasn't so much a decision as more a general inability to organise ourselves. We all just filed out into the hallway, hoping someone else would take the lead.

'Do we really have to go past that . . . body again?' Bridget asked with her usual touching sentimentality.

'You mean my husband?' Marsha was focusing on pulling on a pair of leather gloves with such careful precision it made her look like a surgeon prepping for theatre. Everyone's eyes were on the gloves now.

Marsha paused and met my eyes. 'There's no need to concern yourselves, ladies. We can go into the room above the gatehouse and over the top. The door out onto the drive can be unlocked from the inside.'

Mother frowned. 'Wait a minute, why couldn't Lord Elzevir have used that door last night? Why would he have to be back before the Midnight Gun?'

'Because he'd turn into a pumpkin.' Marsha's eyes narrowed. She took a long, impatient breath. 'Because the door can only be opened from the castle side. Like most castles, it's built to be impenetrable and there's no way of opening it from the outside. Otherwise, we'd be wide open to any old riff-raff and invaders wouldn't we? What would be the point of the blasted gates then?' She gave us a brusque smile.

'I meant you could have left that . . .'

Marsha had already turned to leave.

Mrs Abaddon opened the castle door and we filed out dutifully into the dank air. The wind drove into me, dragging my hair across my face.

'Your Ladyship, I will stay here and tidy away the cups. There's no sign of Lucy yet.'

Marsha nodded.

'Wait,' I said, 'should we leave anyone on their own?'

Mrs Abaddon frowned. 'I won't be on my own. Mrs White is here.'

* * *

The gatehouse sat beneath the cold mist and watched our solemn approach. Only Ron scuttled with any purpose, his eyes rat-keen, his head twitching.

I should have been scared, but all I could feel was the slow, cold spread of exhaustion soaking up through me.

Dad's shape stood sentry at the portcullis, though what he was protecting was doubtful. I hoped it was me, but hope is a silly creature. The low burn of his eyes on me was almost too much to resist, but now was not the time to be weak, to give in or forgive him. Punishment is an essential part of life. I didn't look at him.

Sadly, what my eyes drifted to and landed on like carrion was the dead outline of Lord Elzevir, still in his last moment. His body so conspicuous and solitary. The cannonball rested innocently to the side. Only the glossy pond of blood condemned it. From what I'd seen, what I could remember, he hadn't even had time to look up. I tried to stitch the pieces together, build a story from what we'd seen — a strange and ill-formed little monster of a story. I pictured Lord Elzevir looking towards the gate as it closed him in. The gate lowered before the Midnight Gun went off. So he saw the gates lower. Then bang! His head cracked like an eggshell and all life was gone. Quick and sudden. It made no sense, but death doesn't. It makes all this great expanse of life very senseless.

Dad drifted between me and the sprawled-out body as if he thought his spirit standing there could in some way protect me from death.

'Very ironic,' I muttered.

'What is?' Mother was pin-sharp this morning, noting everything I was doing. She's always bloodhound keen round me when there's a death. It seems to spur her into life.

Aunt Charlotte bent and looked up into my face. 'Don't you go having another one of your turns now, will you, dear? You know what I've told you about looking at dead bodies.'

I sighed.

Ron shot us a concerned glance.

'Up here.' Marsha nodded towards the small door at the side of the gate where we'd seen Lord Elzevir go yesterday evening. She had a flat, almost disinterested look about her. I noticed how she didn't even glance at her dead husband. Not even her basic curiosity had been sparked. She didn't flinch. Perhaps that was her way of guarding herself against death. We all have our ways. The journey over from the world of the unbereaved is long and arduous. She was only just starting out.

Bridget went up the winding stairs first, nursing her wrinkled cat that still stared up at her hatefully. Dingerling was increasingly taking on a bad aura, as if he was Bridget's own little daemon.

Mirabelle followed her.

I edged my way round the narrow, low door. The stone was wet with a dull, tea-coloured sheen, the pungent scent of damp clung to the air. Our footsteps had a cold echo to them. I trod carefully, the steps uneven and worn low in the middle where countless feet had smoothed a path.

We climbed the steps in silence, small white clouds of our breath lingering in the cold morning air. There was a small slit of a window halfway up the stairs, so slim it only allowed a snippet of light to fall on the steps. I peered out like a prisoner and I could see all the way across Dartmoor to where the mist met the land as if the sky had just fallen on it. The fog seemed to be moving closer hinting there was something alive about it, seeking out a way down towards the village. Any traces of early light had been almost completely obscured already. I thought of the tales of a place whose myths still lingered out there. They were just told to scare away outsiders — like us. Well, I was scared enough now to want to leave. The only trouble was how to get out.

I looked at my phone. Still nothing.

Ron was behind me.

'How was the road this morning, Mr MacDonald?' I asked.

'Joe Greengage was out. Says it's flooded bad. Him and Lee are going to try and get a tractor through. There's no way Jocasta could have left the village. She's still here somewhere.'

Another breath of wind circled the stairs and the sound of the rain rose in a river around us. It was beginning to feel like we really were in some sort of production that was being very carefully stage-managed by someone. I looked up ahead but I could only see Mirabelle's back in front of me.

At the top of the stairs, a small room opened out which was only just big enough for all of us. I drew back into a corner and tried to take everything in. Huge chains hung either side of the room. They were the mechanism for the two portcullis gates, the top sections of which were now both visible where they stood open. The chains were on what looked like large cogs that presumably turned round when they lowered.

I slipped through the room, past Mother and Aunt Charlotte, who were both watching me intently. In the centre of the room was the murder hole, covered over with thick glass. Crouching down, I ran my finger round the small window on the floor. Thick, old concrete sealed it in. A layer of dirt and moss had settled there. It hadn't moved in a long time.

'Nothing can get through that.' Marsha was looking at me. 'Thick reinforced glass. The Bradshaws insisted on it so that a person could stand on it. Although why anyone would want to is beyond me.'

I leaned right over and peered through the mottled glass. Directly below was the crumpled body of Lord Elzevir. He looked so small from up here — unreal, as if he wasn't a man at all. I closed my eyes.

When I opened them, a face was peering back up at me just below the glass. The eyes locked with mine, two black stones. I fell back, the air caught in my chest.

'Dad,' I whispered. A dim light sparkled across the back of my eyes. Purple motes drifted in and out of my vision. The stone walls were closing over me. The light dribbled away.

The next thing I saw was Mother's face above me.

'Mum,' I panted. Her hand touched mine.

'Come on,' her voice was quiet.

'He's here, Mum.'

As her face dwindled into the shadows, I thought I saw her lips move around the words, 'I know.' But nothing was clear this morning.

CHAPTER 25: NEVER CROSS A WITCH WITH RUNNING WATER

'What the hell is going on?' were the first words I heard as I came round.

'Nothing that need concern *you*.' Mother was businesslike.

'What do you mean, "Nothing that need concern you?" My wife is missing! There's been a murder!' Ron paused. 'Sorry, Marsha.'

'Don't worry about it.' Still there was that flippancy in Marsha's tone.

'Well, *you* certainly don't sound very worried about it.' Bridget raised her eyebrows.

Marsha shrugged, and I wondered if, from this angle, she could see down the murder hole to the small body of her dead husband. If I looked, would Dad's eyes still be there glaring back at me?

My head pounded.

'It's OK,' Mother said quietly. 'I've got you.' She held my hand and I could feel Aunt Charlotte's arm around my shoulders.

Aunt Charlotte smiled. 'All OK.'

Ron was growing increasingly agitated. 'All I'm saying is, there's a killer on the loose and this young lady has just started talking about someone else being here. Her dad!'

'He's dead,' Mother said flatly. 'That's none of your concern.'

'What? There's been another . . .'

'He died many years ago,' Mother added.

A bemused look spread over Ron. 'Look, I don't know who you people are, but I sense a bad omen. I'm going to find my wife.'

* * *

No one spoke much on the way out of the castle. My legs felt empty, but I'm used to that now. I checked the small door out onto the drive and Marsha wasn't lying, there was no handle, no way in from the outside. There was a bracket each side of the door on the inside and a large beam of wood had to be lifted in and out before the door could be pushed open.

As we crossed the bridge over the moat and down onto the long gravel drive, I noticed two people out on the lane. The Bradshaws.

'Good morning,' they called, as if a man hadn't been killed last night by a cannonball.

They looked along our faces and their cheeriness faded.

'Marsha.' Harriet nodded with a new solemnity as if she'd just remembered the murdered lord under the gatehouse.

'Morning, Harriet. Gerald.' Marsha's face barely moved. 'Out for a walk round the scene of the crime?'

They both looked affronted. 'Of course not! Gerald had a metal detectorists' meeting down by the moat. Which I believe I did mention last night before anyone was . . . before . . .'

'Which I now cannot partake of,' Gerald said stiffly, 'as I have been robbed.'

'Robbed?' Mirabelle frowned.

'Yes, I only noticed this morning. My detectorist equipment has gone from my shed. I don't think anyone has made it up to the village though. The roads are all still flooded, so the meeting's off. Whoever took my equipment is still here!'

'I've told him before,' Harriet continued, 'it's worth a lot of money and he shouldn't—'

'If I may just ejaculate for a moment.' Everyone looked at Gerald.

Harriet cleared her throat. 'You mean interject, dear.'

He looked confused and irritated. 'I know what I mean, Harriet dear. Who was on *Countdown* February 1992?'

'Did you ejaculate there too, Mr Bradshaw?' Aunt Charlotte asked.

'Many times! And Mrs Bradshaw can attest to that.' Gerald folded his arms defiantly. There was pride in this man's face.

'Interject, dear. Interject.' Harriet smiled nervously.

'I'm trying to, dear. I'm trying.' He shifted around uncomfortably. He took a breath to gather himself. 'I would like us all to pause and think for a moment what is different.'

'My husband is dead.' Marsha's face was cold.

'My wife is missing,' Ron added.

'Missing?' Harriet said. 'Again?'

'No . . . . But I meant . . . Well, I meant what is different with the castle?'

'Oh for God's sake, Gerald. My husband's dead. You were intending to have your sad little meeting moments from his body and you're still banging on about the renovations. We haven't done anything since the last set of works you objected to. Does that satisfy you?' Marsha turned away.

'No, no, Lady Black. I'm not ejaculating very well, am I?'

'Interjecting, Gerald. Interjecting.' Even Harriet was growing impatient now.

'Yes, yes, all right Harriet. But look. I was going down to the moat to . . .' Gerald was pointing down the bank towards the moat, his face bunched in confusion.

'There's no time for this!' Ron blurted. 'Jocasta's missing.'

'What do you mean, missing?' Harriet repeated. 'She does like a wander.'

'She is missing! She didn't come home at all and I need—'

'Will you just listen?' Gerald shouted. 'The ducking stool is down.'

The words brought silence. A bemused look crossed our faces and followed where Gerald was pointing to a large wooden pole that looked remarkably like a see-saw with one end of it down in the water.

Marsha started to walk slowly towards it. We followed, almost trance-like, trying not to let any stray thoughts in.

* * *

The ground beyond the gravel drive was boggy. As I lifted my feet, claggy mud sucked them deeper as though it was trying to hold me back. The bank down to the moat looked treacherously steep and slippery.

We neared the strange contraption, and I could see the mud around it had been disrupted quite a lot. Large hollows and footprints were visible in the worn-away grass. Long gouges were cut into the mud. Something heavy had been dragged through it. The central strut of the device was perilously close to the edge where the bank fell away into the black water. The other end of the long, thick pole was sunk beneath the surface. Rain pitted the water's surface and ran down the length of the long, aged beam.

'I've said it before, this is not for use.' Gerald sighed.

We looked doubtfully at each other. It was hard to imagine why anyone would have been trying to use a ducking stool.

Clearly, Gerald's thoughts had not yet made the leap the rest of us had.

'It's sixteenth-century and needs constant maintenance.'

'It is constantly maintained, Gerald.' Marsha shook her head. 'As you well know.'

'Well, if you'll excuse me, Lady Black, that can't be right. The cantilever system is perfectly balanced. It should not fall into the water without a weight on the other end, otherwise the stool will rot in the water. It should be out of the water in its naturally calibrated state.'

I looked at Ron and then quickly at Mother, who was staring into the murky waters.

'We need to raise it.' Mother didn't look for any questions.

'Exactly! Just what I was saying. We need to—'

'Be quiet, dear,' Harriet said.

He looked at her in confusion. 'I . . .'

'If only a weight will sink it,' she kept her voice low, 'then there is something on the other end of it.'

He paused and then realisation flooded his face. 'Oh!'

She nodded and all eyes settled on Ron. He stared at the grim water.

The wind raked through my hair, wet strands flicking across my eyes as I squinted against the rain.

'Right, Gerald,' Aunt Charlotte said decidedly, 'this is your moment! You're up. Raise the ducking stool!'

A moment of solemn duty crossed Gerald's face as if he'd been waiting a long time to hear those words. He looked at his wife, who was all keen encouragement. And he stepped towards the ducking stool. 'With your permission, Lady Black.'

'Yes, yes!' she hissed. 'Get on with it.'

He began slowly but firmly pressing down with both hands, almost as if he was just testing its weight. It didn't move. He glanced over at our group and wiped his hands down his trousers, leaving two dark smears of mud on each leg. He pushed down on the large raised wooden bar again, this time lifting his entire weight off the ground. The first glimmer of defeat started to emerge on his face.

Aunt Charlotte stepped forward, rolled up her sleeves and nodded to Gerald. She placed her hands next to his on the lifted beam. Mirabelle wedged herself in between them and looked straight ahead, her hands firmly set on the wood.

They began to push. It rocked a little and the waters rippled. Again, they pushed down and then each of them began to lean on it until their feet were barely touching the ground. Aunt Charlotte was on the tiptoes of her thick brogues, skidding in the mud, when the stool began to surface. They paused and then with renewed effort, the strain clear on their faces, they pushed.

There was a ripple of movement and something dark broke the surface of the water.

'Push!' Aunt Charlotte commanded.

Ron hurried forward to lever the end of the bar. I couldn't see a space. The strain was evident on all their faces. And slowly they pushed the bar further down and the other end began to rise from the water as if it was being torn out of it.

At first, the slumped mess didn't even look human. The long hair strewn with weeds poured down towards the moat, water raining from the heavy clothes. The shock of it made the four pushing lose their momentum for a second and the stool began to slip. Ron let go.

'Quick!' Mother shouted towards me.

We ran to the wooden beam, desperately trying to nestle ourselves between the others, some of us barely able to get a hand on the wooden bar. Together we pushed down again on the coarse, wet wood. The seat rose up and the long, black cape drained out into the water in a fast stream until finally the body was lifted high up into the air above us. It was a thin silhouette against the slate grey sky, leaking out in a long uninterrupted flow of water as if it was melting.

Jocasta MacDonald's marbled face looked almost serene staring down into her watery grave. She was tied down to the chair with thick coils of rope that gave this scene a very definite purpose. Nothing was vague about this image. Nothing loose about the intent.

'Oh my God,' Marsha breathed in disbelief.

The rope was tied so tight that where the cape was pulled back her clay white skin bulged over the bindings. Someone had stood on the other end of that pole and plunged that trussed up woman into the muddied waters and those slimy depths below. Had she been conscious to see the water rushing up to meet her? Or perhaps she had woken up in her new watery world — alert eyed, then panicked and feverishly struggling. Thrashing inside her bindings, rocking one way then the next, she would have been the very mirror image of the calm, martyred face that looked down on us now.

It hadn't occurred to me until he fell to his knees and groaned, that the woman's husband was there to witness her rising up from those dead waters. She sat above him, her eyes as white as mould, blindly staring down at him. Her expression caught in that last failed attempt to find breath.

'I . . . I can't . . . God . . . No!' Ron's cry seemed to have a new voice.

She hung above us in the sky, unmoved, her dead eyes reflecting the water.

Each of us looked up at her in horrified disbelief.

'Oh my God,' Aunt Charlotte breathed.

'Get her down,' Harriet said. 'Turn it. You need to move it round, then lower it.' She seemed to find it easier to be practical than let the truth of what we were seeing seep in.

We swung her round, the pole pivoting in the centre, as if we were opening no more than a simple gate. The water spewed round her and splattered across us, muddy droplets falling from her among the thin rain. Her cape clung to her back, pulled and gathered in by the rope, glimpses of the grey flesh underneath, battered and bruised.

'Jocasta?' Ron whispered.

'Christ.' I heard Mother's voice as she reached for my hand. I felt her fingers slip between mine.

We set the body down as gently as we could, but she was heavy with water and death. Her head slumped until it rested on her chest. The delicate, ethereal woman who had hovered above us was gone. Stark blue veins rippled clearly beneath the cold flesh, blanched and wrinkled by the water. Long strips of black hair fell either side of her face. Her hands were clenched tight in fear on the arms of the chair where they had been cruelly roped. Her legs were rigid against the wood as if everything about her had tensed in on itself. The water was the merest trickle coming from the tips of her hair now and dripping soundlessly from her clothes. The chair sat heavily in the dirt, its legs sinking into the thick mud.

Her hair parted over the back of her head and I could see the grey skin of her neck. I let go of the bar, my mind numb as if protecting itself from this grim scene.

Ron had stumbled towards her and fell into the mud at her feet.

'I . . . Jocasta . . . Jocasta.'

He breathed her name in and out as if trying to breathe new life into her. He looked up into her face below the curtain of lank hair. His eyes were set wide in disbelief. Kneeling, he clutched his hands tight together until he looked like he was praying up into the face of an angel's statue. As though he was about to start unfolding his soul to this saint. His eyes were pearly with tears.

No one could speak. We watched in fear and awe.

I looked away and saw Dad's shape lingering by the castle walls. Had he tried to warn me, shock me into not coming down here? Standing there beneath the vast castle walls, he was steeped in shadows as if the light of him was slowly going out.

I looked around our sad group. The wind rushed around us in a sea of sound, but no one moved. We stood, such despondent figures, spaced out in our carefully set places. Jocasta on her chair and the broken shape of Ron kneeling before her. A desolate scene, lifted from some poor painting, a pilgrimage or sorrowful gathering to worship or grieve. Who knows what we looked like stranded in that terrible moment?

Finally, Mother cleared her throat. She has always worn silence uncomfortably. 'We need to do something.'

'What can we do?' Mirabelle's voice sounded timid, afraid.

It was Bridget who answered, not Mother. 'Nothing.'
The word was defiant.

'We can't—'

'We can't *do* anything. We've already done enough. Too
much. We should put her back where we found her for the
police.'

Ron looked around at Bridget, his eyes venomous.
There was an eerie calm settling over him. 'You touch her
and I'll sink you.'

'Don't threaten me.'

'Bridget.' Mirabelle held up both hands. 'Leave him.'

'Oh, so you're growing brave now, are you?' Bridget's
face tightened. 'Maybe I should tell them how brave you were
when you first came to me.' As her mouth formed round a
smile, her lips glistened with rain drops.

'Shut up, Bridget. Have some respect.' Aunt Charlotte's
face was set firmly with conviction. 'We're not lowering that
poor wretched woman into the water again.'

'Jocasta. My, Jocasta.' Ron's voice was no more than a
weak chant now.

'That's your rope, isn't it, Gerald?' Harriet's voice was
barely above a whisper as she peered closer.

The thick, blue rope snaked round the black cape,
under the woman's arms. We all looked back at Gerald, who
seemed suddenly stunned. 'Don't . . . I . . .' he stuttered. 'I
told you I'd been robbed.'

'Of your metal detecting kit.' Aunt Charlotte stared at
him. 'Not your murderer's kit! What the hell do you need
that rope for?'

'Pulling up heavy finds.'

'A likely story.'

Marsha stepped between them and held up her hands.
'Right, that's enough. We need to . . .' She broke off and looked
at Ron. 'Someone should go and check on Reverend Vert.'

Ron slowly raised his head as if an invisible string had
pulled it up. His eyes instantly skewered Marsha. 'That bastard? I'll murder him myself.'

CHAPTER 26: THE MISSING VICAR

We decided that, in light of Ron's murderous pronouncement, it might be better if we didn't take him with us to see the vicar.

The Bradshaws offered to stay with him, and as they moved in closer round the ducking stool, I got the distinct impression that their interest might be straying back into historical reconstruction territory.

We walked away, me, Mother, Aunt Charlotte, Mirabelle and Bridget, all following Marsha, all looking shell-shocked.

My thoughts were numb as though the icy rain had melted through into my head and frozen everything. But my stomach knotted and unknotted constantly tying and untying itself. I felt the nausea passing through me in waves.

'Is it wise to leave Ron with Gerald and Harriet?' I frowned.

'It'll be fine,' Mother said. 'He's no more a murderer than I am.' These words brought less comfort than she'd hoped.

'I don't understand it.' Aunt Charlotte sounded weary.

Mother sighed. 'Why does that not surprise me?'

Aunt Charlotte scowled and shook her head. 'We saw her. She was going home. We were all there at Verity's house.'

'Well, clearly she didn't make it home.' Mother didn't add any more.

'But the moat, the castle . . . it's the wrong way from Verity's.' Aunt Charlotte could have been talking to herself.

'What?'

'Think about it. She would come out of the vicarage, and her house, the Lodge, is across the lane over to the left from where she was standing. The castle is across and over to the right — opposite the church. So she wasn't going home.'

'The vicarage.' Marsha spoke as if she disbelieved her own voice.

'Marsha?' There was a moment of genuine concern on Mirabelle's face.

'I need to go.' Marsha stared out at the rain. 'I need to be with Verity. She needs me.' Her eyes had a glazed, unreal nature to them as if they could see so much more than what was in front of them. She looked through us all.

'Well, if you think that's necessary . . .' Mother's voice trailed away.

Marsha was already turning towards the road with a new intent. 'I must go. She needs me.'

'Right,' Aunt Charlotte called. 'Good idea. You go and check everything's all right there and . . .'

Marsha was too far away to hear us even if she'd tried to. She moved with a new purpose, her head lowered and hands shoved deep into her pockets.

We looked at one another. I shrugged. 'She just wants to protect her family, I suppose.'

Bridget's eyes narrowed. 'At the expense of everyone else.'

'I don't see any problem with that.' Mother held back her head disdainfully, rain trickling over her face. 'It's entirely natural for her to be worried. There are two *dead* people here and Verity shouldn't be on her own.'

'Well, it's all a question of priorities, I suppose,' Bridget sneered and cast Mirabelle a sour little look. 'And she's not on her own. Lucy Morello is there.'

'Somehow I don't think that's very comforting to Marsha,' Mother said.

I sighed and closed my eyes as if it might block out what they were saying. 'We need to see if the vicar is all right. He's the only other one on his own, isn't he?' It was a genuine question. I still couldn't work out where everyone lived and should be, and most importantly where they really were. I could have done with that map right now. How could I have misplaced it so easily?

Aunt Charlotte lowered her voice, which doesn't really make that much difference. 'From what the other villagers are saying, she, I mean . . . the dead woman, was probably off to the church, back to the vicar, not on her way home. Her first reaction to the news that there was a killer on the loose was 'I need to get to him.' She didn't mean her husband. I think she was definitely off back to the church. And if that's the case, he's in danger.'

'Or he's dangerous,' I added.

No one answered. I watched Marsha's back disappear into the misty rain, her long hair falling down across her coat. She had a determined walk, which was the very opposite of our brow-beaten group. We were tired, a punishing exhaustion had spread through us all, the rain in some way diluting us. We were being drained. I didn't look back. None of us did. We bent our heads and trudged towards the church. My thoughts were unspooling fast. And again, we found ourselves in this village without any of the locals with us. It was starting to look a little pre-ordained.

We crossed the lane, stepping through the swathes of mud, leaves and sticks flooding down. The rain was a thin drizzle now, but the wind still drove round us. The trees above were black shapes burned by winter. And I was bitter damp in my wet clothes now.

The rusted gate to the graveyard was already open as if it had been expecting us. Aunt Charlotte was right, it was directly opposite the castle. I turned and could still see the small shapes of the Bradshaws, Ron kneeling and the strange outline of the woman roped to a chair at the end of the long construction. It seemed so unreal even from this distance.

Aunt Charlotte caught me looking back. 'All getting a bit *Wicker Man* here now, isn't it?' She spoke quietly, as if afraid someone might be listening. 'Not sure the graveyard's the best place to be.'

'What are you scared of?' Bridget said acidly. 'The ghosts?'

I flicked a look at Dad, who stood solemnly by the entrance. Mother was watching me intently.

'Come on, come on,' blustered Bridget, pushing her way through. 'I thought you people loved the dead.'

A rook called out from the bare bones of the tree over-hanging the church wall. The branches were all bent in sufferance from the constant wind, leaning away from the church. The bird watched us with his smooth pebble eyes before lifting up on the wind in a splash of wings. It wheeled above us then disappeared like smoke.

The graveyard was thick with neglect. Grass had grown so high up round the graves it whispered above some of them like fine grey hair, smothering the long-forgotten names. This fragile decay teetered so very precariously on the edge of collapse.

The church stood by silently, its windows looking down in dark sorrow. A few panes were missing, some cracked. The stonework was crumbling. Everything seemed to be coming to the end of its gentle decline. The path was overgrown at the edges, the gravel full of ragged weeds. We moved slowly past a stone sarcophagus where the lid had slipped down and cracked, leaving a large gaping hole that my eyes were quickly drawn to. A subsiding headstone leaned into it from the side as if the occupants had found some solace with each other.

The cold damp lifted from the ground and burrowed up through my flimsy soled boots, soaking into my skin. I wrapped my coat around me tightly, hugging myself. I could feel Dad's Bible poking into my side and I ached for a sip of its warmth. My head pounded from lack of sleep and I touched the spot beneath my hair where I'd hit it. It was small but still painful. The joints in my neck were grinding against one another. I could so easily just curl up at the base of one of those stones and fall into a deep and welcome sleep.

After Dad died, they found me doing that regularly. After a few months of it, Aunt Charlotte and Mother would know where to find me. They'd bring heavy blankets and flasks of tea as if we'd just embarked on some macabre picnic. We'd drive home in silence past the early shift workers waiting at bus stops, delivery vans and the bundled-up homeless in doorways. I was so disconnected then that it just passed over the surface of my eyes as easily as the reflections on the car window. Mother didn't allow it to continue for too long. She just created a fortress around us, locking us in at night, alarming everywhere in the house — but it wasn't to keep people out.

Bob the Therapist said I'd reconnected a lot. The only trouble is I'm not sure I connected everything in the right order. But Mother is always quick to remind me that I'd been pretty 'dark and morbid' before. Mother often confuses soul-wrenching grief with wearing too much black.

Here, we walked through centuries of grief. Some of the larger, more stately tombs were so old that time had erased their dates. Most of the lids of the larger tombs had in fact fallen in or been dislodged.

At the end of the path stood a small incongruous static caravan. It had a very temporary appearance that had somehow become more permanent, judging by its weather-beaten look and weeds growing up around it. There was a fine spray of something like algae all up the dirty white sides. A light was on. High yew trees cast great shadows round it that presumably meant it was always in perpetual semi-darkness and the lights had to be on all the time. The door was half open in that sort of dark, uninviting, cautionary tale way. We, of course, decided to go in.

'Reverend Vert?' Mirabelle stepped timidly through the door.

Mother pushed through and looked around the place frowning. Mother doesn't do timid.

'Your Holiness?' Aunt Charlotte called.

'He's not the Pope,' I corrected.

'But he's holy, isn't he?'

'Depends if your definition includes sleeping with the local witch,' Mother said.

It smelled damp in the caravan. Even the floor had a spongy texture to it as if it might rot through. The small static caravan looked like it had been abandoned sometime in the 1970s. The fragments of wallpaper had psychedelic patterns that were peeling down onto the mildewed carpet tiles.

A few pans stood next to an old primus stove. Cans of beans and Pot Noodles were lined up behind them, along with empty bottles of cheap supermarket vodka. There was a small unmade bed at one end. Another half-empty bottle of vodka stood by the side of it with two cups. One had a dark-red smear of lipstick across the rim of it.

'Looks like local gossip was reliable,' Bridget commented, her eyebrows raised in judgement.

I took a step further in and Bridget grabbed my arm. 'Touch nothing!' she said. 'We could be dealing with a homicidal vicar.'

I shook my arm free. 'Give it a rest, Bridget.'

'I see no reason to, unless you wish to end up dead.'

Mother sighed. 'Well, whatever he is, he's clearly not here.'

Aunt Charlotte held up a strip of stiff white fabric. 'But his dog collar is.'

'He might have more than one.'

'Or he might have been up to something unholy. Something he didn't feel comfortable doing wearing it.'

Aunt Charlotte put the collar down on the chair and Dingerling instantly ran over and savaged it as if it was a dead mouse.

'Bloody animals — murderous creatures,' Mother murmured.

I stared at Mother. My thoughts seemed to snag on what she'd said but I couldn't fathom it.

'Well, he's better behaved than *your* child!' Bridget countered.

'He's a cat not a child. I'm fed up of you people babying your animals. Dogs, cats, monkeys—'

'We're all animals beneath the skin, Pandora.' Bridget picked up the cat, its pruned pink flesh wrinkling up. She started to wrestle the collar from its sharp mouth.

Mother held up her hands. 'Listen, we've got a drowned witch and a blackballed lord—'

'It didn't hit him there. It hit him on the head.' Aunt Charlotte frowned.

Mother issued *The Look* before continuing. 'The vicar could be on the run. He could have killed both of them and scarpered. He's probably halfway to Bolivia now.'

'Hardly.' The man's voice made us all jump. I turned and saw a sturdy, thickset man filling the doorway. 'Road's still flooded.' His moustache dominated his face. And the only other instantly recognisable thing about him was the unpleasant colour of his dark-yellow jumper.

'And you would be?' Mother raised her eyebrows.

'Lee Colman.'

Perhaps the mustard-coloured jumper and facial hair weren't a coincidence.

'And just how would you know the road's still flooded?' Mother looked at him distrustfully. Mother never trusts a man in disguise, and that moustache certainly didn't look genuine.

He squinted at her, deep lines spreading out from his eyes. They cut cleanly down into his cheeks. His skin had a thick, sallow nature to it. 'Was down there this morning before I went to Verity's.' He started to move away, keen not to look any of us in the eye.

'You went to Verity's this morning?' I asked.

He turned and seemed to have a new look of caution about him. 'Do most mornings. Take eggs.' He was the kind of man who clearly liked a lean sentence.

'Right,' I nodded. I had a sense that there was something else I should be asking, but nothing was forming.

'Just seen Marsha there. She said the MacDonald woman was dead. Thought I should check on the vicar.'

'And why's that then?' Bridget leaned towards him. So did the cat.

His face sank into a frown. 'Shagging her, weren't he.'

Bridget recoiled and covered the cat's ears. 'Please!'

Lee Colman analysed the cat as if he might be considering whether to skin it. 'What you been doin' to that animal? I never seen a cat sheared like a sheep before. Have lice, did it?'

'No, it did not! It was born like this.'

'Ah,' he nodded. 'Devil's cat then, eh? You a witch too? Looking for a bit of Reverend Vert's—'

'How dare you!'

Mother held up her hands. 'This is getting us nowhere.'

'It's a static, lady. Ain't meant to move.'

'Right. Thank you.'

'Ain't gonna get through that flood down there neither.'

'No.'

'My tractor's down out of the village. Can't get to it.'

'OK.'

He nodded sagely.

'I think we should leave now,' Mirabelle said quietly. 'Let's go and find our host.'

I looked around everyone. 'Well, what about the vicar? There's always the church. He could be in there.'

'Checked it.' Lee Colman rubbed his nose. 'He ain't there.'

It was something about his tone or maybe how he glanced over at the church and then back at us that made me feel a little sceptical about this man. Something about his wholesome farmer image didn't sit quite right with me.

I looked out the grimy window at the end, above a table and worn-thin cushions. I could see the church, sitting all dour among the grey morning rain as if it was failing to hold up the sky. I couldn't escape the image of the vicar laying out in front of the altar. Cold with death. Had Lee Colman looked through the door and seen something he didn't want to share? He gave the distinct impression that he was hiding something. But that could just have been the large moustache hanging over his mouth.

He started to turn away from the caravan. His straightforward manner left me with a very distinct feeling that something was being overcompensated for, as if we were being sold something a little bit dodgy that wouldn't work for very much longer.

CHAPTER 27: THE KEY TO IT ALL

There was another path leading out of the graveyard. The vicarage was just at the end of the overgrown gravelly stretch. Having seen where the vicar lived, it wasn't hard to understand the animosity that had arisen from Verity living in the vicarage. That was yet another point of contention in this unquiet little village that seemed to have so many issues, all of which found their way back to the source of Lord Elzevir. He'd somehow managed to create a spider's web of resentment, controversy and mistrust that overlaid everything here. It was so intricate that even his death hadn't lifted it.

Inside Verity's home, a sombre cloud had descended. That glowing welcome had evaporated, and Marsha led us straight through into the dim sitting room. Verity sat motionless, staring into a cold fireplace. The bruise down the back of her leg was even more livid now that she sat in shadow. Her face pallid and drawn. Her eyes raw with tears.

She looked up as Lee entered as if she sensed him before she saw him. A smile caught the edge of her lips before collapsing quickly.

He was instantly by her side, clearly a well-worn path to her chair. Without self-consciousness or awareness that anyone else was watching, he dropped to his knees by her side and held her hand. There was an easy tenderness about him and all that layer of concealment just seemed to fall away. He looked up at her with eyes that were jarringly reminiscent of Ron's as he gazed up at dead Jocasta's face.

'Verity.' His face was etched deep with concern.

There was compassion in her face. She looked almost sorry for him. She somehow seemed to pity him.

'It's all going to be OK?'

She nodded in reassurance. It was so strange to see this self-possessed man looking for his security with this newly bereaved, slight woman.

'Shall I organise tea?' she said.

'Don't worry about that.' It wasn't Verity who answered but Marsha, sitting in a chair by the window, her gaze iron cold. The picture of detachment, there was nothing of her there.

'If the ladies would care to take a seat?' Verity looked at us expectantly. We were caught in an awkward space, watching a scene we should never have been in.

'Yes, yes,' Mirabelle said hurriedly. She scurried over to a chair as far back from the rest of the room as possible.

Slowly, we settled into chairs and this new uncomfortable atmosphere.

'Did Marsha tell you?' Mother said. 'About . . . About Jocasta.'

Verity nodded, deep anguish in her face.

'We couldn't find the vicar,' Bridget said dispassionately.

'Oh, really?' Verity's forehead gathered in concern. She looked round us and then her eyes snapped to Marsha.

'He can't have gone far.' Marsha's voice was cold. 'The roads are still flooded, aren't they?' She looked expectantly at Lee.

He nodded.

We fell into another silence. The room was so taut I could hear the high note of tension ringing in my ears. I could feel the quiet beat of the blood in my neck.

'Where's the girl?' Bridget's voice finally broke the tension.

Marsha frowned.

'The cherry girl.'

Marsha's face drew slowly into a sharp look. 'Lucy Morello? She's resting upstairs. I gave her some . . . one of Verity's sleeping tablets.'

'What?' Aunt Charlotte blurted. 'So, you're drugging people when there's been two murders? Is that wise?'

Marsha pursed her lips. 'She was still hysterical. I don't think that's going to help anyone. The doctors told us they were no stronger than some homeopathic remedies. They're a very mild sedative, aren't they Verity?'

Verity nodded. She looked like she was in dire need of sleep, drugged or otherwise. The sheer exhaustion was crippling us all now. I stifled a yawn and shook my head quickly, trying to throw it off.

'We should try and find the vicar,' I mumbled through the end of the yawn.

Bridget nodded. 'Yes. Either he's the killer or he's dead.'

Everyone took a beat.

I needed a break. The bathroom's always the best place I find when Mother is being overwhelming again. I started to stand. 'Verity, may I use your—'

Marsha was suddenly out of her chair and striding across the room. I hovered just above my seat.

'This is too much,' she said loudly. 'We're sitting around talking and my husband, Verity's brother, is lying dead up the road!' She seemed to have almost dashed across the room and within moments had slammed the door behind her.

Verity cleared her throat. 'I'm sorry. She gets a little . . . emotional. Lee, are you sure the roads are still impassable?'

'Aye.' He looked up at her and then back towards the rest of the room. 'Floods often round here.'

'Oh God, poor Cassandra and Millicent, they've only just got straight from the last flood. I don't think the insurance will pay out again.'

It seemed strange that Verity was still so newborn to grief, not even out of her first twenty-four hours, and yet she had space in her head to think about others. I don't really remember much about the first week of my grief. My brain was so paralyzed that even basic thoughts — eat, sleep, scream — needed the kind of intense concentration I just did not possess.

Lee stood up and instantly stumbled. 'Christ!'

Positioned right by his feet was a large, expensive-looking handbag. He pushed it under the chair with his foot.

'All right?' Verity asked him.

I watched them very closely. He held her gaze for what seemed like a moment too long. Then nodded once.

But I was tired. My mind flickered from one thought to the next. I was starting to read things into every look, every movement, but this did seem different.

There was a string between these two that was invisible to everyone but them.

Marsha was back and she stalked across the room. Her eyes were scanning the floor. She looked increasingly irritated.

Mirabelle suddenly blurted out, 'We need to go and *do* something!'

Bridget eyed her sceptically. 'And what exactly do you propose *doing*?'

'Well . . .'

'Where's my handbag? I left it here last night.' Marsha's words were sharp, casting an accusation across everyone. These quicksilver mood swings of hers were becoming unbearable.

'It's OK. It's OK.' Verity looked at her so earnestly trying to bring her some calm.

There was none. Marsha was growing very agitated very quickly. 'I left it here last night! Someone must have taken it.'

'You mean this?' Lee pulled the big handbag from under the chair where he'd pushed it with his foot. He held it out like it was evidence and waited. 'What you got in here, an anvil?'

She walked quickly towards him and snatched it, thief fast. She held it close to her chest. 'Money, keys, make-up . . .

I don't know. Why?' She shook her head wildly, tears welling in her eyes. 'See!' She pulled the bag open and, with frantic hands, started ransacking it. She held up a purse, then an over-flowing make-up bag and a large set of keys, dropping them carelessly back into the bag. As she did, a large cream-coloured fob was disentangled and fell to the ground. It had two buttons in the centre and was very clearly a remote control, similar to one that might be used for a garage.

Marsha and Verity stared down in astonishment as if a great hole had just opened up in the floor and they were looking down into it.

'Marsha?' Verity didn't look at her. She spoke cautiously, almost afraid of her name.

'What's that?' Aunt Charlotte cut in. 'Is that . . . ?'

'The remote control for the gates at the castle,' Marsha said slowly. Her eyes hadn't moved from it.

'But you said you didn't have one,' Mirabelle said for all of us. 'Only your husband had one and he'd lost it.'

'He had!' Marsha's eyes flicked round us all, appealing to each of us in turn. 'I swear I didn't know it was there.' She paused, grasping for thoughts like a defendant sinking in the dock. 'I know it wasn't there. I'd taken this handbag out especially for the supper. I didn't want to use a good one since it was raining so hard and none of you would notice.

'Thank you so much, Marsha.' Mother's mouth snapped tight as a mousetrap.

'I switched my stuff across and it wasn't there then. That was about an hour before you guys arrived. I brought it out with me but then I forgot it, what with all the stress. I must have left it here last night.'

Bridget stood and unfurled a handkerchief from her sleeve. She bent and picked up the fob. 'I think this should be taken into evidence.'

'Oh here we go again. Vera rides in.' Mother sighed.

'Are we expecting someone else?'

'Be quiet, Charlotte.'

Bridget looked haughtily round us. 'It would appear that Lady Black is insinuating this item must have been planted there to make her look even more guilty, if that is indeed possible. You are, I take it, the sole beneficiary now he's gone.'

Marsha looked appealingly then nodded.

Aunt Charlotte made a strange noise that she does when she's thinking or suffering with indigestion. 'Unless you're found guilty of his murder. Can't benefit then. Remember the solicitor telling you that, Pandora? Like I said, forfeiture rule. A murderer can't inherit from the deceased whom they killed.'

'Did you kill your husband?' Lee said, his mouth hanging slack as he looked at Mother.

'No! Of course I didn't.'

The room fell into an ill-fitting silence.

'Someone put that there!' Marsha shouted. 'Someone is trying to frame me, that's obvious to any fool! Everyone knew I was in the castle alone. I was the only one who didn't need the fob to operate the gates. I could do it from the inside.'

'Yes, that is true, I suppose,' Mirabelle conceded.

Marsha's shoulders sagged heavily. 'I'm sorry. I'm sorry, I just—'

'It's OK, Marsha.' Verity's voice was warm, her eyes full of care.

Marsha dropped the bag and held her head in her hands. 'I just don't know what's happening.'

'Your husband has been murdered,' Bridget said flatly.

Marsha lifted her head and fixed her eyes on Bridget. Neither of them wavered.

Mother cleared her throat. 'Look, why don't we . . .? I mean we should really try and . . .' She was groping for the words.

'Why don't some of us go and look for the vicar again?' Aunt Charlotte broke in. 'You, Pringles Man. You look useful.'

Everyone frowned but our eyes all landed on Lee Colman and his outsized moustache. Aunt Charlotte has never been subtle, but I did have to admit he bore more than a passing resemblance to the man on a can of Pringles.

Bridget kept her eyes on Marsha. 'You should go and check as well if there's any chance of us getting out of the Village of the Damned.'

Lee snorted a laugh. 'No chance, little old lady.'

Bridget looked appalled.

'Took a couple of days last time. Always does.'

'Well, just try for God's sake!' Mother was reaching that point she always does where the customer services represent-ative has to get their manager involved. 'Find a boat! Build a bloody boat! Build Noah's Ark. I don't care. Just get me . . . us out of here.'

'I don't know about building boats, lady. I'm a farmer.'

'Oh my God. Just ride a bloody cow then!'

'Shouldn't ride on cows. They don't like it.'

Mother made a strangled sound of frustration, the kind she reserves for when I have a bit of difficult news for her.

Verity took a long breath and placed her hand over Lee's. She began in a purposeful, calm voice. 'Someone needs to go round the village and tell everyone what's going on. They could all be in danger. Has anyone seen Joseph Greengage and Scarlett Bradshaw this morning?'

Everyone shook their heads.

'What about the magician?' Aunt Charlotte asked.

Mother made a dismissive noise. 'Presumably his second sight means he's already aware of it all.'

'Mrs White's up at the castle with Mrs Abaddon. I told her about Elzevir this morning so she didn't cook his egg. She doesn't know about Jocasta though.'

We split into teams, which immediately made the whole expedition even more dispiriting. Marsha stayed with Verity who was beginning to look quite frail. Lucy Morello was upstairs and didn't come down, presumably due to the fact that our possible murderer had admitted to drugging her.

Along with Mother and Aunt Charlotte, I volunteered to go and speak to the magician. Mirabelle and Bridget went to check on Joseph Greengage and Scarlett Bradshaw. It was very easy to imagine the finely honed disapproval Bridget would be showing them.

Lee Colman was sent to the edge of the village on flood patrol and any boat whittling that he might be able to muster.

'While you're down there, you should tell the Peacocks,' Verity said. She spoke with a such a delicate voice, staring mindlessly as if waves of realisation just kept surprising her. Her brother was dead, and as far as we'd seen, he wasn't what would be described as well liked.

Just as we were leaving and everyone else was distracted with coats and logistics, I quietly asked Verity where the toilet was. I didn't announce it this time, just in case anyone else felt like rushing out ahead of me. She pointed to a small door off to the side of the hallway. Inside, everything was immaculate. I put the lid down and sat staring at the glossy white tiles. I felt inside my coat pocket for the Bible and pulled out the flask of brandy. It had a sour metallic scent and the liquid burned its familiar path down my throat.

I closed my eyes and smoothed my tongue along my teeth, waiting for the glow to spread. Every time it had less of an effect. The past is addictive. The first taste is almost overwhelming, but each sip after that becomes necessity rather than joy. I suppose it could one day even become something unpleasant or damaging.

I waited and finally slotted the brandy back into the book. It nestled there so snugly, all those memories packed in so tight. Like the wink Dad gave me when he'd taken his sip. There was no regret or despair on his face, just a secret little pleasure. This book and its contents had taken on a whole different flavour now they sat in my hands. How sad I had made it. I closed over the front cover and ran my fingers over the embossed word 'Bible'. There was only the memory of gold left in the grooves of the letters.

I shoved the book back in my coat pocket and rubbed the stray tears from my face. I was angry they'd appeared so easily.

I stood and turned to look at myself in the mirror.

The eyes were looking back at me. Floating in his face, with that same lost look as if they didn't know what they were for. Black as two ink blot tests and I never know what I'm supposed to see there.

'Why did you do it, Dad?'

His shook his head.

'How can you do something like that and not even know why? At least have some reason.'

A frown burrowed across his forehead and he still shook his head.

I looked away. He was infuriating now, and if I could have made him disappear right then I would have.

'Just go,' I whispered. But as soon as my brain realised the words were out there, I looked back at the space he'd been in.

He'd gone.

'Oh God.' I touched the mirror but it was just my face there at the ends of my fingertips now. 'No, I didn't mean it. Don't go.'

'Ursula.' It was Mother at the door. I could tell from her voice she was leaning in close. 'We're leaving now.'

I stared into my own face in the mirror. 'Don't go. Please don't ever go. Just come back! Come back to me.'

'Ursula.' She rattled the handle. 'Ursula, open the door.'

I sank slowly. My knees giving way. I was weightless. Ungrounded. As if my tether had been cut and I was suddenly set free. My hands were shaking as they reached for the glass shelf.

As I fell to the ground, a great mess of untidy make-up fell around me. Eyeshadows, lipsticks and creams all unlidded and used, roughly scattered across the floor. They were all dark colours, purple and blacks. Bruised colours.

The world sparkled and dissolved into darkness.

CHAPTER 28: THE MAN WHO SAW NOTHING

Mother was looking directly into my face when I opened my eyes. It was not the best reminder that I was still alive.

'What are you playing at? You stink like a bar towel.'

'Thank you, Mother. At least I know this can't be heaven.'

She was doing her loud whispering that sounded like an angry librarian. But Mother doesn't do libraries.

'Do you want them to think that you're mad as well?'

'Mother, how did you manage to conjure yourself up in here?' I leaned up on my elbows, which brought me uncomfortably close to her face.

She stood up and put her hands on her hips. 'Penny trick. You just turn the lock with it. I used to have to do it all the time when you'd locked yourself in the loo again.'

My mind caught on something but then it was lost.

'Hurry up. Aunt Charlotte is waiting outside and God knows what she's doing.' Mother had become distracted by her own reflection and was pulling her face back to see what she'd look like walking into a force ten gale.

I slowly began to stand. 'But we need to . . .' I looked around at all the mess of make-up on the floor. It seemed strange that Verity had so much of it and it was all so ill-kept.

'Leave it.' Mother made for the door. 'They've got staff.'

'You mean the woman they've drugged upstairs?'

Mother shrugged. She gripped me round the shoulders and guided me out.

'Everything all right?' It was Verity, radiating calm and concern.

'Yes, she's fine. She does this a lot.'

'Mother!'

'Oh, well if there's anything I can do?' Verity glanced round us into the toilet and frowned. 'You've left . . .'

'I'm sorry, but I've got to get her some fresh air.' Mother hustled me out of the door as if we were escaping.

* * *

Tony Voyeur opened the door dressed in his shiny black dressing gown that had more than a passing resemblance to a bin bag. When he turned to lead us into the house, I could see that the word VOYEUR was etched on the back in faded gold lettering. I glanced through into the kitchen as we passed to see a pile of dirty pots in the sink.

The house smelled of grease and dust, like an old run-down chip shop. In the sitting room, there were still the glasses and bowls of nuts abandoned on bookcases from last night's party. Aunt Charlotte's half-eaten sausage roll languished next to the beheaded doll.

The dingy light barely touched the corners of the room. I looked at the washed-up magician as he cleared a few magazines and put them with the rest of the cans and papers that littered the glass coffee table. A plate with a few stale crusts on it and some congealed egg had been left on the sofa. Something had just made this man give up. He'd resigned from life or any semblance of a decent one, at least.

'Please make yourself at home.' He spread out an arm towards the sofa and frowned when he saw the plate.

'Hardly.' Mother sounded particularly tart. She doesn't do mess. She has our house deep cleaned and scrubbed so regularly it's as if she's trying to erase it from existence.

Tony Voyeur hadn't taken in her snub. He was too busy dumping piles of papers from a chair into a corner that already had a small tower of various unopened letters, books and crisp packets. It was all topped off with an overflowing ashtray.

'I've not quite finished tidying from the party.'

'Or started,' Aunt Charlotte mumbled as she lowered herself gingerly into the sagging chair. It creaked and groaned in weak protest.

'Any news on Verity?' He looked around us innocently. He'd already gone home last night when we'd gone to tell Verity of Lord Elzevir's death. This house was next door and only a few minutes' walk. But it would also only have been a few minutes' walk up to the castle. Had there been time for him to leave Verity's, run to the castle, kill Lord Elzevir then run back here? Possibly. Judging from what we'd seen of him so far, he wasn't capable of lowering a duster let alone a portcullis. But he certainly had a motive and it was very clear that this mess of a life was in part due to Lord Elzevir and his revelations.

'Mr Voyeur,' Mother said his name like it was past its sell by date. She was perched on the arm of a small brown chair that had a pair of grey pants dangling from the back of it. 'I'm afraid we have some bad news for you. Well, news — depending on your point of view.'

'OK, fire.'

'Lord Elzevir has been murdered.'

His large, pale forehead wrinkled.

'So has Jocasta MacDonald,' Aunt Charlotte added.

'What?' His expression turned to disbelief. 'Murdered? Are you sure?'

'Fairly sure,' Mother said. 'His Lordship had his head caved in with a cannonball and Jocasta was drowned on the ducking stool. Neither death looked particularly accidental.'

Tony's mouth fell open. 'You're kidding. When?'

'Last night. Lord Elzevir just before the Midnight Gun, we think. But we don't know about Jocasta. We saw her around about twelve fifteen when we went to tell Verity about Lord Elzevir. She left quite quickly and, according to her husband, never came home. You'd already left Verity's by then.'

'Yes, they didn't need me anymore so I thought I'd make myself scarce.'

'Did you go straight home?'

'Yes.' He frowned. 'It was still raining and I needed to clear up from the party.'

I looked round at the dishevelled room. It didn't look like he'd made any effort to clear up at all.

Mother leaned forward. 'Did you see anything of Lord Elzevir? He would have been heading up the road at around five to twelve. Almost exactly the time you were going home.'

'No, no I didn't. You know what it was like, pitch black and bucketing it down. I could barely find my own way. Listen, what is this? I thought you'd come to warn me, not interrogate me! You're not the police.'

Mother stared at him unblinking. 'It was Lord Elzevir who ended your career, wasn't it?'

He stood up. His face increasingly agitated. 'What's that got to do with anything?'

'You had every reason to kill him,' Aunt Charlotte spoke plainly. 'And you were one of the few people on your own at the time of his death.'

'I would never kill someone. I resent the insinuation!' His dressing gown fell open to reveal the large dome of his belly hanging over a pair of Dr Who Y-fronts with the words 'Sonic Screwdriver' emblazoned on them. He quickly grabbed each side of the dressing gown and wrapped it around himself. 'Now please leave.'

'Very well.' Mother stood. 'We thought you should know.'

'That you think I'm a stone-cold killer?'

'We just needed everyone to know there's a possible murderer on the loose.'

'Oh and the vicar's missing,' Aunt Charlotte added.

'The vicar?' He raised an eyebrow. 'Well perhaps you might start looking for Father Brown.'

'Green,' Aunt Charlotte corrected. 'Vert is green in French, not brown.'

'Let's just leave.' Mother was already making her way to the door.

Aunt Charlotte smiled and followed. I made my way out behind them, avoiding eye contact with the hapless magician.

* * *

Back out on the street, the rain misted the air but it was calmer. The wind had lost a lot of its ferocity but it was still biting cold. I shuddered and looked across the road to where the Bradshaws were going through their gate. They had Ron with them. Gerald Bradshaw had an arm round him that might well have been holding the man up. Ron looked so exhausted, spent with the shock and pain.

'We're taking him to lay down,' Harriet Bradshaw called. 'He's collapsed.'

'OK,' Aunt Charlotte nodded. She dropped her voice. 'Poor sod. To lose his wife like that.' She looked at me, then Mother. 'Sorry,' she whispered.

Mother pulled back her hair. Her face looked worn today. She seemed weary, as if she was slowly unravelling. We'd not spoken about Dad since we'd left Scotland last year. The lid had been firmly shut on that little box of horrors, but I could feel it now, wriggling to be set free, for us to release it in a gale of screaming and shouting about disloyalty, misplaced trust and all the things we find it so easy to blame each other for in times of severe stress — at least, that was Bob the Therapist's assessment before he jumped ship. Quite literally. The last we'd heard from the travel company that took him to the remote jungle was that he'd jumped into a fast-flowing river shouting, 'There's still reception! She's calling again.'

But here, now, in this tiny village, there was an increasing feeling that the timer had been set and was running down.

'I think we should head back to Verity's.' Mother's voice was cold.

'Wait, here come Mirabelle and Bridget,' I said.

'Not forgetting Dingerling.' Aunt Charlotte noticeably winced.

The five of us gathered in the bleak street, surrounded by the cute little cottages and homes that harboured all this death and hatred behind their chintz curtains.

'Anything to report?' Mother asked.

Mirabelle shook her head. 'Not really. Scarlett Bradshaw and Joseph Greengage were in there together, as we suspected. They said they were together all night.'

'They would, wouldn't they?' Mother heaved a sigh.

'Well, I don't trust that magician either,' Aunt Charlotte sniffed. 'There's something very odd about him.'

'Fortunately for you, very odd doesn't always equal murderer,' Mother said.

'Surely that's more fortunate for *you* really, Pandora, as it would definitely be *you* who was in the most danger.'

'OK. OK, we're all tired,' I said. 'Let's just say they're all really odd and we need to keep our wits about us.'

'How very kind of you, Ursula.' It was Marsha standing at the end of the path to the vicarage with Verity.

'Any sign of the vicar?' Verity asked, trying to deflect the situation.

I shook my head. 'So what now?'

'We've got to do something!' Mirabelle breathed heavily. 'We've got to get out of here!'

'No chance of that, I'm afraid.' It was Lee Colman trudging up the lane towards us. 'Road's still out and will be for a while.'

Mirabelle's voice cracked. 'There's two people dead and a missing vicar. We've got to get out!'

We stood with the cold wind tracing round us as if it was watching, waiting.

'It's such a small village,' I said. 'There can't be many places where a priest would hide?'

My eyes drifted up to the outline of the castle against the stone sky. More rain was brewing over the moors. My thoughts landed on Lord Elzevir laying there alone on the dead stone — all his pretentions, all his moods and drunkenness washed away across those cobbles. Lord Elzevir Black was nothing more than a name for a gravestone now. A ridiculous name at that.

A cog suddenly seemed to slot into place in my mind. 'Marsha, what was your husband's name?'

She frowned. 'Elzevir — Lord Elzevir Black, as you well know.'

'No, no,' I said. 'I mean the real man, before all this money. When he bought the title did he not have the name to quite match up to it? It's a very unusual name for the kind of man who buys a title.'

She paused as if assessing the various pros and cons. 'His name was Jack.'

'Jack Black?' Mirabelle frowned.

I looked at Aunt Charlotte and gave her my warning eyes. She closed her mouth.

Marsha nodded.

'But why did he change it to Elzevir?'

I watched Marsha's eyes grow keen.

'Or may I guess? The books on the bedside table in my room – were they his favourites?'

She nodded again, this time her face full of resignation. '*Moonfleet*. Elzevir *Block* smuggles barrels in—'

'How my husband made his money is of no consequence whatsoever!'

'And I'm not interested in it either. But what I am interested in is the fact that the barrels in the book are smuggled in under the gravestones through the tunnels. When you told us about the priest hole, you said Nicholas Owen built *many* of the priest holes and tunnels. You didn't mean generically. You meant many in your castle, didn't you?'

She nodded again, keeping her face blank and unreadable.

'I'm willing to guess those tunnels come up near the church, perhaps under the graves, and that's what prompted

Jack Black to become Lord Elzevir Black. Another of his witty jokes perhaps?'

Marsha looked suddenly at Verity. Then nodded again. 'There's many of them — the tunnels.'

All eyes were turning towards the castle. 'There's another way in isn't there?' I said quietly.

Marsha paused and looked at Verity again. She simply said, 'Yes.'

I looked around at everyone. 'We need to go up to the castle.'

'Well, you're not leaving me.' It was Tony Voyeur at his gate still in his dressing gown. 'You're not pinning this on me. I need to be there.'

My thoughts spun out to that castle, the intricate map of tunnels and holes running beneath its stones. Built to protect religious men. Just what did they hide now?

CHAPTER 29: PRIEST HUNTER

Verity insisted on going with us, so there was no surprise that Lee Colman did too. He stayed close to her, almost too close. Lucy Morello came out bleary eyed and groggy. She refused to be left behind as well.

So we formed a macabre little Pied Piper trail up to Black Towers, but just who was playing the pipe wasn't clear at all.

As we set off from Verity's, Ron ran crying into the street. 'I need to see her! I need to come with you. You're going to the castle, aren't you?' His eyes darted frantically between us.

'This is ridiculous,' Mother grumbled. 'It's not a tour!'

'Mother, don't you think it's better if we're all together. We're safer and no one can scuttle off doing secret things.'

She took a deep breath, filling herself up with frustration.

'She's right,' are not words Bridget's mouth is used to. Even the cat looked surprised. 'I have a feeling we might all need to gather very soon in any event.' She ploughed on ahead, looking very pleased with herself as if she'd just said something important. Perhaps she had, but I wasn't going to tell her that.

'Go with Ron.' Harriet Bradshaw was at her gate and almost pushed her husband, Gerald, out into the lane. 'He needs you.'

Gerald looked bewildered.

'The artefacts,' she said through gritted teeth.

His eyes suddenly widened and he scampered on towards Ron, an obsequious look on his face. 'Ron, don't worry. I'm here.'

Ron didn't look worried at all. Insane, yes, but not worried.

So now there were only five people left in the village — Joseph Greengage and his girlfriend, Scarlett, the mysteriously private Peacocks, and Mrs Bradshaw, who wanted to stay just in case Scarlett came back. It felt more important than ever now to keep track of everyone's whereabouts.

My eyes turned towards the castle that had stood ominously over all of us from the very beginning. As our sombre line moved silently on towards it, there was a sense that we were sealing our fates, if they hadn't already been sealed.

We all stood in front of the open portcullis, staring at the broken form of Lord Elzevir, still laying on the floor.

Ron suddenly bolted across the gravel and down the bank towards the moat. We couldn't see the chair where his wife sat, just the tip of the other end of the pole, but it was very clear where he was heading. Gerald called after him but made no effort to follow.

He looked at us. 'He needs to be alone with his grief,' he said solemnly.

I saw Marsha and Verity link hands for a second. Lucy Morello made another of her snared animal sounds that seemed to come from deep inside her.

Unperturbed, Marsha led on with an iron purpose. 'Wait here,' she said. She skirted round Lord Elzevir's body and went up the small stairs by the side of the portcullis. In a moment, she was opening the side gate for us. We passed quickly the way we'd come over the top of the gatehouse and hurried up to the main door of the castle. Marsha opened it and walked in determinedly.

'Mirabelle, you're with me.' Bridget stood firm with Dingerling clutched tight to her chest.

'Why should she be?' Mother shot.

Bridget paused and then let a smile trickle across her lips. 'Because that's how it is now. You made a choice to push her away. No use trying to go back on that now.'

Mother looked at her dumbfounded and then at Mirabelle. 'What?' Her voice was quiet. 'Mirabelle?'

Mirabelle gave her a strained look and turned away.

Marsha paused. 'We do not have time for this! There is a man missing. My husband has been killed and there's a dead woman strapped to a chair. People are dying and you're still doing this! Look, Verity and I—'

'Before we do anything else, I think we should open up the priest hole.' Gerald looked genuinely excited at the prospect of this, although a touch of desperation was edging into his voice.

'OK. OK.' Marsha walked purposefully through the hall towards the tapestry and we followed. She pulled it back as if it was a big reveal moment. I half expected to see the vicar standing there behind the curtain.

'Wait!' Tony Voyeur moved towards her. 'Let me see if I can sense a presence.' He closed his eyes and held out his hands.

Mother pushed past him. 'For God's sake, move out the way, David Blaine.'

'I knew his real name couldn't be Voyeur!' Aunt Charlotte nodded to herself in confirmation. 'Filthy man.'

Marsha bent down and started feeling around behind the wood panelling. After a moment, the small door opened just as before and swung out. There, in the tiny space we'd seen before, was nothing. It was empty. There was no vicar curled up hiding as we'd all started to imagine. I didn't know whether to be relieved or disappointed.

'Now what?' Mirabelle frowned.

Marsha let out a sigh. 'Verity, you know the castle plans. Where are the rest of the priest holes?'

Verity looked confused for a moment and Lee Colman put a comforting arm around her. Some sort of realisation flickered across her face. 'Wait, Lee. Can you help me?'

He nodded.

'Inside, on the right there.' She pointed and he bent to look inside the small space. 'There's a handle. It's a tiny black metal thing.'

He crouched down and looked around before starting to shuffle himself further inside. His wide shoulders barely fit and there seemed hardly enough space for him to even look around. 'I think I see it.'

'Pull it,' Verity said before adding, 'be careful. Hold onto something.' I watched as Verity looked around us all anxiously as if she'd said more than she should. As if she'd revealed a secret.

Lee struggled to pull his arm through into the hole, and after a few minutes there was a dull click and he shimmied his way out of the space.

We all drew round and peered into the dark little cupboard.

It took a few seconds for my eyes to adjust fully but, there at the back of the hole, a section of the floor had fallen away. A small, black rectangle of darkness hinted at a whole new area.

I looked around at the others. Verity didn't seem shocked at all, more anxious.

Marsha, however, did look surprised. 'Well, I suppose you did say this place is riddled with holes and tunnels.'

'Yes.' Gerald leaned into the space, nodding excitedly. 'Imagine how many priests hid there — maybe even died there!' He sounded almost gleeful. He turned to us all, the smile gradually falling with the realisation that his excitement might not be quite appropriate.

Lucy Morello made some more faint sobbing sounds from the back of the group.

'Verity?' Marsha looked at her tentatively. 'Is this . . . ?' she paused.

Verity nodded. 'One of the tunnels.'

'Leading to . . .'

'The graveyard.'

No one spoke. I felt a cold gasp of wind rise up from the tunnel.

'Right,' Aunt Charlotte cut in, 'I think someone's going to need to take a look inside.'

'Well, you're not going to fit in there!' Mother said.

'I don't think many people would.' Mrs Abaddon had appeared at the back of our group. She folded her arms decidedly.

Aunt Charlotte looked ponderous. 'As my sister so kindly pointed out, it's going to need someone slim but also young enough to be quite bendy, so that rules you out as well, Pandora, with your old bones.'

I looked back at Lucy Morello, who was still in a completely agitated state. There was no prospect of her being able to do this. Another gust of wind rose up through the entrance and this time seemed to make a faint whistling sound.

Even Gerald was slowly backing away.

'I can't leave Dingerling,' Bridget said quickly.

Lee Colman had struggled to even get through the door, let alone down through into the passage below. Tony Voyeur was even wider than him.

I was slowly aware that all eyes were settling on me. 'Really?' I said in disbelief.

Mother gave me a resigned look. 'This is going to cost a fortune in therapy bills.'

* * *

As I lay on my belly staring into the dark, small opening I felt a cold little wind in my face. It smelled of the damp stone. An old smell.

I had my phone light but it only revealed the first section of the passage. It seemed to fall away down a steep drop. It was not much bigger than my shoulder width and only a small pocket of space remained above my head.

There was a dankness to the air that stuck in my throat.

I heard Mother's voice behind me. 'This is ridiculous. No, no. She can't go any further. Ursula, come out immediately. It's not safe. What if the priest is in there. I'm not sending my daughter to meet a killer.'

'She's right!' I heard the muffled sound of Aunt Charlotte just before one of them lunged for my legs. But it seemed to push me down further rather than drag me back. My stomach was teetering on the edge of the back lip of the cupboard area, just before it fell away into the passage. I tried to steady myself a little.

And then I fell.

As the board gave way, I slipped fast down through what seemed to be some sort of trap door and landed hard. It knocked the wind out of me and dust filled the air. It didn't feel like I fell far, possibly only the height of a man.

But Mother's voice seemed quite distant. 'Ursula!'

I looked up and could see the light from above. The wooden floor to the cupboard seemed to have given way into a small bare-brick chamber below. It was rough on the palms of my hands. The air was colder here, the walls damp like the sides of a riverbank. There was a fetid smell.

I managed to shuffle onto my hands and knees and turn around to look at the space. I was in some sort of long, narrow cavity with dark-red brickwork all around me.

'Ursula, what is going on?' Mother's face appeared, god-like, from the white square of light above.

'You're blocking the light, Mother. I'm fine.' I shuffled round on the gravelly floor. 'It's another chamber below.'

'Is everything all right?' Marsha called. Her voice seemed further away than I'd imagined. 'What can you see?'

'I'm fine. It's another priest hole, I think, below.'

'Dummy chambers.'

'Who?'

'Quiet, Charlotte!' Mother snapped.

'This top one is a dummy chamber,' Gerald called again. 'To put the priest hunters off the scent.'

'Don't tell me to be quiet! My niece is in there. I'm coming in, Ursula. Get out the way, Pandora.'

'I'm fine! Aunt Charlotte, there isn't room.' I brushed the dust from my face and as I looked down the opposite wall, an outline began to form. Another small, rectangular opening.

'There's something else here,' I called.

'Christ!' Mother cried. 'Get out! Someone get her out! I knew this was a mistake.'

I squinted into the darkness and held up my phone light. 'I think there's a little tunnel leading off it,' I shouted back to them.

'She's right,' Verity called. 'Remember, on the plans?'

'Plans?' Marsha sounded as clueless as the rest of us.

I stretched out my arm and held the torch further towards the small opening. I moved towards it.

'What the hell do you think you're doing, Ursula?' Mother called. 'Get back up here at once!'

'Mother, now I'm down here, I might as well take a look. There's no space for anyone to run at me. You can only crawl down here.' I moved along a little.

Mother dangled further in and shouted down the small passage. 'I warn you, priest, if you're down there and you lay a finger on my girl, I'll crucify you!' Her voice echoed along the tunnel.

I pushed myself forwards. It was a bitter, cold darkness. There was a loneliness to it. How abandoned those men would have felt down here, waiting, wondering in fear. I could see their faces in the gloom, picture them shivering against the walls, half-starved with round ivory eyes peering out from the shadows. The blood fluttered in my chest at the thought of it. I paused to try and keep my breath slow and even.

'Ursula?' Mother's voice had a worried edge to it.

'I'm fine,' I called, although I hadn't really made it sound like that. I was aware my voice came out slightly strangled. I took another long breath. It was just walls around me. Just walls.

I could feel the sweat prickling along my back, the fine dust sticking to my face. I turned my head to the side and looked back towards the small chamber. I'd crawled in quite a way now. I couldn't see Mother's face in the opening anymore. I looked down into the tunnel, as far as I could. The darkness was overwhelming.

I felt something under my hand and brought it up close to my face. A small torch. I clicked it on and a pool of blue light fell on the floor. The corpse candle. The light I'd seen last night dodging through the darkness. It was no ghost, as Tony Voyeur had tried to suggest.

I lay flat in the tunnel and felt a breath of something cross my face. My chest started to feel tight. And the familiar panic began to swill through my stomach. There was a sour taste in my mouth. My heart thumped against the cold floor. What if I couldn't turn around? What if he really was down here?

I closed my eyes for a moment and tried to settle myself. But the black little thoughts came in quickly, landing like birds on a newly sown field. I could feel something there with me in the darkness. Something close to me.

I opened my eyes and his face was directly in front of me.

I drew back fast and banged my head on the roof of the tunnel. My eyes swam.

'Ursula, what's happening?' Mother's voice was frantic but strangely distant.

The eyes were there in the darkness, staring into mine. I smelled the familiar fug of his tobacco. For a brief moment of confusion, Dad was real. I reached out to touch him. My head sparkled with pain and my eyes began to close.

'Ursula,' Mum and Dad both said.

An iron-rich breath of blood filled the air in the small tunnel. The shape of Dad faded and behind where he had been was the unmistakeable shape of a body sprawled on the floor. The face was turned up towards me in an agonised, wide-eyed stare. It was the vicar — already grey with death.

'He's . . . here. The vicar. He's dead,' I rasped. 'Mum. Please.'

I felt a hand on my calf. I was being dragged backwards. 'I've got you.' It was Mother's voice.

CHAPTER 30: INCIDENTS IN THE SITTING ROOM

As I surfaced, little motes of light caught my eye. I was in the hall, laying down next to the entrance to the priest hole. Voices were troubled and indistinct, as though I was looking up from the table in an operating theatre.

Mother's voice drifted in. 'Are you all right?' It sounded so distant.

'Of course she's not OK.' The sound of Aunt Charlotte echoed in my head. 'She's just fallen in the messy grave of a vicar!'

'I can't believe this. How is this happening?' Mirabelle sounded shaky.

Their voices circled me.

'OK, give her some space.' Mother tried to sound in control.

'Space?' Mirabelle took on a firmer note than I'd heard from her in all the time we'd been here. 'There's no space between you. No space for anyone.'

I looked up at her to see her eyes were glossy with tears.

Mother had a look of confusion. 'Is that what this is all about?'

'All what?'

'Excuse me,' Gerald interrupted. 'But I believe the vicar is dead. Could you do this later?'

'What the hell is wrong with you people?' It was Lucy Morello, her eyes hectic, looking round each of us. 'Elzevir is dead! Jocasta's dead! And now the vicar! This place is a morgue and you're discussing if you give each other enough space! I just . . . I c-can't . . .' Her words were stuttered between the tears.

'Get a grip of yourself, girl,' Marsha snapped. 'And it's *Lord* Elzevir to you.'

Mrs Abaddon had an arm around Lucy. 'Let's get you sat down now.'

Lucy almost collapsed onto the elderly woman as she was guided to one of the heavy, dark chairs against the wall.

'Mrs Abaddon.' Marsha sounded very calm. 'Some tea, if you wouldn't mind.'

'Tea?' There was an edge of hysteria to Lucy's voice. '*Lord* Elzevir is dead! You're his wife and you're thinking about tea!'

'Well, it's a little late to be remembering that he was a married man. But then your family never were any good at keeping their hands off other people's property, were they? How long has he been in Dartmoor prison for now? A good few years, I suspect. Is it just your brother who has strayed over to the criminal side?' Marsha smiled. 'You needn't have bothered if you did. I checked his will regularly and there's no mention of you, regardless of what you think he told you.'

Lucy's mouth hung open. 'I . . . how . . . ?'

'There's a dead body down there!' Mirabelle shouted. 'Someone else has been murdered! We need to do something.'

'And what exactly do you suggest we do?' Bridget said calmly. 'We need to leave him where he is for the police. We can't touch anything and no one else is going down there. It's not safe.'

'I found this.' I held out the torch.

'What? You shouldn't have taken it. There could be fingerprints.' Bridget looked affronted.

'It shines blue,' I said and looked at the magician. 'So not corpse candles then.'

He gave a dismissive shrug.

'But what killed him? Was there any sign of what happened?' Verity asked. She held onto Lee Colman's arm to steady herself.

'I smelled blood. It was all around his head. I think he . . .' I saw the image of him so still and staring out of the darkness. 'His throat had been cut.'

Gerald coughed. 'And he's definitely dead?'

I nodded. 'Looked cold, as if he'd been there a while.'

His drained face, so still, so frigid, flashed across my mind again. 'There were scratches. Deep scratches on the side of his face and neck.'

'Scratches?' Mother leaned close to me as if she was checking me for the truth.

'I couldn't really see. But yes, like he'd been slashed at, clawed at by something.'

'Good God,' Gerald whispered.

'Madam, I will go and fetch the tea,' Mrs Abaddon announced.

A sharp, grating sound started. We paused and looked at one another. The grinding continued, a metallic sound that seemed to be coming from outside. Mrs Abaddon walked slowly and calmly towards the door, which someone had left open.

'I will go and see what is happening, Your Ladyship.'

'Maybe it's Lord Elzevir putting the gates down again.' Aunt Charlotte looked ashamed of the comment almost as soon as she'd said it.

We waited in a glowering silence, Marsha and Lucy Morello both sharp-eyed.

When Mrs Abaddon returned, she wasn't alone.

'I found Mr Greengage out in the courtyard, Your Ladyship.' She looked accusatorily at Marsha, as if this hadn't been the first time she'd been called upon to announce his unexpected presence.

'Joseph?' Marsha's face was suddenly a lot more animated. 'What are you—?'

'I'm moving the scaffold, Your Ladyship.'

'What? Why would you be doing that with a dead man there?' Bridget and the cat eyed Joseph suspiciously.

'Well, I was told Verity thought you and His Lordship, God rest his soul, would want it moved for the visit. It had already been moved so I was just making sure—'

'That was all before the ladies arrived, Joseph.' Mrs Abaddon had the distinct tone of someone reprimanding him. 'You don't need to be moving it now.'

'You shouldn't be touching anything out there!' Bridget was appalled again.

'I'm so sorry. We just didn't get to finishing before you ladies arrived. There's always so much to do. It's no trouble, Your Ladyship.' Joseph continued. 'I'll wheel it—'

'Wait.' Mother frowned. 'You just said it had already been moved.'

He nodded. 'Yes, I didn't leave it there. I left it on the other side of the courtyard.'

'It was there when we arrived,' Aunt Charlotte said. 'I remember saying I thought it was a mobile gallows.' She looked around for any sort of acknowledgement.

'Why would someone move it?' Gerald said. 'To tamper with the gates?'

'No one tampered with them, Gerald,' Joseph said. 'They just came down two minutes early.'

'And then he was shot with a cannonball.' Aunt Charlotte crossed herself.

'No, Aunt Charlotte.'

'No?'

I nodded. 'No.'

'I need to leave,' Tony Voyeur suddenly announced from the back of the hall. 'There's too much negative energy here. Three dead people is just really bad karma.' He wrapped his dressing gown around himself and started for the door.

'Three?' Joseph Greengage asked.

'The vicar's dead in the priest hole.' Gerald looked actually excited to impart this news.

Joseph Greengage barely had time to react before Aunt Charlotte cried, 'Stop, Magic Man! You can't just leave a murder investigation.'

'Firstly, it's not a murder investigation — it's just you lot running around shouting at each other and finding dead people. And secondly, I've got to clear up your mess and practice my new trick.'

'Your new trick?' Bridget looked at him coldly. 'Cutting some poor resident of Greystone in half perhaps? Are your knives real, Mr Voyeur?'

He was astonished. 'I don't care for your insinuation! I've never hurt anybody, and any allegations—'

'But it was Lord Elzevir who ended your career, wasn't it?' Bridget sneered.

My mind flew back to their argument last night. Something nagged at my brain and had done ever since then. They were standing in his small cluttered front room. He was trying to do tricks. The flowers came back to me. Aunt Charlotte pulling at them. Lord Elzevir was very drunk by that point. He was staggering—

'Lord Elzevir was rude to you. Insulting you publicly after the flowers trick.'

'*Lord* Elzevir was rude and insulting to everyone,' he said sharply. 'Now, I am leaving.'

'Wait,' I said as if someone had just flicked a switch. 'Then you performed another trick.'

'So what? It's not illegal. It was in my own home. I've done nothing wrong. No one can pin anything on me this time.'

'Would you show us again?'

His eyes darted around the room anxiously. 'What? Now?'

'I'm not sure that's appropriate.' Mother looked at me doubtfully.

'There's a dead vicar in there!' Gerald said pointing to the open hole.

'Please,' I insisted. 'You should really practice with an audience, shouldn't you?'

'Can't imagine why,' Gerald said. 'He never usually has one.'

'Perform the trick,' Marsha said. It had the distinct ring of a command to it. Her eyes didn't leave him once.

He looked around before taking a deep breath. 'Very well.' He unfastened his dressing gown and opened it dramatically as if it was a cape.

'Just exactly what kind of a trick is this?' Aunt Charlotte looked shocked.

'There has to be a little theatre, darling,' he said with a quick shuffle.

'I think there's plenty of that already,' Lee Colman observed, 'especially given that the dead vicar's down there.'

Tony paused. 'Yes, well. This wasn't my idea. I need to be in the sitting room anyway.' He looked at Marsha.

She pursed her lips then nodded once. 'It might be more *appropriate*.'

We walked in deathly silence down the long hallway. No one spoke, the only sound the tapping of Verity's cane on the stone.

Inside the room, the red monkey, Dupin, watched us as if we'd just invaded his space. It's sharp little eyes never left us once.

'Observe and marvel at the great Voyeur!' He swept his dressing gown round him again and knelt down in front of the coffee table. He held up a coin just as he'd done before.

'Tony, how many times have you done this now?' Gerald sighed. 'Every bloody party in memory.'

'Well, if you don't—'

'Carry on, Mr Voyeur, please,' Bridget said, her eyes firmly fixed on him.

'I can't believe we're standing here watching a children's entertainer when Lord Elzevir is dead outside!' Lucy Morello shouted. 'And the vicar's dead in a hole!'

'Be quiet!' Marsha snapped.

'Why? Why should I? Who the—'

'Please, Lucy,' Verity said in her calm voice.

Lucy Morello looked at her and then slumped back into a chair with her bitter eyes still on Marsha.

The monkey made a sound like laughter and we all watched as it performed a little cartwheel of excitement. Its sly little eyes looked at us with amusement. Marsha put her finger to her lips and looked at the monkey. The animal obligingly fell quiet and watched the trick.

'Now, are we ready for the coin trick?' Tony Voyeur had the patient, strained look of a teacher waiting for his class to settle.

Aunt Charlotte frowned. 'Is this the one Pandora uses when you're stuck in the loo again, Ursula?

'No, Aunt Charlotte. Just watch.'

'This is an ordinary coin.' The magician held it up. 'Observe!' He then proceeded to perform the trick we'd seen before, standing up at the end with a look of profound satisfaction on his face, holding the coin in the other hand.

'I don't see how this gets us any closer towards finding out who killed these people.' Bridget folded her arms across her chest.

'Oh, I think we all know who killed Lord Elzevir!' Lucy Morello's face was set with a vicious look.

'Lucy!' Mrs Abaddon admonished. 'Be careful of your manners, young lady.'

'Please.' Verity held out her hands calmly.

'I think Miss Morello has a point,' Lee said quietly and placed his hand on Verity's shoulder. 'Lord Elzevir is dead, Jocasta is dead and no one can get in or out of this village. The vicar was the prime suspect, so now it has to be—' he paused — 'one of you.'

'I suppose it could always be you.' Mirabelle's voice was shaking. 'His Lordship was going to evict you.'

Lee Colman frowned. 'I'm not sure you've got any place to be saying that.'

Mirabelle looked ashamed.

'Hey!' I said. 'You don't know us well enough to speak to us like that.' I glanced at Mirabelle. 'We're all in danger. She has every right.'

'Do I need to be here for this?' Tony Voyeur was slinking towards the door.

'Young lady—' Gerald looked at me — 'I think we should all mind our manners and just remember this is our village and you are guests.'

'Oh and your beloved castle, Mr Bradshaw?'

'I beg your pardon?'

'Well, let's not forget all the deaths involved historical elements very few people would be familiar with.' I listed them off on my fingers. 'A cannonball between the portcullis gates, the ducking stool and the priest hole. It's almost as if someone was making a point, isn't it?'

'I don't know what you mean.' He shook his head. 'Any number of people in this room are very familiar with those things and can operate them. The dead man's wife for one.'

'Oh, well, we all know I'm prime suspect!' Marsha gave a bitter laugh.

'And why would I want to kill Jocasta and Reverend Vert?' Gerald looked confrontational, no doubt channelling his re-enactment face.

'Same reason anyone else would who'd killed Lord Elzevir.' Bridget continued to stroke the cat. 'Because they saw the killer.'

No one moved. Tony Voyeur paused by the door.

Bridget waited, enjoying the moment. 'The vicar and the witch were having a secret assignation at the church. Ursula even saw their torch light.'

She crossed herself and continued. 'They came through the cemetery, from where you can clearly see up the road to the portcullis. We all got to Verity's at roughly twelve fifteen to tell her the terrible news. Jocasta then came to the door. When she was asked what she was doing out in the cemetery she said "ghost hunting". The killer, who was undoubtedly one of us, realised what she'd said and that the witch and

Reverend Vert had been positioned where they may very well have seen them. Perhaps Jocasta ran back to warn the vicar. "I need to get to *him*," she said. She would have said "husband" or even "Ron" there, surely.

'The killer goes out later, when they have the luxury of time, and waits. First Jocasta is killed, presumably on her way home, and the killer indulges in the theatre of strapping her to the ducking stool. The killer then goes to the vicar's filthy little kennel, kills him and drags his body through one of the tunnels that come up under the various gravestones. What better place to hide a dead man of the cloth than a priest hole?'

'This is ridiculous and utterly libellous!' Gerald shouted.

'It's only libel if it's written down,' Aunt Charlotte said absently. 'It's slander if it's spoken. Isn't that what the lawyer said about your blog, Pandora?'

'Not now, Charlotte,' Mother glared.

'You have no proof of anything!' Gerald started to walk to the door.

'Oh, don't we?' Bridget's voice had a devious note to it.

Gerald paused, and a strange, sharp look entered his eyes. Suddenly the twee little local historian had morphed into something entirely different.

Bridget looked around with a self-satisfied smile. 'Mr Bradshaw, you told us you were due to go metal-detecting but you couldn't because your equipment was missing.'

'That's right and it's true. You can ask Harriet.'

'Your wife? You mean the woman who noticed Jocasta was tied up with your rope?' Bridget arched an eyebrow. 'You had a thorough working knowledge of the portcullis, yes?'

He frowned.

'And were aware of the Midnight Gun, the cannonballs and the murder hole, yes?'

'Everyone was!'

The monkey gave a little high-pitched scream and clapped his hands together. He then scampered up and over the top of the pelmet above the curtains. He was no longer fastened to the perch by the lead.

'We have to think about what we've just seen,' Bridget continued.

I watched the monkey tiptoeing along the curtain top, his glassy eyes taking it all in.

'Come down immediately, Dupin.' Marsha was strangely irritated by the monkey. It watched her but didn't move. She mouthed something under her breath before making a strange clicking sound with her tongue. The monkey gambolled down the folds of velvet with ease and sat obediently on its perch, watching Marsha intently.

She looked around us. 'Something Elzevir used to do.'

'I think the key to this is how the cannonball came to be directly above Lord Elzevir's head and drop from mid-air without a person being in there to hold it up,' Bridget said firmly.

'There's the platform, I suppose,' Mrs Abaddon said. 'Joseph's just been moving it around. You could stand on that, couldn't you?'

Joseph nodded. 'But it would take some to get it out of the way. It's not the easiest to manoeuvre. Wouldn't get it out before the gates came down.'

'Lord Elzevir would have seen the platform and the person on top. He'd hardly go and stand underneath and wait for them to drop it on his head,' Aunt Charlotte said.

'Mr Bradshaw can we just come back to your missing e—'

The monkey let out another scream.

'Quiet, Dupin!' Marsha held up her finger. She made the strange clicking sound again and the monkey ceased immediately, as if it had been instantly caught in her spell.

Tony Voyeur was edging towards the door again. I watched him glancing from one person to the next. He had the look of a man worn out by life, performing his cheap tricks to people who didn't want to watch, laughed at routinely by richer, more powerful men like Lord Elzevir, who had just taken everything he ever had without the need for sleight of hand. Lord Elzevir crushed him and moved on nonchalantly. What must it have been like to live in the shadow of this castle, in the shadow of the very man who had led him to this?

The monkey made his presence felt again and Marsha glared at him. The creature was growing increasingly agitated, hopping from one foot to the other. His little squawks coupled with Marsha's rising anger were definitely adding to the tension.

'Shh, Dupin.' Verity held a finger to her mouth. She smiled at the monkey, who instantly grew calmer.

The magician was almost through the door.

'Mr Voyeur,' I called. I stood up.

'Not now, Ursula.' Mother spoke to me as if I might be her pet little monkey that needed controlling. I had that unnerving feeling I have when I know everyone is looking at me. Even the monkey.

'What?' Tony paused.

I walked towards him.

The monkey dropped from his perch and ran across in front of me. He jumped up onto the table and picked up an apple.

'Dupin!' Marsha frantically made the clicking noise. But the monkey did not respond this time.

He ran up the bookcase with the apple firmly in his hand. A collection of swords was perched at the very top of the bookcase in an overlapping display, one sword across another, to form a grid-like pattern. Dupin peered through with his small face and bright eyes. He then carefully, with a concentration that implied he was well practised, climbed through the small metal square formed by four swords. We watched in horrible wonder as he slipped his tiny body through, followed by his back legs, which he hooked through, first one, then the other. The little creature had successfully negotiated the smallest of dangerous spaces without a cut to him. He looked down on us for appreciation before dropping the shiny green apple directly onto the top of Tony Voyeur's head.

'Why you little . . .'

His voice trailed off as the same thought travelled round us each in turn.

'It was the monkey,' Aunt Charlotte announced.

CHAPTER 31: THE TRICK OF IT

We all stared at the monkey as it danced from leg to leg with nervous glee.

'Dupin, down now!' Marsha clicked her tongue furiously.

'You trained the monkey to kill him,' Lucy said as if she was in a trance. 'You trained his own monkey to drop that cannonball. You evil—'

'Don't be so ridiculous,' Marsha frowned. 'How on Earth would you expect anyone to believe that? What absolute nonsense.'

'Marsha?' Verity's voice was quiet.

'Oh come on. You can't possibly believe . . .' Marsha trailed away as she saw the doubt blooming in Verity's face. 'Dupin copies what he sees. He must have seen it happen from the house.'

'You can't see inside the gatehouse from the house,' Gerald said coldly.

'Well, I don't know.' She looked flustered. 'Perhaps he saw it being set up.'

'And he'd assume that someone was going to kill Lord Elzevir, would he?' Mirabelle was growing brave again.

'He's heard us all talking about it.' Marsha clicked her tongue again. 'We've done nothing but talk about it since we got in this room. He's just acting it out. Get down, Dupin.'

Finally, the monkey scarpered down using the books to grip onto. His fast little hands passed from the Bronte's backs down through collections of Keats and Byron, his claws gripping along the spine of Shakespeare and sinking into the finely bound Dickens and Austen. He left a trail of tiny paw prints across their untouched dusty leather, like a fine thread weaving along them. Over encyclopaedias, the French Revolution and map books he scampered, until he made it to the floor.

'You certainly have a lot of control over the beast.' Gerald's eyes filled with suspicion.

Lucy was on her feet, spitting out anger again. 'Surely you don't expect people to believe that the monkey has been listening all this time and is working out the culprit?'

'I don't care what you believe.' Marsha glared at her. 'Isn't it a little far-fetched to suggest I trained a monkey to kill my husband with a cannonball? Wouldn't it have been easier to push him down the stairs?'

'Oh, so you have thought about ways to kill him!'

'Stop!' Mrs Abaddon said sharply.

Bridget put the cat down on Mirabelle's lap without looking at her.

Mrs Abaddon continued, 'We need to keep some grip on reality. No one is seriously suggesting Her Ladyship trained up a monkey to murder her husband. I see that monkey every day. I take more care of it than Her Ladyship. She has no time for the animal whatsoever.'

'Maybe His Lordship trained it to kill someone else and it got it wrong.' Aunt Charlotte attempted to look astute. She looked a little more pained.

'He had less control over it than anyone,' I said.

'Hmm, yes,' she mused. 'Remember the wig.'

'No one trained the monkey!' Marsha said fiercely. 'It's just acting out. It does that. Copied Elzevir. It drinks whiskey. It watches TV. It dresses up in my underwear.'

'What?' I said.

She shrugged. 'Elzevir thought it was funny and then Dupin just kept doing it.'

No one spoke for a moment.

'We're going down some very dark rabbit holes now.' Gerald frowned.

'Or monkey holes,' Aunt Charlotte added sagely.

I looked at her. 'Monkey holes?'

She turned down her mouth.

'I think I shall go and make us all a strong pot of tea. It might bring a little sense.' Mrs Abaddon walked out of the room without waiting for permission.

That's when I noticed Tony Voyeur lingering by the door, intent on his slow exit from the room unnoticed by anyone else.

'Wait, please, Mr Voyeur,' I said.

He paused at the door.

'Can I ask you about your magic?'

'Oh, not this again,' Gerald groaned. 'It's not a trained monkey and it's not black magic.'

Mother looked disappointed. 'Ursula, this is no time for playing tricks with David Copperfield.'

'I prefer Oliver Twist.' Aunt Charlotte nodded trying to look learned.

'May I see your hand?' I said to Tony Voyeur as I walked towards him.

He hesitated before holding it out. Clearly, he knew which one I was asking to see. Carefully, I reached out and held it.

'If you'd like a séance, dear, my rates are very reasonable. We could try and contact His Lordship. Maybe he can help. Table tipping is very good, or Ouija board.' He smiled and I could see his yellowing teeth.

'No, no, no! No more fortune tellers,' Aunt Charlotte said defiantly.

Tony Voyeur gave her a decidedly disgruntled look. 'It's not fortune telling. It's communing with the spirits.'

'They already know all about that,' Bridget said snidely, looking at me.

I ignored her and turned over the magician's hand, and there was the coin, nestled at the bottom of his fingers and wedged into the top of his palm.

He looked at me sheepishly. 'We all have our tricks, dear.' He glanced across at where Dad's shadow lingered in the corner before giving me a knowing look.

My eyes widened. I looked back at his hand. 'How does it stay there? Your grip?'

He looked into my eyes without blinking. 'No,' he whispered. 'It's magic.'

I reached out to take it with my other hand but he pulled back. He then picked up the coin himself and held it out to me. I took it slowly, but before he could take his hand away, I wedged it back into his palm and it stuck.

I looked into his surprised face. 'We all have our tricks,' I said.

Mother looked frustrated. 'Are you going to tell us just what exactly is going on, Houdini?'

Aunt Charlotte opened her mouth to speak, but Mother silenced her with *The Look*.

'Ursula, why don't you make all the attention worthwhile,' Bridget said sourly.

I ignored her. 'It's his ring.'

'Disgusting.' Aunt Charlotte turned away.

'His ring. On his finger, Aunt Charlotte. It's a magnet.'

He stood very still.

'Watch.' I turned his hand over so the palm was facing downwards. The coin didn't fall.

'There are two coins. One he places on top of the glass table and covers with his hand. The other coin is stuck to his ring, holding it in place against the palm of the other hand, which he places under the table. He takes away the top hand and the coin, which he hides. He then displays the second coin, which has come from underneath the table. It appears to the audience that the coin has passed through the table. Am I correct, Mr Voyeur?'

'I hated kids like you.' Tony Voyeur leaned into my face. 'Do you know what it's like for entertainers?'

'Every time.' Mother shook her head. 'Always the child who went up and revealed the magician's trick. Why do we need to expose this sad man quite so publicly?'

'Please, no exposing of him, for God's sake!' Aunt Charlotte flapped her hands.

'Mother! Aunt Charlotte! The crucial point is it's a magnet!'

'So?' Mother stared at me.

'It works through the table.'

'Yes and . . .'

'The *glass* table. If you turn the trick upside down, it still works. He could just hold the coin under the table and his hand with the ring on it would keep the coin in place.'

'Oh my God,' Verity gasped.

'What?' Aunt Charlotte said.

Bridget was looking very smug. 'Oh yes. Yes, I see. Perhaps if we'd taken the time to listen to me earlier, we might all know why this was significant.' She cast a smile around us all.

'Well?' Mother prompted.

'Oh, so you want to listen to me now?' Bridget stroked her villain's cat.

'For God's sake, someone just tell us before there's another murder.'

Bridget pursed her lips. 'Mr Bradshaw.' Her eyes flicked over to him. 'Could you please tell us a little more about your detectoring?'

Gerald Bradshaw looked surprised but somewhat pleased. 'Of course. What would you like to know?'

'About your equipment.'

'Bridget!' Aunt Charlotte looked shocked.

'Quiet!' Bridget said firmly. 'Your equipment went missing, yes?'

He nodded.

I could feel Tony Voyeur looking at me, but I didn't look back.

'And we met you on your way to . . .'

'The moat.'

'The moat.'

'Yes, the moat. I've found coins, shields, bits of armour and . . . What is this? Why am I being cross-examined here?'

Bridget slipped out a smile. 'Oh, this is just an informal inquiry, sir. The cross-examination will come later. Now, tell the ladies and gentlemen. Do you often go "detectoring" around the moat?'

'No.'

'No?' Bridget looked wrong-footed.

'Around the moat isn't very profitable.'

'No,' I repeated slowly. 'That's why Harriet said it! That's the key to it all!' All eyes flicked back to me.

Mirabelle leaned forward. 'What?'

'What do you mean?' Mother sighed. 'What's the key to it all?'

'Shopping trolleys!' I announced.

'Oh, Ursula. Really.' Mother turned away.

'Think! We've all seen the moat. There aren't any shopping trolleys. No one dumps them by the side of a moat. Where do you get shopping trolleys?'

'Wandsworth Bridge Sainsbury's?'

'Yes, Aunt Charlotte, thank you. Now I see why Harriet Bradshaw said "shopping trolleys". I understand! They're not dumped at castles or the sides of moats. Where are they dumped?' I looked around. '*In* the water. Rivers, canals and, it would seem, moats. You're not looking around the moat. You're looking *in* the water, aren't you?'

'In?' Mother whispered.

The monkey made a slight 'oo' sound but fell immediately quiet when Marsha looked at it.

'Yes, that's right. That's what I said, isn't it? There's so much more to find in there.' Gerald was becoming more animated. 'I've found some old coins, a musket and, like you say, there is for some reason always an unhealthy amount of shopping trolleys in bodies of water!'

'I don't care.' Bridget shook her head.

'I do! It's my moat,' Marsha said.

'How quick she is to say "my",' Lucy Morello noted.

They traded venomous looks again.

'I can't imagine why anyone would want to climb in that filthy water. That's suspicious enough in my book.' Mirabelle pushed the cat away and looked guiltily at Bridget.

'I don't get in the water,' Gerald said. 'I don't need to.'

'OK, well, would you like to talk us through what exactly you are doing?' I gave him an encouraging smile.

He looked around us as if some great honour had been bestowed upon him. He cleared his throat in readiness. 'Fishing.'

'Fishing?'

'Yes.'

'But sometimes your "catch" is quite heavy, isn't it?'

'Yes.'

'Yet you don't go in?'

'No, I stand on the bank. Like most fishermen. I use . . .'

'A magnet,' I said slowly.

He nodded enthusiastically. 'Yes, that's it. Magnet fishing. That's how you'd expect to fish for metal, isn't it, young lady? It's all the rage now with detectorists who want to explore underwater. Basically, there's a thick nylon rope.'

My mind snapped to the blue rope wrapped around Jocasta's limp body.

'There's a grappling hook and a super-strong neodymium magnet attached to the line. It's relatively small. Would fit in the palm of your hand. You just throw it all in and see what it brings up. People find all sorts of things. Lots of abandoned shopping trolleys though. Makes you wonder why.'

'Yes, doesn't it?' Aunt Charlotte nodded.

'If we can just bring it back from that,' I said. 'Back to the trick.'

'What?' Gerald looked genuinely affronted.

'Your magnet is very strong, yes?'

'It was, until it was stolen. I told you, my detectorist's kit was stolen.'

'Could it work through glass?'

'Yes, of course it could.'

The room paused. I spoke slowly and deliberately. 'And just as Mr Voyeur's magnet can hold a coin through the glass, so your very strong magnet could perform Mr Voyeur's trick but with a cannonball suspended on the other side of the glass, yes?'

I heard Verity take a sharp breath. The whole room seemed to glisten with interest now.

He nodded once. 'It could, but it would just hold it there. It won't drop.'

'Until the strong nylon rope was pulled away, yes?'

'That's correct. You'd still need someone to gather the rope in. You'd need to pull the magnet away from the glass.'

'Or you could use a mechanism, a very strong mechanism built for lifting something heavy, if someone wound the rope around that mechanism — say, as the gates descended?'

The monkey made a small, excited noise again.

Gerald nodded and everything was replaced with silence.

'So, someone could go up into the gatehouse and place your fishing line magnet on top of the glass in the murder hole and secure the rope around the portcullis mechanism. Then, if they came down the stairs and pushed Joseph's trolley over in order to climb up to the ceiling, and held up a cannonball to the glass, it would stay there. And could stay there all day?'

Gerald nodded again, more slowly this time.

'Once the cannonball is held in place by the magnet on the other side of the glass, they climb down and move the trolley away. Then, when the portcullis fell, the rope would be pulled back, pulling the magnet away and releasing the cannonball, while both gates came down. Yes?'

'That would work, yes.' He spoke quietly as if the full meaning of his words was still percolating.

'You would be left with a man on his own, with the gates down and a cannonball that had fallen from a solid, immoveable glass roof, yes?'

He didn't need to answer.

'And anyone could clear away the magnet, which you said was as small as the palm of your hand, and the rope.'

'No one went up there until the next day,' Marsha said.

'Only we know that they did, because Gerald's rope was used to tie up Jocasta.'

'Anyone could have taken that stuff away,' Mother added. 'There would have been plenty of time for someone to slip up there. We'd raised the portcullis and gone to Verity's. Then we separated out. Plenty of people were on their own. It would have been so easy for someone from the village or any of the rooms in the castle to slip out at any time, get the magnet, kill Jocasta and then head off to the sleeping vicar.'

'It could be anyone,' Aunt Charlotte said in wonder.

'Ingenious!' smiled Bridget. 'And to think I cracked it!'

'Woah there!' I stammered. 'I worked out the trick. The magnet behind the glass.'

'To be fair, I worked that out first,' Tony Voyeur offered.

'Yes, you did know how to do it,' I said.

'Oh, come on, everyone here's seen that trick a hundred times. I freely admit that.'

'Stop! Stop!' Bridget commanded. 'It means the portcullis operation is the focal point. To put the scheme into operation and pull back the rope that had to move. There were only three ways that it could be lowered — the remote, the override and the control panel up in the castle. Only one person had access to all of those.'

Everyone turned to look at Marsha, and the monkey let out a scream of excitement as if somehow his scheme had worked. And in that very strange moment, it seemed as if the monkey had framed the lady of the house.

CHAPTER 32: ANNOUNCING A MURDERER

'So, we're all just coming back round to it being me then, is that it?' Marsha glared.

'You see, it's often the most obvious person,' Aunt Charlotte nodded confidently.

'Motive is a very powerful clue.' Bridget was looking very self-satisfied again, so we braced ourselves.

'That bitch hated him,' Lucy Morello spat. 'That's motive enough. He was trying to divorce her and leave her without any money or her precious castle. This way she could get rid of him and have everything she wanted.'

I looked round the room. 'Surely if she was planning that and such a complicated way of killing him, she wouldn't leave herself as the only person here, with the remote control in her bag. She's left herself as the ridiculously overwhelming main suspect.'

Lucy Morello tightened her mouth.

'You thought you might benefit from his will, didn't you?' Mother added.

The girl sniffed and flicked her head dismissively. 'I did not. She's the beneficiary. It's a lot, all this.' She waved her hand round the room. 'She's not so old. Maybe she thought it was worth doing the time for.'

'We know that's not a possibility,' I said. 'Remember? The Forfeiture Rule? Aunt Charlotte's favourite — a person criminally responsible for the death of another person cannot inherit as a result of their criminal act.' I waited.

And then the darkest part of my thoughts lit up with an idea. 'We go back to the beginning and we look at it from another angle. We turn the trick around and look at it upside down. The remote control is in Marsha's bag — very visibly. Why is the platform with wheels there? Who knew the secret system of tunnels that led under the graveyard and beyond to move around and dispose of the vicar's body?' I thought back to the scratching and dragging I'd heard in the walls. 'How is it that Lord Elzevir ended up on his own? Why are we here?'

'We were invited.' Mother frowned.

'Some of us were.' Bridget couldn't help herself.

'By whom?' I asked. 'The lady who plans to kill her husband? She could have done that any day of the week and looked a lot less guilty than this!' I shook my head. 'No. We must start to look at the questions fairly. We must see each person as equal and then the answers come flooding in.' I bent down and tapped my fingernail rhythmically on the table until it was the only sound in the room. I carried on, everyone just watching. Listening.

'By the tapping of my finger something wicked this way comes,' Bridget said, as if a light had just turned on for her too.

'What the hell are you talking about?' Mother doesn't like other people understanding things when she doesn't.

I stopped tapping my finger and the room was quiet. 'There was no tapping.'

'What?'

'Mother, listen. Something has been itching at me since the beginning of all this. I see it now. I hear it. Or at least I *didn't* hear it. There was no tapping, but there should have been, shouldn't there, Verity?'

All our eyes travelled towards the woman sitting calmly in the chair with her cane by her side.

'When we surprised her by going back there, when Marsha took us there and hammered on the door, it was Verity who answered — very quickly, I recall. And there was no *tap, tap, tap* of her cane on the stone floor as there had been everywhere else she'd walked previously. Marsha lunged forward towards Verity in front of everyone else. She embraced her, and I remember Verity's hand was on hers, meaning Marsha's was under Verity's. Marsha's hand would not have been under Verity's if Verity was holding the cane in the first place. Verity, you'd put your hand on top of Marsha's as she handed you the cane, hadn't you Verity? You'd walked to the door quickly and without a cane. Because you don't need a cane, do you?'

Lee Colman stood close by her, looking down at the woman. 'Verity?'

She didn't answer. She didn't look at him. She stared straight ahead, tears flaring in her eyes.

Bridget continued now with relish. 'Yes, oh yes,' she beamed. She clapped her hands. 'I knew it! This makes so much sense now.'

I continued, vaguely off-balance from Bridget's enthusiastic agreement.

'Marsha looked so clearly guilty. She always has — *ridiculously* so. In fact, she's always looked so guilty that it started to look to me as though she was being framed. Surely no one would leave this amount of evidence pointing to themselves. No one would leave themselves so obviously as the suspect — alone in the castle, the only one with access to any of the means to lower the gate. So I asked myself, why is Lord Elzevir dead? Everyone seemed to have a motive but they were all tied up in vengeance for past misdemeanours. The Peacocks hadn't been paid their money, the Bradshaws were cross about the perceived loss of heritage, even you, Joseph Greengage, had an affair with his wife.'

'Hey, wait a minute, that was a one-off—'

Mother held up a silencing hand. 'But I don't think we're looking at vengeance here, Ursula.'

'No, Mother. It all makes sense now. Someone set this up *and*, in the process, set Marsha up too. This took a lot of planning didn't it, Verity?'

She sat still, quietly staring.

'So we go back to the beginning with my questions but now armed with the knowledge that Verity is able-bodied and does not need a stick to walk. It all looks very different, indeed.' I nodded to myself.

'Verity?' Lee Colman repeated. 'Say something.'

She looked up at him. 'What can I say, Lee? The girl is right. I don't need the stick anymore. I . . .' Her head collapsed into her hands. 'I haven't for a long time.'

'Bloody hell,' Gerald said, wide-eyed in disbelief.

The monkey agreed with another sound of intrigued wonder.

I took a deep breath. 'Firstly, why is the platform with wheels there? Yes, Joseph Greengage put it there, but it was Verity's redecoration plans and she designed the structure to have wheels. Secondly, who knew the intricate system of tunnels and priest holes that led in and out of the castle? We were told Verity knew all the castle plans and now, of course, we know that she can use them easily to move around and store dead vicars. Thirdly, how is it Lord Elzevir ended up on his own at just before midnight? Because Verity "fell" and needed assistance from Marsha. She then sends Marsha home, insisting she be there to let Lord Elzevir in, meaning that Marsha is there on her own at the relevant time. Meanwhile, all the servants needed to be with Verity, which had been pre-arranged as an absolute necessity for her to take part in the evening. Look at her leg. The bruise. I saw all that dark make-up in the downstairs bathroom.' I paused for breath.

'And you forget, of course—' Bridget held up her finger — 'your last question, Ursula. Why are we here? Because it was Verity's idea! She brought us all here to *witness Marsha killing her husband*.'

Verity looked round us all, her face desperate with anguish. 'Why would I do such a thing?' Her voice had fallen to a fragile whisper.

'Well,' Aunt Charlotte smiled. 'Of course, we come back to my old friend, the forfeiture rule, which I have mentioned several times and that now actually becomes much more useful. If he's dead and Marsha is found guilty, she cannot inherit, so the money goes to the next of kin — you, Verity. And you'd be free to marry the man you love, who Lord Elzevir was trying to evict from his farm. Lee Colman.'

He looked at her with desperate eyes. 'Verity?' he whispered.

'It's true,' Verity began. 'I do love you, Lee. But I would never kill my brother, not even for you. I loved him. As hard as everyone else may find that to understand.'

'But you were lying to him, weren't you?' Aunt Charlotte nodded towards Verity's leg. 'You were pretending to need a stick.'

'Yes, yes. God, yes.' The tears overwhelmed her for a moment. 'I was, and for that I am very sorry. He paid for me to live here. I have no income. When I fell from the horse, *his* unruly horse, I lost everything and I truly was crippled for months. It just became easy to carry on like that. He showed me love and affection. He looked after me in a way he never had before because he felt guilty.'

Her eyes shone with a film of tears. 'I liked being his favourite. I loved being in his light. It was like being near the sun. I just didn't want to lose that. And I certainly would never have killed him.' She looked around us pleadingly. 'You've got to believe me!'

'Why?' Lee Colman said flatly. 'You lied.'

The monkey made a low-pitched sound of dismay and shook his head.

Mother leaned forward in her chair, her eyes sharp. 'But tell us this, Bridget, how she could have performed this feat? Mrs Abaddon and Lucy Morello were in the house with her. She would have had to get out somehow to operate the gate.

Even if she had access to the remote, it wouldn't work from there. No way.'

Bridget was silent. A hole had appeared.

There was an eerie quiet about us now.

'The punch bowl,' Mirabelle spoke quietly.

'She used a punch bowl? What rubbish.' Aunt Charlotte slumped back.

'No, it smashed. Full of punch. But there was no flood of punch as you'd expect. Within minutes, there was nothing more than a damp floor. It drained away almost immediately. There was nothing there. Why would that be, Verity?'

Verity looked around the room with panic stricken eyes. 'I . . . I . . .'

Marsha's face fell. 'Verity?'

Verity looked at her, a look of realisation spreading. She was clearly very aware that Marsha must know what she was about to say. Verity looked down with shameful eyes. 'Because one of the priest tunnels surfaces under the vicarage as well.'

'Oh, of course!' Bridget announced. 'I mean, that just makes sense doesn't it? If they needed to escape from the church, they might need to escape from there too. Jocasta told us there'd been priests living there for hundreds of years. When we got to Verity's house to tell her about Lord Elzevir's death, Lucy Morello emerged from her room with her AirPods in. She wouldn't have heard any movement in the hallway. Mrs Abaddon told us she'd been downstairs in the kitchen clearing away.'

Mother folded her arms. 'But how did she bring the gate down?'

Bridget pretended to look confused. 'With the remote control, of course. You will note that it appeared in Marsha's bag after the bag had been left there under the chair. Why would Marsha let it be so obvious and fling it out of her bag? She would have hidden it, not flaunted it. She didn't know it was there.'

'Verity?' Marsha's voice was low. Her mouth barely formed around the words. She looked at her in disbelief. 'You were my friend. I would have kept you here. Looked after you even if your injuries had mended. I would always have been here for you. I would always have loved you.'

Tears escaped from Verity's eyes. Her face crumbled. 'I know I've been lying. I know. I'm so sorry. Marsha, you've got to believe me. I never meant to cause any harm. I never meant . . .' She swallowed her words and paused. 'I didn't kill him, Marsha. I swear it.' She looked around at everyone.

My mind tumbled with all their words. Thoughts hammered away in my head.

'Marsha, *please*! You have to believe me.' Verity cried.

'Why should I? You've lied to me about your leg, about everything. It's all been a lie. All this time, Verity. All this time.'

I glanced across the room at where Dad's shadow stood solemnly watching me. He shook his head slowly. No.

CHAPTER 33: REVELATIONS

'No?' I said cautiously. My eyes stayed fixed on Dad.

'Oh, Ursula, for God's sake. When we have a solution, why not just accept it?' Mother was exasperated, which is never good for her. She doesn't do patience.

'Because it's not right.' Mirabelle didn't look at anyone. She sounded so detached now.

'I beg your pardon?' Bridget's voice had a precise edge to it now. She stared at the side of Mirabelle's face.

'Oh God, here we go again.' Tony Voyeur landed in the chair as if he was intending to crush it. 'Three people are dead and someone not that far away killed them.'

'That is precisely what we are trying to work out, Mr Magic Fingers.' Mother remained poised. 'Whoever killed Lord Elzevir was seen by the witch and the vicar who were cavorting around together.'

'She just said who it was — Verity,' Tony Voyeur answered. 'And she certainly has been lying for a very long time.'

Verity sat quietly sobbing in the corner, her head in her hands, rocking slightly. 'Oh God,' she uttered intermittently.

I looked at Dad. He shook his head.

Bridget hadn't stopped staring at the side of Mirabelle's head, as if she was drilling her way through into Mirabelle's thoughts. Mirabelle must have been aware of it but she didn't turn to look at her.

When she started talking, Bridget's voice had a threat nestled in among every word. 'I looked after you when they all cast you off. I took you in when you were breaking down and now — now, when they are here in front of you — you just fall on your knees in front of them? Pathetic.'

The monkey let out a long slow noise of intrigue and put his hand under his chin, leaning in closer.

Mother frowned. 'What on Earth is she talking about, Mirabelle?'

'Now, isn't the time for this!' Aunt Charlotte held the sides of her head.

Lee Colman nodded. 'The old woman's right.'

Aunt Charlotte looked around bewildered.

'Look,' Marsha cut in. 'A lot has been revealed.' She looked pointedly at Verity. 'I think we need to take a moment. We need to try and calm down and take it all in.'

'Calm down?' Tony Voyeur wrapped his dressing gown around himself tightly. 'Calm down? There's a body in the walls. A body in the moat. A body in the gatehouse—'

'Good job they got rid of the library,' Aunt Charlotte added.

Marsha was at the door. 'I will go and ask Mrs Abaddon to bring that tea and perhaps something a little stronger to settle our nerves.'

Before she left, she looked at Verity. A sadness filled her eyes. 'We'll see if we can't get some phone signal or something now. I think the rest is a matter for the police. We should leave it to them.'

'Marsha? Marsha please,' Verity pleaded. 'You've got to believe me.'

She and Verity looked at one another. All the complicated strands were there between them on full display and neither seemed to be aware that the rest of the room could see them. All that care and attention Marsha had lavished on Verity thrown back at her in one swipe. To discover she'd

246

never needed the walking stick at all, never needed her constant assistance and all that devotion we'd seen. It must have burned. But probably not as much as the fact that it was quite possible that Verity had been trying to frame her for the murder, and what other way was there to see it?

She'd carefully made sure Marsha was alone and the only person who could have done it. She'd put the key visibly in her handbag. She'd even organised a man to put in place a decorating platform on wheels. She'd set everything so carefully down to the last little detail to kill her own brother and frame Marsha for it.

If there were any doubt whatsoever as to her guilt, all that wholesome innocence was instantly wiped away by the great lie she'd been living under. Lord Elzevir had died believing in her. All the care and attention lavished on her had been pointless.

A new sadness had invaded Marsha's eyes. That's what betrayal does — it poisons everything, polluting all the good until nothing but the betrayal remains. It defies everything else.

'I'm so sorry,' Verity whispered.

Marsha turned and walked out of the room.

It had gone very quiet, very still in the room, as if we were poised for something else. As if something was missing.

Verity sobbed quietly.

I looked over at Dad, his head hung low in dejection. I couldn't see any one of my memories without the filter of his unfaithfulness over it. He hadn't just cheated on Mother — he'd cheated me out of the memory of a good and honourable father.

I looked over at Lee Colman, who watched Verity with a new suspicious look. Had he known about the lie? He looked pretty surprised, but then they all had their secrets here. I pictured Ron, bent double by pain, somewhere out there in the rain and mud, looking into the slack face of his dead wife. Did he weep for her death or her infidelity that led her to it? The bitterness would infect every breath from that moment onwards.

Even Joseph Greengage, quiet and solemn in the corner, had indiscretions he regretted.

I glanced over at Mirabelle. She still wore that sorrowful expression — that strange penitent's look.

'Mirabelle,' I began.

Bridget cleared her throat. I ignored her.

'Mirabelle, why isn't it right?'

The monkey cracked a nut and sat back on his perch as if he was settling in for the final scene.

Mirabelle's face crinkled. 'I'm sorry?' Every time she spoke it had a defeated note to it. But there was more than that. It was as if she felt the need to apologise for the words.

'Mirabelle, you said "it's not right." What's not right?'

Bridget sniffed. 'Well, you might ask now, lady.' She held up her nose as if the cat had done something unspeakable. I looked down at the animal. It had — in her open handbag, but she hadn't noticed yet and I wasn't about to start telling her.

I looked quizzically at Mirabelle. 'What's going on here? Why are you Bridget's lapdog?'

'It's a cat, dear.'

I ignored Aunt Charlotte and continued. 'Why is Bridget making all these pointed little comments?'

I saw Mother shift in her chair.

'No. When I said it's not right, I wasn't talking about me,' Mirabelle sounded frail. 'I was—'

'But you should!' Bridget sounded as if she was ordering Mirabelle. 'You should tell them! You should talk about you.' She folded her arms defiantly.

'Tell them what?' Mother looked disorientated.

Aunt Charlotte was on her feet, dominating the room. 'Right, what exactly is going on?'

'Ha,' Bridget scoffed.

The monkey imitated her. Then looked pleased with its mockery.

Bridget's face iced over. 'You don't like being on the outside, do you, you Smart Women? None of you do. Well, it's your turn now. Where were you when she came to me desperate, ruined, a mess?'

Tears pricked Mirabelle's eyes and she looked away quickly.

'It's OK.' Bridget put an overprotective hand on Mirabelle's lap. 'Don't cry.'

Tony Voyeur stood up and smoothed a finger along each black eyebrow. 'Who cares? There's a murderer! Most likely in this room.' His eyes flicked to Verity. 'You've just accused someone of killing her brother, something's apparently "not right" and now we're doing this? I'm getting whiplash!'

'Disgusting,' Aunt Charlotte murmured. She looked at him squarely. 'Some things are more important than death. And we should know. We've seen enough of it.'

'Oh, that makes us feel much safer,' Gerald said.

'This is madness!' Tony Voyeur shook his head with the look of a defeated man.

Mother looked him up and down. 'So speaks the man parading around in a dressing gown with his name on the back and a house full of headless dolls.'

'Tony, just let the ladies speak,' Verity said quietly, wiping away the tears. 'They have something they've needed to sort out from the beginning.'

'Oh, and we're listening to you now, are we, when you lied about your injury?'

'And don't forget, she's probably the killer,' Gerald added decidedly.

'I didn't kill anyone.' Verity looked up at Lee Colman with pleading eyes. 'You have to believe me. Please Lee. I didn't kill anyone. I wouldn't hurt Elzevir.' She spoke so earnestly it was as if in that moment she was laying out her soul to him for inspection and judgement.

Everyone watched her and Lee intently, waiting. The monkey clapped as if this was some sort of show he was watching.

'It's . . . It's not up to me.' He turned away.

Bridget didn't wait. She cleared her throat, brushing aside their conversation. 'If you must know, Pandora, you always kept Mirabelle on the outside. She could never get between you and your wretched daughter. Before that, it was your precious George.'

'Wait a minute, Bridget. You don't get to talk about him.' My eyes locked on her but I was aware of Dad's shadow flickering at the edges of my vision.

'That's it! Just exactly what Mirabelle was talking about. Just that. Right there. No one's allowed to talk about you or your precious father.' Bridget gave a decisive single nod towards me. 'That's why she lied and you deserved it. All of you. But Mirabelle didn't deserve the breakdown afterwards.'

'Lied?' I repeated slowly.

'And you were so quick to believe her. Shows how much you really did care about precious Daddy. A philanderer indeed.'

The room seemed to contract around me. The air was being squeezed out of me.

'What the hell's she talking about, Mirabelle?' It was Mother I could hear in the background of all the new noise.

Everyone's voices seemed to grow muffled as if I was listening to them underwater. The only thing that grew clearer was Dad's outline.

Mirabelle looked straight at Mother. 'I lied.' She said it simply as if it was just nothing.

'Well, it seems like it's confession time again,' Gerald said with a large grin that he instantly dropped when he saw our reaction. 'Lots of liars in the room.' He raised his eyebrows towards Verity, who looked away.

Mirabelle began in even words, thinking each one through carefully. 'It was a lie. I told you George had an affair because I was sick of hearing what a saint he was. Sick of all the bullshit eulogising *she* did.' She nodded towards me. I heard her breathe in heavily through her nose. 'So, I told you a little white lie. I told you he had an affair. It was just to take the edge off his gleam. Make some light fall on me. I didn't know you would turn so far against him. I didn't know it would have such an impact on you and Ursula.' Her words fell fast like spent cartridges.

Aunt Charlotte's mouth was hanging open. 'You're kidding, right?'

Mirabelle shook her head, and in that moment, I imagined hitting it so hard it dropped from her shoulders onto the ground as easy as one of Tony Voyeur's dolls. But she carried on talking, sound carried on coming out of her mouth as if she was desperate to get rid of it.

'Do you know what it's like to stand in the shadow of someone else's adoration?'

I heard Mother. 'How could you? All those years.'

Their words were circling me now, filling up the air until the room felt swollen with them. But my eyes turned to Dad. He slowly lifted his head and looked at me. And then he smiled. And it wrapped around me like arms drawing me in. A pure smile. His face softening back to what I always remembered. And my head went blank.

Mirabelle's voice chattered away at the edges of my thoughts. 'I didn't mean . . . I . . . just said it. You just believed it, Pandora, and then the years rolled by and it was such an easy lie. But then Ursula knew and *she* started all the fire-and-brimstone suffering and you just got closer and closer to her. And I lost you. I lost *me*.' There was nothing left of her voice now. She was making great stuttering sounds, forcing the words out through the tears.

When Mother spoke, it was in a flat voice that sounded so detached. 'He died with me believing a lie. He died with all my jealousy and hate on him.'

Dad shook his head frantically.

'No, he didn't,' I whispered, still staring at him.

Mother's face wrinkled with confusion. She stared at the space where his shape lingered. He looked at her and smiled.

I don't know if she saw him in that moment. Maybe. But her eyes turned to Mirabelle.

'I just wanted you to love me as much,' Mirabelle pleaded.

Mother's smile was just a thin, sharp line. 'Well, now I hate you as much as you made me hate him.'

Aunt Charlotte held up her hands. 'OK. Let's stay calm.'

'Stay calm? She destroyed everything.' Mother spat the words out.

I was suddenly very aware of the rest of the room, the outsiders watching us. Their excruciating little eyes on us, judging us. I put my hand on Mother's sleeve.

'That wasn't what I wanted!' Mirabelle shook her head.

'Who the hell was the woman at the funeral?'

'No one.' Mirabelle looked down shamefully. 'Just someone I asked to come along to support me, and then I said it was time to go.'

'Jesus, Mirabelle,' Aunt Charlotte breathed.

'I can't . . . I don't . . . I'm not coping so well now and I just . . .' Mirabelle was crumbling in front of us, drowning in guilt. And then she was on her feet, looking around us rabbit fast with fear. She bolted from the room.

Mother held up her finger. 'Don't fucking speak, Bridget.'

Bridget shrugged.

We stood in an empty silence. No one moved.

I watched Dad, his face soft with sympathy. His outline was more blurred. He was no more than a pale grey shape. His eyes never left me. His smile didn't flinch.

And then he was gone.

I saw Mrs Abaddon enter as if I was on the other side of the window staring in. The big ring of keys by her side jangled against her hip.

'She did everything for her,' I whispered. 'Looked after her.'

CHAPTER 34: THE ART OF FRAMING A LADY

I could hear people talking as if they were very distant. Sweat trickled down my temples. The newborn air rushing into my lungs.

'Are you all right, dear?' Aunt Charlotte's firm hands pressed into my leg. I could smell Mother's hairspray, her head near mine.

Lee Colman spoke in a sombre voice. 'She doesn't look well.'

'We need water.' It was Verity by my side, her eyes full of concern. There was no walking stick in her hand now.

'Well, I'm not doing anything for any of you anymore,' Lucy Morello said viciously. 'You're all liars and murderers.'

'I'll fetch some, madam,' Mrs Abaddon said calmly.

'What happened to the tea you were making?' Tony Voyeur grumbled.

'Tea, *sir*. Right away.' Her keys rattled with irritation.

'She looked after *her*,' I said into Mother's face.

She stared at me.

'Who, dear?' Aunt Charlotte spoke softly.

'Verity.'

A vague memory of Dad was there, shaking his head. 'No.'

'Mirabelle said, "it's not right".' Cobwebs of doubt were spinning out fast.

Verity's face tensed. I turned my head to look at her. 'She did everything for you, didn't she?'

She looked away, her face hot with shame. 'I know. I know I lied.'

'Lot of it about,' Aunt Charlotte said pointedly.

'But I didn't kill anyone. I swear.'

Behind her, I could see Gerald Bradshaw was making for the door. 'I need to go and check my wife is safe. And my daughter. I can see exactly what's happened here. It's very easy to see.'

'Wait,' I said. 'What if they died because of what they *didn't* see?'

'Oh, attention seeking again,' Bridget said.

'You've said enough, Bridget.' Mother stared at her. 'Don't make yourself the next victim.'

I turned to Verity. 'Where does your tunnel go?'

She looked confused. 'From my home to the church-yard. It comes up under one of the graves.'

'And the castle tunnel?'

'Well, that's a different tunnel and a different grave. It's quite clever, really. They're purposefully not linked, so if one tunnel was discovered, another could remain in operation.'

'So, Verity, if you'd passed through your tunnel, you would have come up in the graveyard and had to use a different tunnel to get to the castle, yes?'

She nodded.

'If Jocasta and the vicar were in the graveyard at that time, which she said they were, they would have seen you move between the graves. But she didn't see that. She came to your house and she never mentioned seeing you there. She said she'd been "watching the ghosts", meaning there was no one else there to watch. Jocasta and the vicar had to die because they *didn't* see you there. They saw no one in the graveyard.'

Everyone was looking. Waiting. Gerald was paused at the door.

'Your daughter, Scarlett Bradshaw.'

He frowned. 'She's got nothing to do with this.'

'She told us the Peacocks were flapping about the lightning hitting the exchange. Joseph Greengage, you were with her?'

He nodded. 'That's right. She wanted to check on her mum and dad. We'd just seen Lee Colman and he said the road was flooded too.'

'But you see,' I said, 'that makes no sense.'

'It's true!' Joseph said. 'We've got no need to lie.'

'Other than sleeping with Lord Elzevir's wife.' Lucy Morello watched him suspiciously.

'No, no,' I held up my hand. 'The Peacocks had no reason to be flustered about that if it was all true.'

Lee Colman coughed. 'It's all true. I ain't no liar.' He stared meaningfully at Verity, who winced.

I sat up straight. My stomach was roiling. 'Four corners square, this. One, the panic of the Peacocks; two, the vicar and the witch saw nothing; three, the key; four, Verity's lie.'

Verity looked down.

'The Peacocks wouldn't have panicked.'

Tony Voyeur sighed. 'They're quite old and this is an isolated place. You don't know what it's like when we're cut off.'

'I think we do now!' Bridget said indignantly.

I ignored them and continued. 'The Peacocks wouldn't have panicked because the exchange was already down. They didn't expect to have any signal. Add that to the facts we know. Jocasta and the vicar would have seen Verity pass through the churchyard if she'd been there. Jocasta, when she stood at Verity's door and made her quip about "watching the ghosts", was unwittingly telling the murderer she was there and saw nothing but ghosts, no humans.'

They were silent.

'Then add the fact that Mrs Abaddon has the keys to the castle.'

'But not the portcullis, miss.' Mrs Abaddon stood at the door. Again, without the tea.

'No, but you did lock the main door before we left, yes?'

She nodded. 'I always do.' She rattled the large set of keys at her side.

'Verity, your leg is fine?' I asked.

Lee Colman stepped forward. 'Enough. We know that.'

'We do now, but up until this moment only Verity knew.' I looked round them. 'Oh, and the murderer.'

They stared.

'You see, all the little details were put in place to point us Verity's way. She organised the party. She wanted it. She organised the decorator and the moving platform. She was the reason Lord Elzevir was alone. She has a tunnel under her house leading to the graveyard. She had the bag in her home and planted the fob. So when her big lie about her leg is finally revealed and we discover she is able to move around and she's been lying for so long, well, we would obviously think she was guilty. But to set all this up and then allow for the big reveal, the murderer would have to know you had that big secret. That you could have committed the murders because you could walk very well.'

'No one knew,' Verity said quietly. 'Not even Lee.'

'You *told* no one. But someone else did know.'

She frowned.

'The only other person who knew was the one who took such good care of you and took you to all your hospital appointments. Lady Marsha Black.'

Gerald Bradshaw sighed. 'We're going round in circles. You've just told us Marsha was framed.'

'She was.'

'Well why would someone frame her if they weren't the murderer? Who would go to the trouble of framing the murderer?'

'She would.'

'Who?'

'Marsha.'

Their faces seemed to gather as one.

'Think! Marsha wants to kill her husband. He's awful to her. She hates him. That much is public knowledge. It's also well known by enough people that he intends to divorce her and make sure she receives nothing. But how can she kill him when she would be the obvious suspect? Everything points to her. Then it occurs to her, if it is so obvious and becomes so improbably so — it could start to look like she's being set up. She can use it to her advantage and make it look like someone is framing her. She just needs to tweak the edges of the picture, and rather than looking overwhelmingly guilty, she looks overwhelmingly framed. All she needed was the framer for this particular portrait of a sad woman. Someone she could back into that role.

'It was done very subtly but constantly. Who told us everything we knew about Verity's involvement? Marsha did. The party was Verity's idea, so Marsha *said*, out of earshot of Verity, who would no doubt have corrected her. The decorating project was Verity's, as was the platform with wheels and its placement — so Marsha *told* us when Verity wasn't there, Lord Elzevir being alone because Verity fell.'

I pushed the bruise on the back of Verity's leg and she winced. 'Perhaps it's on the back from where someone else kicked you down. The make-up planted in your bathroom — I was in the middle of saying I was going to the bathroom when Marsha jumped up and ran in there.

'It looked like Verity was moving us all around and creating situations she wanted. Verity sends Marsha back to the castle to make sure Lord Elzevir can get in and ensures she's alone there. Verity wanted the staff with her that night. Verity wanted Marsha to take everyone back to the castle after the death, presumably giving her a chance to kill Jocasta and the vicar. But all these things we "know" about Verity because we were told them by Marsha. We never *heard* Verity say this party was her idea. We never *heard* her make demands about where the staff should be or send Marsha home to be there on her own. Everything we know that makes Verity the framer comes from the person she supposedly framed. Marsha Black.'

'What about the remote control in Marsha's handbag?' Tony Voyeur pointed out.

'Mrs Abaddon,' I said, 'where did you leave Marsha when you walked her up?'

She didn't hesitate. 'At the gates.'

'So you didn't walk up and unlock the main door. The key is the *other* key. Marsha would have had to unlock the door with the large bunch of keys she kept in her handbag. There was no room in her skinny clothing to hide that. She took the bag because it had the keys. It was never left overnight at Verity's. She couldn't have got in the castle otherwise.

'She knows when he'll be back — just before midnight. After all, she told him to be. *She said* Verity had reminded her to tell Lord Elzevir, but again we never heard that. Marsha waits. Flicks the remote control. The portcullis lowers and the rope tightens and pulls back the magnet. The cannonball falls and Lord Elzevir is dead.

'She has all along followed a careful two-pronged plan — first, frame herself, and second, make it look like someone is framing her. Then all she had to do was set up the pieces to make it look inescapably like it was Verity who framed her. And it all falls into place because . . .' I paused to breathe.

'She knows the big secret Verity has. That she has lied. She knew Verity could easily have committed the murders and has hidden behind a lie. And it's such a big lie that when revealed alongside all the times she has "framed" Marsha, there can be no other answer than that she is the murderer.'

'This is some trick!' Tony Voyeur said quietly.

'Ah, but it started to derail a little when Jocasta turned up at Verity's and announced she'd only seen ghosts in the graveyard. She would, of course, have seen Verity if she really had been up to the castle via the tunnels. Marsha had to eliminate anyone else who knew no one was there. And she was cunning and daring enough to commit two more murders later that night when we had all gone to bed. She even had the luxury of time to be grotesquely creative.'

The sound of an engine ripping into life made me pause. We listened.

'So where the hell is our murderer?' Mother said.

We looked around stupidly as if we'd just misplaced her.

'She went to ask Mrs Abaddon about the tea.' Gerald looked down the hallway. 'And perhaps something stronger, she said.'

'I didn't see her,' said Mrs Abaddon.

The crunch of gravel mingled now with the sound of the engine.

There was a pause before the room spun into movement.

I glanced back only momentarily to see Dupin smiling at us and holding out the map as if he was studying it. I frowned at him and I could have sworn he winked.

We ran through the long hallway, past the weapons and armour, our feet echoing around the high ceiling.

I watched Verity racing on ahead, she looked so odd unencumbered by her cane. Lee Colman was watching her too, with sad eyes. Big lies leave big marks. Deceit is a stain that will always leave its outline behind.

I looked for Dad. He wasn't there.

Outside, the pulse of the engine filled the air. It was a small sports car, the smoke from its exhaust clouding the dirty grey courtyard. Marsha sat gripping the wheel with both hands, staring resolutely, angrily at the small gatehouse. She glanced over towards our rapidly assembling group at the door to the castle. She smiled as if we were in some way ridiculous to her and nodded towards Verity.

'Wait!' Verity called and began running towards the car.

Marsha turned and looked straight ahead. With a sudden jolt, the car burst into life, racing towards the open gate.

'Surely she doesn't mean to run over his body?' Aunt Charlotte looked horrified.

Bridget shrugged. 'She killed him, I suspect damage to the corpse isn't a worry for her.'

We stepped out into the courtyard, Lee Colman running ahead with Joseph. All of us scattered out.

As I crossed the courtyard, I began to slow and I watched the slim, dark shadow of my father rise up in the centre of the gates. He stood there, motionless. The car was accelerating towards him.

'*No!*' The word exploded out of me.

Mother turned to look at me in confusion and saw my eyes widen as Mirabelle ran from the side of the gates and held out her arms in front of the speeding car as if she could in some way stop it.

She could not.

Marsha did not stop.

When the car hit her, Mirabelle's body rose up in a fast arc through the air, thrown out to the side as easily as water. It ended in a dull thud.

The air erupted with a riot of noise, shearing metal and shattering glass against the stone as the car veered to the side with the impact and the front end smashed into the wall of the gatehouse. Screams echoed round the courtyard. The car came to an immediate standstill, a buckled mess pushed up against the unmoved stones. Then silence. Stillness. Disbelief.

The portcullis began to slowly descend and I looked back to see Mrs Abaddon holding the remote control in her hand. It was perhaps unnecessary, as Marsha's body was slumped over the wheel, unmoving.

'Mirabelle!' Aunt Charlotte was the first to reach the unmoving bundle. She fell to her knees and shouted out again, 'Mirabelle!'

I watched Mother slow to a stop in front of me. The world seemed to snag on those seconds, caught unawares as if this wasn't part of the preordained plan. Something shifted in that moment, recalibrated.

Mother looked all around as if she didn't understand.

'Oh my God. Oh my God. Oh my God.' Bridget was scuffling in shocked breaths towards them.

We gathered around Mirabelle — me, Mother, Aunt Charlotte and Bridget — and we knelt down as though praying. But we weren't. We looked down at the broken parts of her, her blood-smeared face and twisted arm. Her leg was against mine. I took her hand, holding it in both of mine. It was still warm with life. She couldn't be dead because it didn't feel like she'd gone. The touch of her was too real. Could she feel my hand? She felt of life. But her eyes told a different story. They didn't flicker. They were set open and wide, drinking in some view that those about her couldn't see.

I turned desperately to Mother, who in one slow blink closed any idea that this wasn't death. Her head fell and her body sank into itself.

Aunt Charlotte called her name again, this time with annoyance as if she wasn't listening. 'Mirabelle! Don't be silly. Just get up.'

Mother grabbed at Mirabelle's arm. 'Mirabelle! Mir-a-belle, listen to me.' She looked up at my face pleadingly.

Bridget lifted Mirabelle's head and placed it on her lap. A thin red trail trickled out of Mirabelle's nose, curving round her lips. Bridget pulled back the matted hair, thick with sticky blood.

'Oh Mirabelle.' Mother's words were being suffocated. 'Don't go. Please don't go away. Not now. Don't leave. We've so much more to do together.'

'We need to get an ambulance,' Aunt Charlotte said.

I could see the others, holding back in disbelief, Joseph trying his phone.

Bridget rocked Mirabelle's head a little in her lap. 'Shh.'

The cool wind touched Mirabelle's face and her eyelashes seemed to move as if she was blinking, as if she might flutter back to life. I tried to imagine her lips breaking into a small smile. But she was very calm. A stillness had entered her face as though all her thoughts had suddenly relaxed, all the words and anger had just slipped away. She was empty.

'Mother?' I whispered.

She took steady breaths as if she had to remember to breathe.

Bridget's hand moved down to Mirabelle's throat and her finger pushed into the flesh.

Aunt Charlotte looked up at her. Bridget was biting her lip so hard her teeth were leaving deep imprints. She shook her head slowly and dislodged a tear.

Bridget pulled in a long breath and said, 'She's gone.'

CHAPTER 35: WE FALL INTO SHADOWS

We remained, kneeling by Mirabelle for quite a while, waiting for all of her to go. In the silence, I could hear the air moving around as though it was gathering something up, sweeping up around us in small circles until my hands were pale with cold and my feet numb.

The rain had dwindled and now a dark, oxblood sun hung low behind the mist. It brought no warmth. I was aware of the others moving beyond our tight group of mourners, the villagers whispering nervous questions and hurrying over the stones. Lee Colman was striding around at the edge of my vision, Verity crying. These people had, in an instant, become nothing to me anymore. Some of them were clustered around the hissing car. They didn't seem to move with any urgency. I didn't even care to ask the outcome there.

After some time, I don't know how long, sharp lights clouded the grey air and everything blurred at the edges. The only thing shining out clear that I remember in that picture was Mirabelle and her perfectly still, abandoned face.

* * *

That actual moment of death, when life stops, is so fleeting, but it is a note that plays beneath the surface for many years and days to come. It may fade into the imperceptible sound of memories, a remembered old relative, a funeral long ago. Or it may be a ferocious tide that washes everything else away in its wake. When you finally surface and it spits you out, you may have been so lost beneath those violent waves that everything else just seems so quiet and still. Everything else, the normality of life, is just dull. Life can be pale beside the vibrancy of death. It is easy to be lured in. Grief is a hydra. Take off one head and another grows up in its place. Screaming desperation is so easily replaced by anger. Sorrow slips over to bitterness.

I didn't just lose Mirabelle that day. I lost Dad — again. He's not come back yet. I look for him in windows, reflecting back the empty streets. I search dark, forgotten corners for just a glimmer of movement, but there is nothing. He is consigned to memories for now.

There'd been two losses that day, Dad and Mirabelle. Not three. Not Marsha. She survived. Harriet Bradshaw had finally managed to get some phone signal down in the village and called the police. They had arrived in two small dinghies at the outskirts of the village, already prepared for three murders.

The semi-conscious murderer, Marsha Black, was taken out first. There was a flurry of people, voices, photographs. Areas taped, blankets, notes — while Mirabelle just lay there serenely. She was not troubled by any more of it. But she would have enjoyed all the reporting of events — she always liked that part.

Our theories didn't need too much proving. The case was short and bitterly fought. Marsha threw all the mud she could and dragged her beloved sister-in-law's reputation through the papers until all Verity Black could do was hide away in her castle, alone. Lee Colman kept his farm but not his regard for her. Too many lies pollute even the clearest stream.

Greystone was finally allowed to go back to being a sleepy, cosy little village. They just harboured more jealousy and resentment than they did before our visit. But we're no strangers to that.

We buried Mirabelle on a cold morning beneath a crushing sky. It wasn't love on display but pain. Mirabelle's death took pieces out of Mother that I could not replace. We would never 'get over it', just bend around it. I waited for her to bend, not break.

Mother and Aunt Charlotte were both trapped in disbelief.

Bridget wore her grief extravagantly, but I did not resent her for that. Grief is bespoke, cut to fit perfectly and so different for each individual person.

Mirabelle was gone and she'd taken parts of my mother away with her. I should have hated her for that, but it was pity that overwhelmed me. She'd gone trying to take the lie off her lips. I should have despised her for that as well but I didn't. It just confused everything. Now the lie was gone and so was Dad. Why, I didn't know. Was he somehow redeemed? Had she set him free? That was something I could hate her for, I suppose.

Mother didn't talk about the lie. And when we mentioned Mirabelle's name, it was as if some shame had attached to it. Whose shame though, was still unclear.

Aunt Charlotte insisted on coming round more often, which irritated Mother, so that at least provided some welcome familiarity as they bickered their way around the kitchen. We even suffered Bridget's increased attentions, but Mother drew the line at animals when Bridget adopted Dupin the monkey, so that vastly reduced the visits.

We found some solace with each other in those quiet months until the next invitation landed on the mat. It's fair to say, that threw us all into disarray, especially when a name from the past reappeared and changed everything.

THE END

ACKNOWLEDGEMENTS

This is the first book I've written that won't be launched into lockdown. So if your name isn't here, I can finally thank you in person when we catch up for a drink. I've got three books' worth of celebrating to do!

It takes a lot more than me to write three books, which means there's a lot of people to thank. Firstly, a huge thank you to everyone at Joffe Books. To the wonderful Emma, whose editing is so fabulous and makes the books sing, thank you for all your work and patience! Thanks to Laurel as well for your fantastic editing. And thanks to the lovely Nina and Annie, for your endless support and help. And to Jasper, thank you so much for believing in these books, for your endless encouragement and for giving me the chance of a lifetime. It means the world.

Thank you also to the Crazies for the fabulous parties and gifts. These are so special. Jill and Bev, you're amazing! I can't wait to meet the gang and all the Joffe authors in real life! You guys are the most supportive bunch of authors and I feel very privileged to be with you. To all those wonderful readers, reviewers and bloggers, thank you for all your amazing support.

Thank you also to the D20s, my wonderful co-convenor at the CWA, Bonnie, and all the other authors who reach out and offer endless support and advice. It's mind-blowing how fantastic the writing community is.

Also, I need to thank the wonderful people of Devon, especially a small place I know! Thank goodness you're all so much lovelier than the people in this book. Thank you for all your support and kindness. You guys are brilliant! There will be a party!

Thanks also to Venetia Vyvyan and all the team at Barnes Bookshop. Your support is so fantastic.

Finally, a massive thank you to my wonderful family, who show endless enthusiasm and support. To Sarah, thank you for reading everything, even the scary stuff! To my mother who keeps the library. Delilah and James, you are so understanding of when I have to lock myself away. Your opinions, thoughts and plot devices have been invaluable. Your murder board work, countless hours discussing ideas and Lego builds are legendary! So many characters would have been lost without you.

And finally, darling Kev. Thank you for all your limitless patience, support and love. You make this possible. I can never thank you enough.

ALSO BY VICTORIA DOWD

SMART WOMAN'S MYSTERY SERIES
Book 1: THE SMART WOMAN'S GUIDE TO
MURDER
Book 2: BODY ON THE ISLAND
Book 3: THE SUPPER CLUB MURDERS

Thank you for reading this book.

If you enjoyed it please leave feedback on Amazon or Goodreads, and if there is anything we missed or you have a question about, then please get in touch. We appreciate you choosing our book.

Founded in 2014 in Shoreditch, London, we at Joffe Books pride ourselves on our history of innovative publishing. We were thrilled to be shortlisted for Independent Publisher of the Year at the British Book Awards.

www.joffebooks.com

We're very grateful to eagle-eyed readers who take the time to contact us. Please send any errors you find to corrections@joffebooks.com. We'll get them fixed ASAP.